**Their eyes locked momentarily
and a rush of heated desire
rippled through them both.**

"You should put me down," Marie said, her voice barely above a whisper. "At some point, I'm going to have to learn how to use my crutches, unless you're going to carry me around until I don't need them."

"No, I'm not going to do that, but your shoes and your crutches aren't going to work, and when you traverse this parking lot with one shoe on and the other inside your purse, you're going to say, 'Devon Harris could've helped me inside, damn it.'"

Marie laughed as Devon leaned into her and their lips touched briefly, gently, sending a jolt of electric yearning coursing through her system . . .

Also by Cheris Hodges

JUST CAN'T GET ENOUGH

LET'S GET IT ON

MORE THAN HE CAN HANDLE

BETTING ON LOVE

NO OTHER LOVER WILL DO

HIS SEXY BAD HABIT

TOO HOT FOR TV

Recipe
for
Desire

CHERIS HODGES

Kensington Publishing Corp.
http://www.kensingtonbooks.com

DAFINA BOOKS are published by

Kensington Publishing Corp.
119 West 40th Street
New York, NY 10018

All Kensington Titles, Imprints, and Distributed Lines are available at special quantity discounts for bulk purchases for sales promotions, premiums, fund-raising, and educational or institutional use. Special book excerpts or customized printings can also be created to fit specific needs. For details, write or phone the office of the Kensington special sales manager: Kensington Publishing Corp., 119 West 40th Street, New York, NY 10018, attn: Special Sales Department, Phone: 1-800-221-2647.

Dafina and the Dafina logo Reg. U.S. Pat. & TM Off.

ISBN-13: 978-0-7582-6572-2
ISBN-10: 0-7582-6572-7

First mass market printing: March 2012

10 9 8 7 6 5 4 3 2 1

Printed in the United States of America

Acknowledgments

There are so many people I'd like to thank on my journey to completing this novel and I hope I don't miss anyone. First, I'd like to thank all of the readers who have reached out to me through social media and e-mail. Your kind words often brighten my day. I especially want to thank Tamika Robinson, Yolanda Gore, Tiffany Strange, Wendy Covington, LaSheera Lee, Altonisha Johnson, Illai Kenney, Tasha Martin, Tashmir Parks, Connie Banks Smith, Keehanna Williams Avinger, and you, holding this book in your hands.

To the book clubs: Without you this would not be possible. Thank you. Especially SistahFriends Charleston, SistahFriends Atlanta—SistahFriends worldwide! The PWOC of Jacksonville, Lavender Lilies Book Club, and Round Table Readers Literary Book Club.

I'm thankful for my friends and family who listen to my rambling about ideas and characters. Beverly McDuffie, thanks for being my Starbucks buddy and listening to me reading to you. Amesia Huntley; Erica Singleton; Adrienne Hodges-Dease, the best big sister ever!; Briana Dease, my favorite and only niece; and my parents, Doris and Freddie Hodges: Thank you just doesn't seem to be enough.

Author's Note

My Sister's Keeper is a fictional place, but in Charlotte, North Carolina, there is a place for homeless women. It's called My Sister's House. Their mission is powerful, yet simple: "To stabilize and strengthen our sisters through counseling, stability in living arrangements, and education as we guide them on the path to self-reliance."

In these times, anyone can find herself in need of help. Learn more about My Sister's House by logging on to www.friendshipcdc.org/mysistershouse.htm.

Chapter 1

The only thing Marie Charles enjoyed more than being the center of attention at someone's party was hosting one of her own. Either way, she was instantly the center of attention. Charlotte's resident party girl was always on the cutting edge of fashion, dressing in clothes that were always tailored especially for her svelte body. And she knew how to keep everyone's attention—by either walking into a venue exchanging air kisses with the most high-profile man or woman who caught her eye so that she could get her picture snapped, or by dating the hottest ball player, singer, or actor she wanted. She was a professional public-relations maven, so it was her business to be in the know. But if you asked the right people, Marie Charles—daughter of civil rights attorney Richard Charles III—was just a girl seeking the wrong kind of attention.

Tonight, she was playing hostess at Mez, where her public-relations and event-planning company, M&A Exclusive Events, was sponsoring a party for the Charlotte Bobcats' second playoff win in franchise history. She'd checked the VIP list and kissed a couple of the players on the cheek, telling them congratulations. And, of course, she basked in the compliments the men lavished on her and how she filled out her gold Alexander McQueen dress. As Bobcats center Drayton Neal reached out and grabbed Marie so that they could take a picture, she turned to her intern, Hailey, and said, "This is how you host a party."

Hailey, a shy Central Piedmont Community College student, offered her boss and the six foot nine basketball star a slight smile as the *Carolina Nightlife* photographer snapped photos.

"Have some bubbly," Drayton said to Marie as he held out a glass of Ace of Spades Champagne Blanc de Blancs. She happily accepted the flute of six-hundred-dollar champagne and sipped with Drayton. He palmed her bottom as if it were a basketball and brought his lips to her ear. "You know you're sexy as hell. What do I have to do to make you my good-luck charm?"

"Get your hands off me," she replied through her smile. While most women would've welcomed the advances of an NBA baller, it was just another night on the town for Marie. "I'm not a trophy."

"Umm," he said, taking a step back and watching her sip her champagne. "You look like one to me. You are wearing that gold, baby."

Marie drained her glass and turned to Hailey. "We all look amazing when they're drunk."

"Okay."

Marie took Drayton's bottle and refilled her glass. "Thanks for the bubbly and good luck in New York," she said with a flirty wink. As she and Hailey walked away, she told the intern, "When you're hosting an event, don't spend too much time with one group of people. You have to make everyone feel special so they'll come to your next event. I need you to check the table and make sure everyone has drinks. Have you seen Adriana?" Marie glanced at her watch and fingered her curls. It was almost time for DJ Chill to start his set.

"She was talking to the DJ," Hailey said. Marie nodded.

"I'm going to check on the bartenders and make sure they're making the Bobcat rum punch," she said, then strutted downstairs to the wraparound bar. Marie had carefully selected the drink menu and had worked with the bartenders to make sure everything was perfect. Landing the Bobcats as a client had been a huge get for M&A. *Tonight has to be perfect,* she thought as she crossed over to the crowded bar. Smiling, a half an hour into the party, Marie was sure that everything was going to be . . . wait. Was that William Franklin, her fiancé, walking in the door with *that woman*!

William was holding hands with his ex-wife, Greta Jones, looking at her as if they were still together. "Oh, hell no," she mumbled. She started to stalk over to them, but a hand on her shoulder stopped her.

"Marie," Adriana Kimbrell, the *A* in M&A Exclusive Events, said. "Please don't trip."

"Do you see this? He came to *my* party and brought her!" Marie hissed.

"DJ Chill is about to start and we don't need to have a scene," she said. "Let's just sit down, and you need to calm down."

"I simply don't believe this bull," Marie snapped as they sat down at the bar.

Adriana waved for the bartender. "Patrón and two glasses. Leave the bottle." Turning to Marie, she said, "Ignore them. She's only sniffing after him again because you two are together," Adriana said as she poured Marie a glassful of tequila. "She can't beat you in any other way, so she wants her loser ex back. Let her have it."

Marie downed a shot and then snatched the bottle off

the bar and took a big swig. "If either of them thinks that I'm going to let this go, then they don't know who the hell I am."

"Marie, this isn't just about you and Willie. Our name is on this event. Do you know what I had to do to get Mez to agree to let us have this party here after what you and Tia did during the last event we hosted here?"

Marie took another swig. "We had a good time and got all kinds of press for this place, so they need not trip. I made Mez a hot spot."

"Neither should you," Adriana said as she tried to take the Patrón away. Marie quickly moved the bottle out of her friend's grasp.

"I'm cool," she said. "Look at this outfit." Marie stood up and twirled. "Not trying to mess this up by slapping that slut silly." She glanced out on to the dance floor and watched as William and Greta danced closer than close, but when they kissed, she felt a tug of embarrassment. Everyone knew that was her fiancé, and there he was pretending that she didn't exist. Sure, she wasn't in love with him; her relationship was simply a means to an end. Respectability in her father's eyes. But the longer she watched him, the more the alcohol began to kick in. Marie took a shaky step, with the liquor bottle in her hand, toward the dance floor, shaking off Adriana's hand and ignoring her as she said, "Don't do it, Marie!"

Marie thought she'd saunter over to William and Greta, but the Patrón made her stumble, bump into patrons, and cause quite the scene before she grabbed Greta's shoulder.

"Oh, shit, Marie," William said. "Look . . ."

"This is pretty cozy," Marie slurred. "Funny that you're kissing her when I'm wearing your engagement ring." She threw her left hand up in the air.

Greta shook her head and giggled, which infuriated

Marie to the point that she took a swing at her. But, in her drunken state, she stumbled and landed on the floor flat on her bottom.

William bent down and helped her up. "You're embarrassing yourself and you're drunk."

"And you're kissing this bitch as if you're still married," Marie shouted, bringing the music and movement around them to a halt.

Greta shook her head. "And this is what you left me for? Have you gotten it out of your system?"

William turned to Greta and shot her a look that cried for silence. "Marie, I wanted to tell you that Greta and I had been seeing each other, but . . ."

"You know what! Go to hell. Both of you go straight to hell!" Marie yelled. She fumbled with the ring on her finger, trying to pull it off and toss it in William's face. But the ring slipped off and flew across the dance floor. "It was a cheap-ass stone anyway. It wasn't even flawless. So, kiss my flawless ass good-bye, loser!" Marie turned on her heels and nearly lost her footing as she pushed her way through the crowd. As she passed the bar, Adriana grabbed her arm. "Where are you going?"

"Home."

"You're not driving."

She snatched away from Adriana. "I'm fine and I can drive myself home. It's three blocks."

"Marie, you need to sit down, drink some coffee, and sober up," she warned as she frantically waved for Hailey. "You're only going to make matters worse if you try to drive."

The intern walked over to the bar and glanced from Marie to Adriana. Before she could utter a word, Marie launched into a rant.

"And I'm supposed to sit here and watch them?" Marie

nodded in Greta and William's direction. "I will not. He doesn't even realize he needs me more than I need him."

Adriana rolled her eyes and then reminded her friend, "You said you were going to dump him anyway. Why are you acting like a donkey?"

Marie tore her gaze from William and Greta. "Because I was supposed to dump him! I messed up. I thought getting engaged would get my father off my back, but it hasn't worked and that . . ."

"Hailey," Adriana said, "you're going to have to drive Marie home."

"Bu-but," she stammered as Adriana pressed Marie's car keys into her hand. Marie glared at the women. "I said I can drive," Marie slurred.

"Right," Adriana retorted. "Hailey, don't let her talk you into allowing her to drive. As a matter of fact, go get the car now." Turning to Marie, she continued, "I can't leave because I have to smooth things over after that scene you just caused. You're going to be all over the blogs, again."

Hailey tore out of Mez to get Marie's Jaguar. Marie sighed and shook her head. "Do what you have to do," she said as she took a last look at William and Greta.

Marie furrowed her eyebrows and pointed her index finger at Adriana, "You'd better hope that damned girl knows how to drive. I just got that Jag."

Adriana sighed. "Don't do anything *else* stupid."

Marie threw her hands up and stomped outside, feeling as if she was sobering up. As she stepped out into the cool night air, hot tears streamed down her cheeks. How was she going to show her face on the party scene again? Losing her man to Greta Jones, a nobody who didn't have an outfit that fit her chubby frame?

"I can't believe what happened in Mez," Marie heard a

woman saying. "Marie Charles looked like a damned fool out there. Drunk as a damned skunk and she tossed her ring. William Franklin isn't worth anyone making that big of a fool over."

Marie turned and faced the woman, who was reporting her business over her cell phone as if she was a correspondent for CNN.

"Girl, I got to go," the woman said as she locked eyes with Marie. Marie started to say something, to read Miss Information the riot act, but she didn't have time for that. She was going home. Marie stumbled down the stairs as she spotted Hailey pulling out of the parking deck. She looked over her shoulder and saw a small crowd had gathered and was watching her every move. Trying to put more glide in her wobbly steps, Marie crossed over to her car and opened the passenger-side door of the Jaguar XK. "All right, Hailey," she said. "Thank you for driving me home. I'll make sure a car comes and gets you."

"Marie, I'm not sure if I can do this," Hailey said. "This car is expensive."

"Just drive, Hailey, it's only three blocks," Marie said as she leaned her seat back and closed her eyes. Her mind wandered to her relationship with William and why she'd even agreed to marry him. She'd only wanted to satisfy her father's archaic notion that a proper Southern woman should be married and starting a family by thirty.

She was twenty-seven and still young enough to have fun. That's why she had the job that she created. That's why she spent her time at every party on the East Coast that she could get into—and that was every one of them that wanted press. Marie knew how to make a scene, good or bad. Tonight was bad. She'd make up for it tomorrow. Maybe even have a bachelorette auction for some needy group and put herself on the block as a way to announce to

Charlotte that she was back on the market. That's right, Marie Charles would be back and William would be a distant memory.

Marie had closed her eyes for only a moment when she felt the car jolt and then a hard impact. Her eyes flew open as Hailey screamed. The car hopped the curve and slammed into a one-hundred-year-old oak tree. The explosion of the airbag shocked Marie and knocked the breath out of her.

"Oh my God," she and Hailey screamed. Marie struggled to undo her seat belt as Hailey scrambled from the car. "Are you all right?" Marie called out as she kicked the door open and stumbled out of the car.

"I'm so sorry," Hailey said.

"Were you drinking too?"

"No, no. But I don't have a driver's license," Hailey cried. Tears ran down her cheeks. "I can't get in trouble. I have to get out of here."

Marie crossed over to Hailey as well as her drunken legs would take her. She placed her hands on the young girl's shoulders. "Calm down," she said. "You take off. I can talk my way out of this."

"But what about your car?" Hailey asked as she wiped her eyes.

Marie shook her head. "That's what insurance is for," she said. The last thing Marie wanted was to get her intern in trouble. She'd taken Hailey under her wing because she saw a lot of herself in the twenty-year-old. Hailey, like Marie, had grown up without her mother and wanted to go into public relations. Marie had met her when she'd spoken to a group of marketing students at the college. Seeing her standing there sobbing uncontrollably, she knew that she couldn't allow Hailey to face charges. Besides, she was Marie Charles; she could possibly talk her way out of this mess.

"Get out of here; I'll handle this," she told her.

"Are you sure?"

"Yes," Marie replied. "Hurry up." She noticed a few passersby pulling out cell phones and she assumed they were calling 911. As Hailey dashed away, Marie headed back to the car and climbed into the driver's seat. She tried to back the car up, but it wouldn't move. Before she could get out of the car, swirling blue lights and sirens froze her in place. This was going to be bad. Inhaling deeply, Marie hoped that she knew the officers who were approaching her; maybe she could just talk them into calling a tow truck for her and this accident nastiness could be put behind her.

"Ma'am," one of the officers asked as he pulled the driver's side door open, "are you all right?"

Marie stumbled out of the car as the officer opened the door. The other officer grabbed her arm, holding her up. "Have you been drinking?" he asked.

Marie looked up at the officer—not recognizing him as an officer she knew—and smiled, then she held her index finger inches from her thumb. "Just a little, but this has nothing to do with that."

The officer who'd been holding her arm called for a medic and a tow truck, while his partner questioned Marie further.

"Can you stand up?" the officer asked her.

"These shoes are just a little painful," she slurred, then leaned against a sign post.

"Can you perform some field sobriety tests?"

Marie sighed and rolled her eyes. "Do we really have

to do this? Why don't you just give me a ticket and we call it a day?"

"Ma'am, you hit a tree. This can't disappear with just a ticket," the officer said as he watched his partner direct the approaching tow truck and the medic ambulance. "You're obviously drunk."

Marie folded her arms across her chest and stomped her foot on the cement. The officer shook his head, knowing that he didn't need her to breathe into a Breathalyzer to know she was over the legal limit. "Come on, ma'am, either perform the tests or I will have to arrest you for suspicion of DWI."

"Arrest me?" she snapped incredulously. "Do you know who I am?"

"No," he said. "I don't know who you are. Do you have your driver's license?"

Marie slapped her hands on her hips and focused her indignant stare on the officer. "I'm Marie Charles. You're not going to arrest me. No one got hurt and you don't have to arrest me."

"Yes, I do," he said as he reached for his handcuffs. This wasn't how things had played out in her mind when she'd sent Hailey away. The drunk part of Marie considered running; she didn't want to be put in handcuffs. When it came to dealing with handcuffs, she wanted to be the one in control. But with her shoes and the splitting headache she had, running was not an option.

"Come on, officer"—she paused and squinted at his name tag—"Wiggams. Ooh, just like *The Simpsons*. Can't you just give me a warning?"

"Ma'am, place your hands on your head," the officer barked. Marie rolled her eyes again, ready to tell Officer Wiggams how sorry he was going to be, but she simply did what he told her.

"You're so going to lose your job," Marie said with a giggle.

"You have the right to remain silent," he said. "I suggest you use it."

"Go to hell," she snapped as he locked the cuffs on her wrists. The officer read Marie her Miranda rights and then stuffed her in the back of the squad car. She threw her head back and groaned. Marie knew her father would be livid when the news of her arrest reached him.

Six A.M. was the magic hour for celebrity chef Devon Harris. He stood in the kitchen in the middle of his loft, creating a savory meat pie recipe for the women at My Sister's Keeper, the homeless shelter where he volunteered and taught a cooking class for some of the women who lived there. The meals that his students made became lunch and dinner for the sixty-five residents who lived in the shelter. Devon placed the top crust on the pie and gently wrapped it in wax paper. He needed to head to the kitchen of Hometown Delights, the restaurant where he ran the kitchen for his friends, Jade Goings, Serena Billups, Alicia Michaels, and Kandace Crawford. Over the last three years, the restaurant had become one of Charlotte's premier eateries and meeting places. Fans of the Food Network flocked to the restaurant because Devon filmed his weekly show, *Dining with Devon*, there, and every month, Devon debuted a new dish to go along with a social event hosted at the restaurant.

Devon was proud of the work he did at the restaurant and was thinking of writing a cookbook. Hell, he didn't have anything else to do. Since he'd been in Charlotte, he had grown tired of women looking for a wedding ring after two dates or who thought one dinner date meant they were in a committed relationship. Devon couldn't deal with that or the women who felt as if they had to compete with everything he did all in the name of being independent. He didn't mind a woman who had her own thing going on, but did she have to keep throwing it in his face?

Maybe that's why he threw himself into his volunteer work with My Sister's Keeper. Working with those women made him happy and took his mind off the fact that his bed was colder than the top of Mount Everest in the middle of December. Still, he'd rather have a cold bed than share it with a woman who didn't mean a damned thing to him. He'd indulged in a few meaningless flings, which Serena and Alicia gave him hell about, and he was tired of the empty feeling.

"You know you're just trying to replace Kandace," they'd say to him when he'd complain about it.

"Don't let her husband hear you say that," he'd always reply. Back in college, Devon and Kandace had dated until he made the mistake of cheating on her. Any hopes of rekindling their romance had been dashed when Kandace met Solomon Crawford, a rich guy who always got his way. Devon was genuinely happy for Kandace, even if he didn't like her husband. But with Kandace and Solomon expecting their first child, he'd made more of an effort to get along with Solomon.

That wasn't easy, though. Solomon still didn't trust that Devon was over Kandace and often made snide remarks about Devon still wanting his wife.

Yawning, Devon decided that he'd make himself some coffee, since he couldn't shake his sleepiness, before heading into the restaurant to bake the pies and take them over to the ladies at My Sister's Keeper for lunch.

While the coffee percolated, Devon scrambled two eggs and tossed in some of the leftover meat from the pies to make a quick breakfast burrito, then flipped the TV on to watch the morning news.

"Charlotte socialite Marie Charles was arrested on suspicion of DUI after police say she crashed her car into a tree on Elizabeth Avenue early this morning. The accident followed a dispute at The EpiCentre, where Charles attacked a man on the dance floor at the popular eatery Mez," the newscaster stated. Devon glanced at the picture of Marie Charles and shook his head.

"Everybody wants to be famous for all the wrong reasons," he mumbled as he poured himself a cup of coffee. Devon changed the channel to ESPN and watched Sports-Center while he ate his breakfast. After eating, showering, and dressing, Devon dashed out the door and headed for the restaurant. He wanted to make sure that the pies were hot and delicious for the women at the shelter before he started lunch for the restaurant.

Chapter 2

Marie's mouth was dry; her scalp felt as if thousands of ants were crawling on it. And the polyester jail jumpsuit made her skin itch as if the ants had jumped from her scalp to her skin. All she wanted to do was get out of this cell and into her garden tub with some jasmine oil and her cell phone by her side. The court was waiting for the results of Marie's blood test, since she hadn't taken a Breathalyzer test overnight. And, because she'd hadn't been seen behind the wheel of the car, she was able to hold on to her driver's license pending the results of the blood test. Not that it mattered, because her beloved Jaguar wasn't drivable. Marie had to find out if this incident made the news. If it did, she'd have to spin the story to make herself look like another victim of the police; after all, no one likes a drunk driver. She stood up and scratched her head, wishing for a hot oil treatment.

"Charles," a jailer called out. "You've made bail."

"Thank God!" she exclaimed as the woman opened the door. "This was hell."

The jailer didn't say a word as she led Marie to be processed out of jail. Marie smiled happily as she signed for her belongings, but then she realized that she had no way to get home.

"Marie Clare Charles," a voice boomed, vibrating off the walls of the jail's lobby like thunder or the voice of Jesus himself.

She dropped her head. "Hey, Daddy," she said quietly. Marie looked up and stared into her father's chestnut brown eyes; there was no warmth in them. Not today, anyway. His eyes screamed disappointment, dismay, and anger. Richard Charles III was a formable man, standing at six-five, with his hair graying at the temples.

"Don't you 'hey, Daddy' me. Have you lost your ever-loving mind?" he asked as he folded his arms across his massive chest. "There I was sitting in my office drafting a brief for a case that's going to trial in a week and my phone won't stop ringing. I'm hopeful that it's the district attorney's office, and it's Steve Crump, Jason Stoogneke, and some reporter from *Creative Loafing*."

"Wow, channel three is talking about me?" Marie said with more cheer in her voice than should've been there.

Richard slapped his hand against his thigh. "This is *not* some damned joke. You're facing a serious charge, Marie! If this isn't the wake-up call you need to grow up, then I don't know what it's going to take."

"It's not as if I hurt someone," she said flippantly. "It was a rough night and I wasn't even . . ."

"Shut up!" he snapped. "Don't admit to anything in here. We're going back to my office and we're going to have a serious talk."

"Can it wait?"

Richard squeezed his temples and sighed. "Marie, ever since your mother died, I've done you a grave disservice. I've given you everything you wanted. Maybe I should've been a stricter disciplinarian, given you punishments, and stuck to them. But no more. I'm not saving your ass this time, because you obviously need to learn a lesson."

"What are you talking about?" Marie asked, shrugging her shoulders. "I made a mistake. It was only a tree, Daddy."

Richard pointed his finger in his daughter's face. "You keep making mistakes; you keep doing foolish things that make sense to no one but you. When you go to trial on these charges, you're going to accept whatever punishment the judge hands down."

"Why can't you just make this go away?" She was tempted to tell her father the entire story, but that would've led to another lecture about honesty.

Richard shook his head. "I've made too many of your problems go away. That's why you think it's all right to get wasted and drive around Uptown, crash into a tree, and expect me to make it go away. Not this time, baby girl. Go on and go home, but we will have that talk."

Marie smiled sheepishly. "I kind of need a ride home," she said.

Richard dug into his pocket and handed her three one-dollar bills. "Take the light rail." He stormed out of the jail as Marie stood there speechless. Did he think she was going to get on public transportation? A second passed before she ran out after her father.

"Daddy, come on, give me a ride. I'll go to your office and we can talk now," she said, though all she wanted was a hot bath and her bed.

Richard stopped as he got to his car, and glanced at his daughter. The older she got, the more she reminded him of Cela, her mother. He'd doted on his wife, who had told him not to be so permissive with Marie. But after Cela's death when Marie was ten, he'd forgotten about not being permissive and became a welcome mat for his daughter.

"Get in," he said as he unlocked the doors of his Mercedes CL Coupe. They drove for about five minutes in silence. When they stopped at a red light, Richard turned to Marie.

"What was last night about? Please don't tell me it had anything to do with that slime you're engaged to."

Marie tossed her head back. "That's over," she said with a snort. "I just had too much to drink and I thought I could drive home."

"That was very dangerous and stupid. Why don't you think before you act? Two months ago, you almost got a public indecency charge for hopping into the fountain on the square wearing nearly nothing. You need to start acting your age. How are you a public relations whatever when you make a scene every time you go out?"

Marie sighed. "Because you have to crack a few eggs to make an omelet," she said. "This isn't old-school Charlotte where you have to . . ."

"Your reputation is all you have and all that matters. You're ruining it and . . ."

"Is it my reputation or yours that you're worried about?"

Richard frowned at his daughter. "I have built my reputation and people know who I am and what to expect from me. You're the one who's going to wish she made better decisions in her life when you're my age."

Marie yawned and nodded as if she was really paying attention to the lecture she'd heard time and time again. Richard glanced at his daughter, and he knew it was time for a serious change if she was going to stop being a destructive party girl.

* * *

"That's right," Devon whispered over her shoulder. "Just pinch the edges gently. Yes."

"Mr. Harris," Skylar Thomas said happily. "Check mine." Devon turned from the student he'd been working with and told Skylar he'd be right there. Then he focused on the young woman in front of him.

"What's your name?" he asked.

"Bria," she said softly.

"Your first time making a pie crust?"

She nodded and smiled. "Well," Devon said, "you're doing a great job."

Again, she smiled, beaming under Devon's compliments. He crossed over to the other students, checking the progress they were making with their pie crusts. He glanced back at Bria, wondering what her story was. She was so young and seemed passive and afraid. Perhaps she was running from something, or maybe she was like many of the other women here, having just fallen on bad times and at the end of hope's rope.

Over the last six months since he'd been volunteering with My Sister's Keeper, Devon learned that homeless didn't mean hopeless. These women were fighters, especially his new best friend, Shay. She knew computers like the back of her hand, but, when she was stricken with a rare blood disorder, spent eight months in the hospital, and everything began going downhill. She lost her job and her health benefits, so when she was released from the hospital, she had nowhere to go.

The women at the shelter came from so many different backgrounds; some of them had college degrees, were former professionals, or were escaping abusive relationships.

"You ladies are doing great," he said, then glanced at

his watch. "Now that we have the crusts done, let's work on the filling."

"That's what I'm talking about," Shay said as Devon pulled a bag of apples from underneath the counter. He glanced at his watch again and saw that he needed to get to the restaurant to prepare for lunch.

"All right, ladies," he said. "I need you to peel these apples and then I'm going to have to leave. But I do have something special for lunch." He walked over to the oven and pulled out the tray of meat pies he'd made that morning. "Pie doesn't always have to be dessert."

Bria nodded. "My grandmother used to make potpies for us," she whispered.

"This looks good," Shay said as Devon set the pies on the counter. "What's in it?"

"Beef, cabbage, carrots, and corn, with a special cheese sauce," he said. "You ladies will be the first to taste this. I made enough pies for all of the residents."

The women smiled at him. "When I get back," Devon said, "we'll make dessert."

"All right, ladies," Shay said. "Let's get these apples peeled so that we can have dessert for a change."

"Yes," Adele replied, then smiled at Devon. "It's so nice having you around, Devon."

He returned her smile and nodded in her direction. "I'm happy you guys let me come around. I have to go, but I'll be back so we can make dessert and talk about you ladies making lunch and dinner next week. I'm going to turn you all into a kitchen staff," he said.

An excited murmur rumbled through the kitchen as Devon waved good-bye to the ladies. On his way out the door, Elaine Harper, the director of the shelter, stopped him. "Devon, I have to tell you that your work here is doing wonders with these women."

"Thank you," he said.

"I have a favor to ask you, though," she said.

Devon tilted his head to the side and looked at Elaine. "What's that?"

"Well, we've been asked by the Mecklenburg County Probation and Parole Department to take in some of their nonviolent female offenders to do their community service. I just want you to supervise some of the women when they start coming here."

"What will I have to do?"

"Sign their papers and make sure they reach their hours, nothing hard. I would put a staff member on it, but we had to let two people go and I can't afford to hire anyone right now," she said.

"I'll do it," he said. "But, I have to go right now. Will you be here at five?"

"Yes," she said. "Will you bring me some dessert from the restaurant?"

Devon laughed and closed his hand on Elaine's shoulder. "I sure will. I'm making a chocolate cake for dessert today."

"I don't know what I did to deserve you, but I thank God for it every day."

Devon smiled at the older lady and wished that he had that effect on a woman he could start a relationship with. As he headed for the restaurant, Devon thought about the work he was doing at the shelter and how it gave him a feeling of peace. He wished he could do more. Then it hit him like a ton of bricks; Hometown Delights could host a fund-raiser for the shelter.

When he pulled into the restaurant's parking lot, he parked his classic Ford Mustang next to Alicia's Lexus Coupe. Rushing into the office, not even checking on his lunch staff, Devon called out Alicia's name.

"What's going on, Devon?" she asked as she returned the phone to its cradle.

"I have an idea for you and the ladies," he said, smiling at her.

"The way you were screaming out my name, I thought there was some kind of emergency out here. You can't scare me like that!"

"There's no problem, but an opportunity for us to make a difference."

"I'm listening," Alicia said as she leaned back in the leather seat behind the desk.

"I've been working with My Sister's Keeper and the women who live in the shelter."

Alicia nodded. "You're doing a great thing over there," she said.

"I think we can do more," he said as he leaned against the wall. "What if we hosted a fund-raiser for the shelter? Times are tough and they're having a hard time keeping the staff together and providing for the women."

"I bet. The economic news makes me count my blessings every night. We can do that, but I'd better run it by Jade and Serena just to make sure," Alicia replied. "Maybe we can get Maurice and some of his football buddies involved."

"That would definitely ramp up the amount of donations," Devon said as he nodded.

"Let me ask you a question, though," Alicia said as she ran her fingers through her hair. "Is this new and improved socially conscious Devon Harris doing all of this charity work because he can't get a date?"

"Getting a date isn't the problem. Finding a woman in Charlotte who doesn't have more issues than *Ebony*, *Essence*, and *Jet* is."

"Thankfully, I don't fall into that category," Alicia

quipped. Devon raised his right eyebrow as he looked at his friend.

"Alicia, lie to yourself, darling; don't lie to me."

She folded her arms across her chest. "And what's that supposed to mean?"

Devon cocked his head to the side and laughed. "The scowl on your face says it all. Brother to sister, you are the kind of woman that makes a man feel as if he's never going to measure up."

Alicia fanned her hands and sucked her teeth. "Whatever. You're just mad because your perfect woman is married to someone else and about to have his baby."

"Let the Kandace thing go. I have, and God knows Solomon doesn't need to think I'm hoping to rekindle the romance with his wife."

"I can't help but tease you about that; it makes my day."

Devon wagged his finger at Alicia. "You need to get a life," he said. "Let me go check what the staff is doing for lunch, and I have to make a dessert."

"What are you making for dessert?" Alicia asked with a gleam in her eye.

"Nothing for you. Oh, you're going to have to come by the shelter and try the pies the ladies and I are making."

"Sure," Alicia said. "As long as you give me some of what you're making for lunch."

Devon sighed and winked at Alicia. "Do I need to make enough for your non-cooking married friend?"

"Are you talking about me?" Serena Billups asked from behind Devon. "Because I did come to get lunch for my husband and his crew."

"How do you all make a profit when none of you can cook and you're always eating like this is your own personal kitchen?" Devon said when he turned around and hugged his friend.

"Please," Serena said when he let go. "You've been cooking for us for years."

"Yes, I've spoiled you all terribly," Devon said. "Have you ever cooked for Antonio?"

Serena shrugged. "I boiled hot dogs once," she said.

Devon shook his head. "And on that note, I'm going to the kitchen." He turned and headed for the kitchen to get ready for the lunch rush.

Chapter 3

Marie stared listlessly as her father continued his lecture about responsibility once they made it to his office in south Charlotte. Was she twelve or an adult? Richard paced the floor as if he were trying to walk a hole in the carpet.

"I've made some calls," he said. "But with the publicity that you've garnered, we can't keep this quiet. You're going to be punished."

"With all of your contacts in Charlotte, this is the best you can do? This isn't just about me, Dad. I just don't want to get. . . ."

Richard glared at his daughter. "Marie, what you did was dangerous and you do need to face that. Why didn't you just allow someone else to drive? You're lucky that no one was killed. Why do you think that I'm going to try and absolve you of the consequences of what you did?"

"Isn't that what you do for your clients every day? I'm your daughter. You can't do the same thing for me?"

"You sound like a spoiled brat, and I've already said I'm partly to blame for that, but you obviously didn't hear me when I said that I wasn't going to continue to feed into your delusions of entitlement," Richard boomed. "I told you a long time ago, William Franklin wasn't good enough for you. But you had to involve him in your life, and now, you've allowed your emotions to make you act like a damned fool. Am I supposed to just give you a hug and make it all go away?"

Marie closed her eyes and sighed. Part of her wanted to tell her father that's exactly what she wanted him to do. She wanted to tell him that if he would stop expecting the worst of her, maybe it wouldn't keep happening. But Marie also knew those were excuses and that if she expected her father to help her, she was going to have to be honest.

"Daddy," she said, "I know what I did was potentially dangerous. It was stupid and it was a mistake. But I have my business to think about. I can't go to jail. If you help me, I will turn over a new leaf, stay out of trouble, and nothing like this will ever happen again."

Richard shook his head. "I wish I could believe you. I wish I felt as if you weren't trying to work me over to get what you want."

"I'm not doing that," she said. "Daddy, do you know how hard it is being the daughter of the great Richard Charles III? So, yes, I've lashed out in the past. I've tried to carve my own niche in Charlotte."

"By acting like a silly party girl? Stripping and drinking too much? Yes, you're separating yourself from the career and image I've built for myself, and you're doing a damned good job of it," he snapped caustically. "If you really want to change and want to turn over a new leaf, the first thing you have to do is take responsibility for your actions. Take a plea. I'll work with the DA's office to see what we can do. If you have to do jail time, then you will do it."

She groaned at the prospect of spending another hour in jail. "Do I really have to go to jail?"

"Honestly, I'd love to see that. But realistically, this is your first offense and you probably won't go to jail. Probation, most likely. But with me, you're going to have to show and prove. No more stunts, no more publicity for all the wrong reasons."

"Fine."

"Don't say fine, just do it."

"Is it too soon to ask you if I can borrow one of your cars since mine was totaled?"

Richard sighed and shook his head. "The last thing you need to do is to be seen driving. I will have a car service take you wherever you need to go."

"And that's going to look so much better, me riding around in a limo and getting out looking like a superstar. I know about image, Daddy, and rolling around town in a car service is a one-way ticket to jail. Unless that's a part of you teaching me a lesson."

"Marie, I want you to change who you are and how you act, but I don't want you to continue down this path of self-destruction. What's going through your mind when you do these foolish things?"

Marie sighed and rolled her eyes at him. "You've made your point and I've heard you, but the last thing we need is for some photographer to snap a picture of me getting out of a limo. Can you imagine what the papers will say and how that will change the way a judge will treat me. As you said, image is everything."

"Last night was when you should've called the car service or paraded around in a limo," Richard said, then he handed Marie his car keys. "I will be coming for my car at five thirty; don't make me have to track you down."

"Yes, Father," she said, then grabbed her father's keys

and tore out of the office. Once she hit the fresh air, Marie almost felt civil again. All she needed was a spa treatment, a manicure, a pedicure, and something delicious to eat. As she hopped behind the wheel of her father's car, Marie pulled out her cell phone and called Adriana.

"Hello?"

"Adriana, it's me."

"Marie, oh, my goodness, you're out of jail. Are you all right?" she asked. "I thought Hailey drove you last night. I know you didn't put her life in danger along with yours . . ."

"I don't need another lecture and I wasn't driving. I need a shower, a good meal, and a hairdo. Last night was hell, and my father put me through some more hell just moments ago. But Hailey is all right. I wish you would've asked her if she had a driver's license before handing her the keys to my car, which is totaled."

"Are you ready for more bad news?"

"If I say no, can you make it disappear?" Marie groaned as she pulled up to the intersection.

"We've been banned from Mez."

Marie muttered curse words under her breath as she listened to Adriana tell her that the management ended the party and told Adriana that they would no longer host events by M&A.

"We also lost the location for two of our upcoming events and one of our CIAA parties. Marie, you messed up royally, and it's costing me money."

"Listen," Marie said. "We can make things right. Shit happens, all we have to do is wait for the next news director to get caught stealing from Harris Teeter, or another city council member to get accused of sexual harassment."

"And how am I supposed to pay my bills? Marie, I love

you. But I don't have a rich daddy willing to stick his neck out for me."

"Then what are you saying?"

"You need to take a step back. Stop being in everybody's face all the time."

Marie groaned as she pulled up to the Aveda Institute on South Boulevard. "You know what, if that's how you feel, then fine. I have to go." Marie tossed her phone in the backseat and pounded her hands against the steering wheel. Did Adriana think she could run M&A on her own? Whatever!

Marie was the one with the contacts, who knew the right people, and who grabbed headlines. Well, most of the time that was a good thing, but did Adriana think she was going to be the new "it" girl?

She slammed her car door and stormed inside the salon. "Oh, my goodness," her stylist, Rodricko, exclaimed. "Look who they let out of the slammer. Girl, get in my seat right now. Did you smile in your mug shot like all the little starlets do?"

Marie marched over to his seat, every eye in the place following her, but no one said a word. "You know I had to ban Greta from my place because I thought that garden tool was lying about your arrest. Imagine my surprise when I found out it was true. What happened, girl? Did Willie the Leech really leave you for Greta?"

"They walked into *my* event together as if they hadn't signed divorce papers a year ago."

"But, honey," Rodricko said as he gently combed Marie's tangled roots. "Are you hurt? You didn't really love him, did you?"

"No, but I'm not going to let him get away with playing me. Does he know who I am?"

"A damned fool," he snorted.

"Excuse me?" Marie said. "Did you just call me a 'damned fool'?"

"Yes, I did," Rodricko said as he led her over to the shampoo bowl. "From the moment you announced you were engaged to Willie the Leech, I knew it was a mistake. You're free now and you should celebrate that with a new haircut, color, and dance a jig. And if you have to celebrate with some spirits, you got enough in the bank to call a whole car service."

"But he embarrassed me and I'm not going to take that lying down."

"So, taking bullshit standing up is supposed to do what? Marie, you're being stupid. The next thing I know, you're going to be telling me that you want that Rihanna redness in your hair or some Lady Gaga-esque hairstyle."

Marie leaned back and folded her arms across her chest. "Well, I thought that red would look good on me."

Rodricko threw his hands up. "Lawd, child, you need more than a hairdo!"

"But, no, no," Marie started, "removing William from the equation, Adriana is tripping, too. We lost Mez, and she thinks that I should take a step back."

Rodricko sighed as he massaged a deep conditioning serum into Marie's hair and scalp. "Well, if you were the client, what would you tell yourself?"

Marie wiggled her nose and exhaled. "Maybe I would suggest lying low for a little . . ."

"Marie, I hope you know this isn't going to be as easy to get out of as when you and your girls got naked in the Square for PETA or whatever fake cause y'all had gotten involved in. Daddy might not be able to fix this."

Marie crossed her ankles and smiled. "One thing about having a name in this burg is that it never lets you down."

As Rodricko slapped a plastic conditioning cap on her

head, he had a feeling that things were going to get a lot worse for Marie before they got any better.

So, the pie wasn't restaurant quality, but it was damned good, Devon thought as he sampled another one of the pies from the women at My Sister's Keeper. These women had talent, and all he had to do was teach them not to be afraid of spices.

"How did we do?" Shay asked Devon, looking hopefully at him for a critique on the pies.

"The pies were good, but we can make them better. We have to get our spices down," he said. "That's going to come with timing and more practice. I wanted to talk to you ladies this afternoon because the restaurant where I work, we've decided to host a fund-raiser for this place. I wanted to know how many of you wanted to help me with this. We can find out where you're strongest and . . ."

"Hold up," Shay said. "You're talking about that restaurant where all the crazy stuff keeps happening?"

Loriene nodded. "First it was Solomon Crawford's stalker–business partner, then the movie producer tried to choke one of the women, and . . ."

Devon waved his hands. "That's neither here nor there. This is going to be a chance for you all to learn some life skills, and those psychos you named won't be on the guest list," he said. "But, here's a chance to get your face out there to some employers and possibly make some connections with people who can help you prepare for the future."

"We don't want to be looked at as if we're a charity case, either," Shay said.

"I don't want to be a part of this," Bria said as she rose from the table where she and the other women from

Devon's class were sitting. "I know we're in a bad situation here, but it's not as if we haven't tried to help ourselves."

Devon threw his hands up. "And I understand that, but this place here is special, and so are every last one of you. All I want to do is let other people in the city know what I already know."

"That's not a bad idea," Shay said. "But why don't you and your rich friends just write a check if you want to clear your conscience so badly."

"It's not about that," Devon said. "When I said I was going to work with you ladies and this program, I meant more than write a check. What I've learned from you ladies is that anyone could end up in a situation like this. I'm glad to be a part of this team, and when the right people find out what's going on here, they are going to want to help as well. We all have to pay it forward."

Shay propped up on her elbows and looked up at Devon. "You know, if my ex-husband was anything like you, I might not be in a place like this."

Devon smiled at Shay. "If my ex could fix a computer the way you can, then there is no way I would've allowed her to marry a multimillionaire," he quipped as he tapped his laptop lid. "But, ladies, we can raise a lot of money, show a lot of people how much heart Charlotte has. Who knows what this could mean for the other women around the city who may need the services of My Sister's Keeper."

Shay looked at her fellow culinary arts students. "We should do it. Devon hasn't led us wrong before."

A ripple of mumbling went through the crowd while Devon focused on Bria, who looked as if she wanted to bolt right out the door and never return.

"All right," Shay said, "I'll help. I did work in public relations before; maybe I can help the people who will be promoting the event."

"That's the spirit," Devon said. "I want you ladies to feel like this is your event; I want you involved in every aspect of it."

Shay and everyone else, but Bria, nodded and seemed to be getting excited about it. "We'll talk more about this next week," Devon said as the women began to file out of the room.

"Bria," Devon said as she approached the door and the others were out of earshot. "Can we talk for a second?"

"I really have to go," she said nervously. Devon placed his hand on her shoulder and forced her to face him. He'd seen that look before, only it was in his mother's face when he'd seen it last. Bria was running from something just as his mother had spent years avoiding the spotlight and questions when Devon Sr. had gotten out of hand with his anger and slapped her. He'd tried not to leave a mark, because the wife of the Atlanta Hawks' star center couldn't be seen around town with the marks of an abused woman.

When Devon Sr. would get a lick in too good on his mother, Devon and his mom would head out of town for about a month, pretending they were on a big adventure until he had grown up enough to know what was going on. By the time Amelia Harris had been diagnosed with ovarian cancer and Devon Sr. had decided to play the doting husband as she died, Devon had decided he hated his father enough to turn his back on everything his father had designed for him—the basketball career, the education at Georgia Tech, and becoming the crown prince of the hardwood. Instead, he'd taken up his mother's dream and discovered that being a chef made him happy. What he hated about himself was that in the process of finding himself, he'd hurt Kandace when he'd cheated on her with a throwaway groupie who his father had sent to "greet" him before he headed off to Paris. That had been the dagger in his relationship with Kandace.

Devon couldn't recall her name, but he'd never forget walking upstairs and finding a cocoa beauty lying in his bed with nothing but a white teddy on. His father and Kandace had gotten into another argument at the party and he'd grown tired of playing referee that night. Especially when Kandace had known that him becoming a chef would be the biggest tribute he could pay to his mother. He'd felt as if she'd allowed Devon Sr. to ruin his party, where he'd done all of the catering himself to show his father and his friends that he had culinary skills. Devon had overindulged on the scotch and champagne, and all he'd wanted to do had been to go to sleep. Until she'd licked her lips and stroked her double Ds. He'd needed a release, and Miss No-Name seemed willing to do whatever he'd wanted.

The moment he'd joined her in bed, they'd started kissing, she'd grabbed a condom, unzipped his pants, and began giving oral sex. Devon had closed his mind to his father's constant belittling of his career choice and girlfriend. But at the time he'd lost himself in the cheap thrill of the nameless groupie, he'd heard Kandace scream from the door. Devon had struggled to pull away from the woman and had chased after Kandace. He'd wanted to explain why. Then again, he hadn't quite understood why he'd cheated himself.

Looking at Bria, he knew the look in her eyes: pain, disappointment, and fear. "What's really going on with you?" he asked her quietly. "If you're here to get away from some jackass who has been putting his hands on you, then let me know. I can talk to Mrs. Harper, and we can get you the help that you need."

"I don't want to talk about that. And I don't need everyone in my business. He can never find me." Before Devon could say anything else, Bria tore out of the room and disappeared into the residential section of the shelter. As much as he wanted to follow the young girl and get her to talk to him, Devon knew from his experience with his mother that he couldn't force her to talk. When she was ready, she'd get the help she needed.

As Devon packed up to head back to the restaurant for dinner service, he wondered if Bria would feel more comfortable talking to someone like Serena or Alicia, maybe even Jade. Definitely Jade, he surmised as he got into his car. She'd be able to reach Bria and would be a lot nicer than Serena.

Chapter 4

Two weeks later, Marie found herself standing in the district court dressed in a Chanel skirt suit, trying not to tell the pompous judge passing down her sentence to shut the hell up. Was this man simply trying to make the evening news or was this what really happened in court?

"Driving under the influence is illegal and stupid," Judge Tracy O'Conner said. "Ms. Charles, you're fortunate that no one was hurt when you decided to take a spin in your sports car after drinking all night."

Marie fought the urge to roll her eyes. Could he just suspend the sentence already? This was only her first offense. "I don't think you've learned a true lesson," the judge said.

"Excuse me?" Marie turned to her father. "What's going on here?"

"Look at me," Judge O'Conner bellowed. "What lesson have you learned?"

"Not to drink and drive again," Marie replied, trying to keep her voice even and respectful. "I'm fully aware of how lucky I was to not hurt myself or anyone else. What I did was a mistake that will never happen again." She could feel Hailey looking at her from the gallery. She'd told her intern that she didn't have to show up in court because she was sure that the judge wouldn't sentence her to a jail term. And Marie planned to keep her word and keep Hailey out of trouble.

"That's not enough. Everyone says that when they're in front of me after causing an accident because they weren't smart enough to call a cab when they had too much to drink."

"But, your honor, what more do you want from me?" Marie asked as her father squeezed her left hand, signaling for her to be quiet.

"I want you to take full responsibility for your actions, don't just say what I'm sure your father has told you judges want to hear. You may not have hurt anyone, Ms. Charles, but I see you as being a spoiled young woman who thinks an 'I'm sorry' will fix everything."

"I don't think that, your honor," Marie said. "I want to . . ."

The judge held up his hand. "I've come to a decision. Your license will be suspended for thirty days and you will perform five hundred hours of community service with a women's facility in the city. This will be coordinated with the Mecklenburg County Department of Probation."

Marie turned to her father. "What does this mean?" she whispered.

He nodded toward the judge, who wasn't finished with his dressing-down of Marie. "And furthermore," the judge said, "in reading the background on your case, I feel that you have gotten away with a lot of things because your father has the means and the connections to keep you out of trouble. All of the citizens in this county don't have those benefits. It will do you some good to take your community service seriously. I don't want to see you in this courtroom again. You can have a bright future, but your selfish actions may dampen that."

Marie cocked her head to the side and eyed the judge as if she wanted to leap across the bench and slap him. Instead, she simply nodded and listened to the judge's rant.

"I hope that you will learn something more than never driving under the influence again."

"Yes, sir," Marie said, struggling to keep the sarcasm out of her voice.

"Next case," the judge called as Richard began gathering his papers. Marie had started to charge out of the courtroom, but her father stopped her.

"You have to talk to the probation department and get the community service set up," Richard said as he grabbed his briefcase.

"I really have to do that?" Marie whispered. "Can't I just write a check?"

Richard glared at his daughter. "Did you hear anything the judge said? You have to follow the letter of your probation. I'm glad you went before Judge O'Conner. I almost tried to get this moved, because he's tough. But you're on your own, Marie. I'm tired of this attitude of yours."

"Daddy," she whined.

"Don't 'Daddy' me. I told you before that you were acting like an out-of-control party girl and I was sick of it. Your actions in there with the judge could've landed you in jail."

"How?"

"You don't speak to a judge like that in open court or ever. You think you can just do what you want and get away with it. Judge O'Conner was right, you need to learn a real hard lesson here, Marie," Richard said as he pointed down the hall. "The probation office is that way, I'd suggest you get in there and get your paperwork done."

"Where are you going?" she asked.

"I have another case."

"How am I supposed to get home?"

"Well, there's Charlotte Area Transit, there's a taxi cab, or you could walk, since you live four blocks from here," Richard said. As her father left her standing in the hallway alone, Marie knew she had to follow these rules and talk to the probation office about community service. Who did they think she was? Chris Brown? *Please, God, don't let them put me on trash pick-up duty or something. This is horrible,* she thought as she walked into the probation office. Marie ignored the other people waiting in line and walked up to the front desk.

"I'm Marie Charles and I have to see a probation officer about community service," she said to the clerk at the front desk.

"You're going to have to take a number and wait like everyone else," the surly and obviously overworked woman replied.

"But, you don't understand, I have an appointment at Neiman Marcus in an hour. I don't . . ."

"Take a number and sit down. Do I look like I give a damn about Neiman Marcus? You're no different from anyone in here!" The woman grabbed a plastic sign that read BACK IN FIVE MINUTES, slammed it on the desk, and tore out of the room.

Marie turned and looked at the people she was waiting with and sighed. She wouldn't be trying on the new Louboutins today after all. She plopped down on a vinyl chair and fumed. The clerk had no right to be mad! Marie was going to miss out on her chance to get a brand-new pair of Louboutins. Folding her arms across her chest, all

Marie could think about was making William suffer for this. How could he come to her event with that cow of an ex-wife? Marie chewed on her bottom lip, realizing for the first time that she hadn't heard from him since that night and she really didn't care.

Damn, she thought, *I really did create this mess for no reason.*

It was an hour and a half before Marie met with her probation officer, another overworked civil servant with a bad attitude, at least in her opinion. Tito Parker was his name, and Marie wondered if the overstuffed man knew that his shirt was three sizes too small.

"So, you have five hundred hours of community service that you have to complete as a part of your plea agreement." He sighed, then coughed. Marie fanned his germs away and groaned. Was this her life? Sitting in front of a probation officer like a common criminal because she made a little—well, pretty big—mistake?

"Yes. Can we get this over with?" she said.

He glanced up from her file with a perplexed look on his face. "Ms. Charles, I don't know if you think this a makeup counter or a shopping mall, but we will be done when we go through the judge's orders."

Marie leaned back in her chair and folded her arms across her chest. "Fine."

"Now," he said. "The judge wants you to do something significant with your service and has already outlined where you're to complete the order hours. I guess you're happy that you won't have to collect trash on Independence Boulevard in that traffic."

"Great," she said sarcastically.

He narrowed his eyes at Marie. "Weren't you in the papers over the summer for leading a protest about nothing in Center City?"

"It wasn't about nothing," Marie retorted. "Animals are important."

He looked down at her shoes. "Are those leather?"

"What's your point?"

"If you care so much about animals . . . never mind. Anyway, the shelter where you will be working caters to single women who are homeless."

"A soup kitchen?"

Tito ran his hand across his face. "You know what, Ms. Charles, I'm trying to work with you and you're making it very difficult." He slammed a colorful brochure on the desk in front of her. "This place is for women who, unlike yourself, weren't born with a silver spoon in their mouths and fell on hard times. Maybe you can make a difference in their lives with your abundance of riches."

"So, I can write a check and be done with this?"

Tito shook his head. "You know, I'm so sick of people thinking they can just throw money at a problem and it's supposed to be all better."

"Anyway, what am I supposed to do when I get there?"

"You will be working under Devon Harris; he'll give you your instructions and report back to me about your progress. Ms. Charles, make no mistake, if you don't do what you're supposed to do, you will be in violation of your probation agreement and you will face jail time and a hefty fine."

Marie shuddered at the thought of spending more time in jail. The one night she'd spent there had been more than enough for a lifetime. "Fine," she said. Tito handed her a folder.

"Your time sheets are in here and I need to have them in by Monday at noon or I will have to consider you in violation," he said.

Marie flipped through the folder and sighed. Maybe

Devon Harris would just sign the timesheets and let her go without actually putting in the work. Then she could focus on something much more important: rebuilding her own image. That was the best service she could give to the community. And that would show William's trifling ass that she was still a winner.

Serena smiled as Devon finished teaching the ladies at My Sister's Keeper a lesson on making pasta sauce. He was really into what he was doing, and she was proud of her friend.

"All right, ladies, I have a treat today. This is Serena Billups, one of the owners of Hometown Delights and sponsors of our fund-raiser. Serena is going to talk to us about how to present ourselves in a business situation," Devon said. "While she's talking, I'm going to can our sauce and get the lasagna ready for dinner. Let's give her a hand."

The women clapped as Serena stood in the middle of the kitchen. "Thanks for having me here," she said. "I think I want some of the lasagna."

The women laughed and Serena began her speech about business etiquette. As Devon began to line the pans, Elaine Harper walked into the kitchen. "Devon," she whispered, so as not to interrupt Serena's speech. "May I see you for a moment?"

He nodded and followed her out into the hallway. "What's going on, Mrs. Harper?"

"Well," she said. "I just got a call from the Mecklenburg County Probation Office."

"This sounds serious," he said.

"Kind of," she replied. "We're going to have a woman coming in to do some community service."

"What did she do?"

"It was a nonviolent offense," she said. "I have her file in my office. I know it's asking a lot, but you're going to be the one to make her schedule and sign her time sheets."

"That's fine, I'll just have her come in when I do. I do want to see her file, though," Devon said, thinking about Bria. The last thing he wanted was someone coming in that may have a connection to her past. She was slowly opening up to him, quietly telling him about how she'd moved to Charlotte after her mother died and her father's new girlfriend made living at home very uncomfortable. Every time he'd ask her about a boyfriend, she'd grow silent. But he did notice that she was meeting with one of the counselors from the Mecklenburg County Women's Commission.

"It's in my office," Elaine said.

"I'll follow you," he said. "How's Bria doing?"

"Oh, Devon, she is making very good strides. She's a good girl with some really big problems for someone so young."

He nodded as they walked into the office. "But," Elaine said, "these women really enjoy working with you and they trust you. I can't believe that you've been working so closely with us."

"I'm doing it for my mother," he said as she handed him the file marked MARIE CHARLES.

"Your mother?"

"She needed someone for her, and there was no one there to listen to her," he said.

Elaine nodded. "I understand," she said as Devon flipped though the file.

"DUI, huh?" he said. "Wait, is she that public-relations chick who got into trouble a few weeks ago?"

"One in the same, and the daughter of attorney Richard

Charles III. He actually represented us when we were in a dispute with some of the neighbors here about rezoning this land. He's a good man, but from all accounts, Marie is a spoiled brat."

"Well, we'll try to get some of that out of her. We have plenty of work she can do."

Elaine smiled. "Yes, there is a lot of work to do here. Have I thanked you for this fund-raiser that you're organizing? Everyone is excited about it."

"I'm excited as well," Devon said. "Maybe Marie Charles can help, since the court has ordered her to be here."

"Not a bad idea. She sure does know how to get media attention."

"Yeah, but we want to make sure that we're getting the right kind of attention," Devon said, and Elaine nodded in agreement. He waved good-bye to her and headed back to the kitchen, catching the tail end of Serena's speech—which had obviously captivated the women.

"And remember," Serena said, "a setback is just a setup for the biggest comeback." The ladies erupted in applause and Serena smiled brightly at them.

After they settled down, Devon directed the women on how to can the pasta sauce and told them to finish the lasagna. He turned to Serena as they worked and shook her hand.

"I have to say, I'm impressed."

Serena punched him on the shoulder. "You should be, jerk. Jade told me that you weren't even going to ask me to come. If Jaden hadn't gotten sick and Jade hadn't begged me to take her place, I would have left *you* hanging."

"Come on, Serena. You know I'm still not used to the kinder, gentler Serena Jacobs," Devon quipped. "I owe you and I will cook for you and Antonio. Something special and simple that you can recreate."

"Funny," she replied. "I keep telling you people, Antonio didn't marry me for my cooking. But I will take you up on your offer. Seriously though, I'm really proud of what you're doing with these women. When you were teaching them how to make the sauce, you weren't talking down to them or anything like that. This is really personal for you, isn't it?"

Devon nodded. "I think about my mother when I come here. What if my father didn't have money and she didn't have the means to get away when things started getting rough?"

Serena patted him on the shoulder. "I wonder if I wouldn't have been in a place like this if Emerson hadn't left me at the altar and we'd gotten married, but Emerson's movie failed." She shuddered and hugged herself tightly. "But for the grace of God go I," she quoted.

"I'll see you at the restaurant for dinner," he said.

"Umm, not tonight," she replied, with a naughty twinkle in her eye. "A. J.'s going fishing with Norman, so . . ."

Devon threw his hands up. "Save the details. I get it."

Serena bade the women good-bye and sauntered out of the shelter, still proving to Devon that the Serena Jacobs he knew still existed.

Chapter 5

Marie kicked off her shoes when she walked into her Uptown condo and promised herself to never take a cab again. The driver seemed to be driving with his eyes closed, barely following traffic guidelines. And then he had the gall to ask her if he could pick up another fare while she was in the car! Shivering, she grabbed her BlackBerry, which her father had insisted that she leave at home, to check her messages. Of course there was a message from her personal buyer at Neiman Marcus, asking where she was. But the next message caught her off guard. Maybe it was the bass in the caller's voice or what she'd taken as a seductive timbre that made her knees quiver and her heart jump and skip a beat. Who was this man? And, boy, did she like the sound of her name coming out of his mouth. Sitting on the edge of the sofa, Marie listened to the message again—this time hearing every word he said.

"Good evening, Marie Charles, I'm sorry to call you so late. But I just got your file from My Sister's Keeper and I understand we're going to be working together. My name is Devon Harris and I'll be supervising your community service. We should get together so that I can tell you what I need and expect from you. Please give me a call at seven-oh-four, five-five-five, two-three-four-four."

Marie pressed the End button on her BlackBerry. This was about her damned community service? Ugh! "But Devon Harris, that name sounded so familiar," she said as she lifted her iPad from the edge of her coffee table. She typed his name in her Google search menu and waited for the links to populate.

When the Web site for Devon's cooking show came up, Marie remembered where she knew him from: the Food Network and Hometown Delights. That restaurant was almost as notorious as she was, with it being the scene of a murder involving mogul Solomon Crawford, and where director Emerson Bradford lost his mind and tried to kill his ex. She clicked on a picture of Devon, drinking in his chocolate brown skin, short wavy hair, and big hands. Of course he had big hands; he was a chef and probably knew how to knead a body just like bread dough. Still, it wasn't as if they were meeting for a social engagement or to have a nice dinner. He was going to be her community service supervisor. He probably had all kinds of negative thoughts about her. *Why do I care?* she thought as she tore her eyes from his picture. It was five minutes after eight, so Marie figured it wasn't too late to return Devon's call. But did she really want to? The last thing she needed was to be judged by this man. Again, she wondered why she cared what Devon Harris thought about her. She'd never met the man. Marie dialed his number and waited for him to answer.

Devon looked down at his cell phone, trying to see if he knew who the number belonged to since a name didn't pop up with it. Shrugging his chef's jacket off, he answered the call.

"Devon Harris."

"Mr. Harris, this is Marie Charles, returning your call," the woman cooed.

Marie Charles, he thought. *Right, the chick on probation.* "Miss Charles, yes. Thank you for calling me back."

"Just call me Marie. So, you said we should get together and talk about the community service project," she said. As Devon listened to her, he had to admit, she had a hell of a sexy voice.

"We do need to go over your schedule, because I want to get you started with us at My Sister's Keeper as soon as possible. We're in the middle of a fund-raiser and I know you have a background in public relations, so . . ."

"You expect me to work for free?" Marie shot back. "I will peel potatoes in the soup kitchen, but there is no way in hell . . ."

"Hold up," Devon said. "You have to calm down. From what I understand, you have five hundred hours of community service to fill, and there is a lot of work that needs to be done, and you really don't have a choice as to what you're asked to do."

"So, you're going to take advantage of me because I have to perform community service? You do know who I am, don't you?"

Devon fought back his caustic comment. "Look, Miss Charles," he said. "You have to fulfill your community service hours, I don't care who you are. But if you think you're going to dictate how this works, then you're wrong."

He heard her suck her teeth and imagined her head wagging back and forth as she talked. "This is getting off on the wrong foot," Marie said. "I'm a little tired; it's been a long day."

"OK, then we can talk about your schedule now. I want you to get started tomorrow morning," Devon said.

She sighed into the phone. "Can we meet somewhere Uptown. Maybe the bar at the Westin?"

"Are you sure you want to go to a bar?" Devon asked snidely.

Marie mumbled under her breath before saying, "What would you suggest, Mr. Harris?"

"The Westin is fine. I can meet you there in fifteen minutes," he said. Before Devon could say another word, he heard Marie's phone click off. He glanced at his phone, shaking his head. "This is going to be a long night," he mumbled.

"Talking to yourself?" Alicia asked as she passed him in the hall. "Not a good sign."

Devon looked at her and grinned. "Where are you off to?"

"Why?" she asked when she stopped and looked at him. "You need a ride somewhere?"

"I drove today," he said. "You're dressed up, though. Hot date?"

Alicia shrugged. "I wish. Just a boring business meeting. Why were you having a conversation with yourself earlier?"

"Marie Charles."

"Who? Wait. The party girl?"

Devon nodded. "One in the same. It seems as if she's going to have to do her community service at My Sister's Keeper, and I can tell already it's going to be nothing but a headache. She had the nerve to tell me what she wants to do. She's the one under a court order."

Alicia shook her head. "Wow. Better you than me."

"We're meeting at the Westin to get her schedule together," Devon said, then groaned.

"Before you go, I do have some good news about the fund-raiser for My Sister's Keeper," Alicia said. "Concrete Jazz has agreed to play the dinner for free."

"Yes!" Devon exclaimed with a fist pump. "Shay is going to be happy about that. She had been talking to their manager about them performing here."

"She is a hell of a negotiator," Alicia said. "I spoke with Nathan, their manager, and he wasn't trying to do anything for free."

Devon nodded, then looked down at his watch. "I have to go. I'd hate to keep the princess waiting. She might leave before we get the business handled."

"Good luck," Alicia said as Devon dashed out the back door. He sped to the hotel, since he was about five minutes late for his meeting with Marie Charles. But when he arrived at the bar, it was clear that Marie was even later than he was. Of the three people sitting in the Westin, not one of them looked like the young woman he was supposed to meet.

Marie walked into the bar of the Westin and glanced around the sparse crowd until she locked eyes with a scowling Devon Harris. He looked a lot better in person than he did in his online photo. She sauntered over to him with a smile on her face. "Sorry to keep you waiting," she said to him.

"This isn't going to be a habit of yours, is it?" Devon asked as he extended his hand to her. "Devon Harris."

"I know, I've seen your show once."

"Only once?" he asked with a smirk.

Marie shrugged. "I'm not interested in cooking," she said, then waved for a bartender. Devon furrowed his brow.

"Miss Charles, I think the fact that you're twenty minutes late means we don't have time for a drink and small talk," he said.

"Excuse me?" she questioned. "I had to walk here, so I'm sorry if I didn't make this last-minute meeting in a fashion that satisfies you."

Devon slammed his hand on the bar and shook his head. "This isn't going to work. You're sitting here acting as if I'm inconveniencing you when you have to work with My Sister's Keeper because a judge told you to do so."

"And," she said, "it doesn't mean that I'm going to jump when you say so or be your freaking slave. I need something to drink."

The bartender stood a few inches away from Marie and Devon, unsure as to what to do next—pour a drink or run. Devon nodded at the bartender. "We're going to need something strong," he said. "Just keep pouring."

Marie smiled at the bartender and said, "I'll just take Cîroc red berry cosmopolitan and he's paying."

Devon rolled his eyes. The sooner he got this schedule worked out with Marie, the sooner he could get away from her. "Listen," Devon said. "I start teaching over at the shelter around nine A.M. Maybe we should go over there now so that I can show you the area where you will be working. This is serious to me and I need you to take this seriously as well."

"I'm willing to do what's expected of me," she said. "I don't want to go to jail. But, you don't have stand in judgment over me."

"Judgment?"

"I hear it in your voice," she replied. "There's more to me than what you read on the Internet."

Devon's attitude shifted from wanting to drink to showing Marie just how serious her work would be. "I don't have time to read about you and your exploits on the Internet. Let me show you what's important," he snapped, then slid off the stool. "Do you have time to take a ride with me?"

Marie sipped her drink and peered at Devon. He wasn't going to just sign her time sheets. He actually wanted her to work those five hundred hours of community service. Setting her glass aside, she rose to her feet. "Fine."

Shaking his head, Devon paid for their drinks and then led her outside. Marie walked behind him, typing on her cell phone. Devon stopped and glared at her. "Cell phones aren't going to be allowed in the kitchen," he said.

Marie looked up from her text message and offered him a plastic smile. "Sorry, but if I'm about to get into a car with you, I need to inform someone just in case I don't come back."

"Paranoid much?" Devon asked.

"You never can tell these days," she said as they approached the Mustang. "Your work at the shelter must be doing wonders for your ratings, chef with a big heart," Marie said.

Devon frowned as he opened the passenger-side door. "What I do for the women at My Sister's Keeper has nothing to do with my career."

Marie smirked and arched her right eyebrow. "Sure it doesn't. You're telling me that you're volunteering because you just have a good heart? I don't think so."

"I really don't give a damn what you think. I'm going to need you at the shelter by eight thirty," he said in a surly tone. "You can see the shelter tomorrow."

"Excuse me?" she snapped as she held on to the open door. "You got me out here and now you're dismissing me?"

Devon moved her hand from the door and closed it. "That's right. See you in the morning, and you need to be on time. You're going to help me prep my lessons and get the supplies that the women need to cook lunch to start with. I expect you to put in a full day of work and wear a hairnet," he said firmly.

Marie started to laugh. Just who did he think he was talking to? "Let's get one thing straight," she said as she slammed her hand against the door, causing Devon to cringe. "I will not let you talk to me as if I'm some common criminal, I . . ."

"No," Devon said as he threw his hand up. "You're not straightening out anything; there's a court order that says you have five hundred hours of community service to fulfill. My Sister's Keeper has opened its doors to you so that you can pay your debt to the community for whatever foolishness you've done. Show some damned respect or I will let your probation officer know that you're not in compliance. And don't you ever slam my door like that again!"

Marie narrowed her eyes at him. "You know, this probably isn't going to work. Why don't . . ."

"You want to go to jail or you want to follow the rules? I'm not one of these people who hang out at The Epi-Centre and need your approval to get on a party's guest list. Helping these women is a serious matter; if you're not going to take it seriously, then you need to find someplace else to conduct your community service," Devon said.

She folded her arms across her chest and glared at him. As angry as she wanted to be at Devon, she could not deny that he was sexy as hell. Those brown eyes would make her melt had they been meeting at a party or at the bar for another reason. The fact that he wasn't overly impressed with Marie Charles gave her a sensation that she'd never felt before. He was a chef, but he didn't have the body of a man who ate decadent food all day. He obviously spent a considerable amount of time in the gym.

"Miss Charles?" he asked, breaking into Marie's thoughts. "Are we clear?"

"Crystal," she replied after clearing her throat. "What's the address of the shelter?"

Devon handed her a pamphlet about My Sister's Keeper. "Will you need a ride in the morning?"

"No," she said. "I'll make sure I get there on time without having to walk."

Devon nodded and Marie started down the sidewalk, mumbling about how Devon should watch his tone when talking to her. She glanced over her shoulder and watched as Devon zoomed from the curb in his red sports car. "He's not all of that," she mumbled as she headed back to the bar to finish her drink and call a cab.

Devon shook his head as he got behind the wheel of his classic Mustang. Marie Charles had been everything he'd thought she'd be—arrogant, pig headed, and stuck up. But there was something he hadn't expected: She looked a lot better in person than she did on TV or in her mug shot. If he had to describe her skin, he'd say butterscotch smooth with chocolate-chip brown eyes. Though he wasn't sure if her silky shoulder length auburn hair wasn't a weave, it fit her perfectly. Especially the way her bangs skimmed her perfectly arched eyebrows. And that body, small waist, an onion booty, and curves that he'd be interested in riding if she wasn't such a wannabe diva in her own mind. So what that she was well known in Charlotte; didn't she realize that her little act only made her a big fish in a small pond? Maybe he should've told her not to come to the shelter at all and that she needed to find someplace else to do her community service. How would the women react to her? Moreover, was she going to bring that diva attitude with her? He could immediately see her clashing with Shay. And then there was Bria; she already had so much she was dealing with. Would Marie push her deeper into her shell?

Maybe Marie's bark is worse than her bite. Hopefully she will come in, do her work, and get along with the women. They could learn a lot from her, if she's willing to share, he thought as he headed to his loft. *Hopefully, this won't be the disaster that I think it will be.*

Chapter 6

Marie smiled sweetly at the cab driver and offered him a sizable tip for driving like a normal person as he stopped in front of The EpiCentre. She was only a block away from her home and decided to walk so that she could wrap her mind around her encounter with Devon. Looking up at the glowing building, her mind wandered back to the night of the party. She'd acted like a fool, and if she was honest with herself, she'd admit that she had been simply following a well-defined pattern. Self-destructive behavior. That's why she'd started dating William and accepted his engagement ring, because she knew the relationship had no chance of going anywhere. Marie was afraid of love. She didn't want to feel the pain that her father carried on his broad shoulders since her mother died. She knew that love didn't last forever. William had been a means to an end. He'd given her father the illusion of his daughter being that proper Southern woman he'd always talked about.

Truth of the matter was, Marie didn't want to work hard at love only to find herself hurt in the end. She'd ruined relationships that would've been meaningful, much to the ire of those closest to her. Adriana had labeled her as *Le saboteur* and even had a T-shirt made for her with the French saying on it.

"Marie?" Adriana said as she approached her friend. "What are you doing out here?"

"Just leaving a meeting," she said, then looked at her friend closely. Adriana was wearing a brand-new pair of Louboutins. "I guess you made it to Neiman's."

"What happened to you? We waited for . . ."

Marie shook her head and threw her hand up. "I don't even want to talk about it. I'm starting my community service in the morning."

"Wow. What will you be doing? Picking up trash or something?"

"You'd love that, wouldn't you?"

Adriana sighed and shook her head from side to side. "Are you mad at me or something? I take no pleasure in your misfortune."

"Why would I be mad? I mean, my best friend is pushing me out of the business that I created."

Adriana stroked her short curls and cocked her head to the side as Marie ranted. "That's what you think I'm doing? I'm trying to save our business, Marie. People don't want to work with us because of you. But don't you worry, I'm still lining up clients for us. You're still getting paid; just what are you angry about?"

Marie sighed. "Adriana, I'm sorry. This is new to me, being a pariah in my city. People think I endangered lives by driving drunk, and it was just an accident with a nervous little girl driving. I told Hailey I would keep her out of trouble because I thought I'd get out of this without a scratch."

"I guess you haven't heard about William," Adriana said quietly.

"What about that bastard?" Marie asked with a snort.

"He and Greta are back together. They're getting married again."

For a brief second, Marie was angry. Then she made peace with it. "Those jackasses deserve each other."

"Thank the Lord! You've come back to your senses! So, you're not going to go after them and do something else crazy, are you?"

"I don't give a damn what William does or that he's going to remarry that woman," Marie said. "I'm done with the lame men of Charlotte anyway."

"Where are you heading now? Want to grab a drink at Whisky River?"

Though Marie wanted to pump Adriana for more information about what people were saying about her, she said no. "I have to go home. The guy who's over my community service is a hard ass, and he's already laid down the law about me being late. And I have to prove to him and Richard the third that I'm trying to learn a lesson."

"That's great," Adriana said. "Want a ride?"

"Hell yes! And I hope you have some shoes for me in your trunk."

Adriana frowned. "Come on, now. Do you think I would forget my best friend?" The women headed to Adriana's car in the parking deck, but Marie wasn't thinking simply about the shoes; she couldn't get Devon Harris off her mind.

Was he really that altruistic, helping those women because it was the right thing to do? Maybe he had something going on with one of them or the director of the place. *Why do I care with whom the chef is dipping his spoon? All I have to do is perform the community service and then I'm out of there. Still, there has to be something behind why he's so dedicated to that shelter. Maybe it will be fun to uncover and expose his judgmental ass.*

"Marie," Adriana said as she popped the trunk of her car open. "Did you hear me?"

"What? Huh?"

"I said, the two boxes on the right are yours. What are you plotting over there?"

Marie shrugged as she picked up one of the shoe boxes. "I was thinking about something. You know who I met with earlier?"

"Your community service supervisor, and?"

"It was Devon Harris."

Adriana's mouth dropped open. "The Devon Harris from the Food Network? Is he as fine in person as he is on TV? I watch that show just to see his sexy behind. Nothing like a smooth black man who can cook and look that good at the same time. Between him and G. Garvin, I love cooking shows. You're lucky to be working with him."

"Lucky? To be stuck in a homeless shelter with him? He was insufferable," Marie said. "I don't care how unbelievably sexy he is, I'm not going to allow him to treat me as if I'm some derelict."

"A derelict? Well, I guess you can understand why he would feel that way," Adriana said.

Marie shot her friend a chilly look. "That's not the point. He was talking to me as if I was some hood rat with a mile-long criminal record. I'm Marie Charles, he'd better recognize it."

"That's right, so you have to show him who you are and who knows what will happen after that. Knowing you, he'll be eating out of your hand once this thing is over." Adriana and Marie climbed into the car.

"I want to uncover why he's so into taking care of the people at this shelter. Now, he claims that he's not doing it for the ratings on his show, but no one is that caring. Not in Charlotte and not for nothing. So, the more he treats me like garbage, I'm going to dig until I find his secret."

"What if there isn't a secret?"

"Then maybe I'll let him buy me dinner," Marie said with a laugh.

"Better still, let him cook you dinner," Adriana said. "So, how are you going to find out what his secret is, Nancy Drew?"

"I figure something out," she said. "Even if I have to be sugary sweet to him."

"You, sugary sweet? Please let someone have a video camera around when this happens."

They took the short drive to Marie's home in silence, and Marie tried to wrap her mind around what Devon Harris was really doing. She had to get her plan ready, arrive at the shelter on time, cozy up to Devon, and pretend that she was interested in whatever was going on there and watch how he interacted with the women. Then, if there was something unsavory going on, she'd use it to her advantage.

"How long will you be at the shelter?" Adriana asked when she pulled up to Marie's building.

"Until after lunch. Why, what's up?"

"Well, we need to talk about some of the campaigns we still have, and we need to caress some of our clients, who Greta's trying to poach."

"What?"

Adriana nodded. "I know we can't have you out front being the face of the company right now, but I think you need to help me make some of the phone calls."

"Glad you've admitted that you can't do this without me. I'll call you when I'm done at the shelter and we can get busy. I'll be damned if Greta actually takes something from me that I actually want."

Marie gave Adriana a brief hug and then headed inside to get herself together for her first day with Devon.

When Devon woke up the next morning, he realized that he needed to stop by the restaurant before heading to the shelter, because he had to take a look at the setup for the show. When it came to doing live shows, Devon was a bit OCD. Today he would be cooking in front of an audience for the first time since he'd been filming the show at Hometown Delights. He was thankful that Alicia, Serena, and Jade were as excited about the filming as he was. Of course, Serena wanted a seat in the front row, although he wasn't sure why because she still couldn't cook.

Now he was regretting that he'd told Marie to come to the shelter today for her community service, since he'd told the ladies who took his class that they could come to the taping. How did he forget that? It was probably because Marie Charles had pissed him off with her haughty attitude and her accusation of him volunteering for ratings. He didn't understand why he was so offended by Marie's charges. Serena had suggested the exact same thing when he first told them that he'd be working at the shelter. Alicia had told him that he was working at the shelter because of his poor dating luck. There was something about Marie, though, something that infuriated him as much as it turned him on. She was sexy, there was no denying it. But she was everything that he was trying to get away from. Now, he was going to be working with her every day. If he was lucky, she'd prove him wrong and not be the diva that he assumed she was.

He took a quick shower, dressed, and headed to the restaurant to check things out. Looking at his watch once he entered the restaurant, he saw that he was going to be late getting to the shelter if there were problems on the set. The crew, to Devon's pleasure, had everything under control, turning half of the bar into a cooking area.

"What's up, guys?" Devon said to the crew.

"Hey, Devon," the producer, Noah Clark, said. "Came to check things out, huh?"

"Yes, I can't remember the last time I cooked in front of an audience, and I have some special guests coming." Devon looked out at the seating arrangements. "We need to add some more seats."

"Yes, sir," Noah said, then spoke into his radio for someone to bring chairs. Devon walked around the side of the bar and checked out the cooking equipment. Everything was in place and he was worrying for nothing. Glancing down at his watch, he saw that if he left now, he'd make it to the shelter on time. "Noah, I'm leaving this in your capable hands. But I need another electric skillet over here."

Noah shot him a thumbs-up sign as Devon headed out the door. When he hopped into his car, he ran right into a traffic jam. This wasn't going to look good. *Why am I worried about impressing her?* he thought as he sat in the traffic.

Marie stood in front of My Sister's Keeper with her hands clenched in angry fists. This man lectured her about being on time and she was five minutes late and he still wasn't there. She rocked back on her Jimmy Choo heels as her resentment grew. "That jerk," she groaned as she started pacing back and forth. "He'd better give me credit for every minute that he was late."

A young woman walked toward Marie and stopped short when she seemed to realize that she didn't recognize her. "Ma'am," she questioned as she gave Marie a cool once-over. "Are you lost?"

"No," Marie said. "I'm here to do some consulting with Devon Harris, but he seems to be running late."

The woman looked down at her watch. "He is a few minutes late. Would you like to come inside and wait? All you had to do was ring the doorbell and they would've let you in."

"So, you work here?" Marie asked.

"No. I live here," she replied as she punched a code in the front door and opened it.

"But you look so . . ."

"Honey, what did you think we were going to look like here?"

Marie honestly couldn't answer that question because all she had been focused on was seeing Devon again. She glanced at the woman again. She didn't look like what Marie thought homeless women would look like: tattered clothes, dirty and matted hair, and holey shoes. This woman looked like someone she'd pass on the street, neatly dressed, hair pulled back in a ponytail, and she was smiling. Marie didn't expect to see smiling faces in the shelter, that was for sure. The woman at the front desk motioned for Marie to sign the visitors' registry.

"I'm here to work with Devon Harris," she said.

"Oh, you're the lady who's on probation? I'm Lydia Thompson; I run the front desk. Mr. Harris called and said he's sorry that he's running late." Lydia opened the desk drawer and handed Marie a folder. "This is for your time sheets so that you won't lose them."

"When is he getting here?" Marie asked. "I don't have all day to wait for him."

"The wait is over; I'm right here," Devon said from behind her. His baritone voice made her shiver. Whirling around, she drank in his wickedly sexy image clad in a white T-shirt showing off his sculpted arms and his blue jeans that hugged his thighs. Boxers or briefs? she wondered as her eyes roamed his body.

"Well, you're late," she said, her voice taking on a breathless tone.

"Yes, and I apologize, but we have a busy day. Our lesson is going to be short today because I'm taking the ladies to a taping of my show. I'm going to need you to help with transportation."

"Excuse me?"

Devon motioned for her to follow him into the kitchen area. "First Baptist West is going to provide a van and driver. You can come along and observe and make sure we get to the restaurant and return here without losing anyone."

Marie folded her arms. "So, how long am I going to be here today? I do have work to do, work that I get paid for."

"Miss Charles, you're scheduled to be here for five hours today. You've been here all of twenty minutes and you're trying to leave?"

"You don't know how long I've been here, since you've just arrived."

Devon placed his hand on Marie's shoulder and she felt her skin sizzle. "Can we not make this difficult?"

Before she could reply, a group of women entered the kitchen. "Good morning, Devon," one of the younger women said as the other ladies sized Marie up.

"Who is this?" another woman asked with a nod toward Marie. Devon looked up at the women and smiled.

"Ladies, I want to introduce you to Marie Charles," he said. "She's going to be helping us for a few months. I think it would be nice for us to introduce ourselves."

"I'm Shay," said a woman with her hair pulled back in a ponytail.

A younger girl with a skeptical look on her face nodded at Marie. "I'm Bria."

The other six women introduced themselves as Andrea, Rita, Yolanda, Deidra, Skylar, and Thelma. Marie smiled and waved at the ladies. She had to admit, they were nothing like what she'd expected.

"So," Skylar asked. "You're a chef or a business woman like Serena?"

"I'm in . . ."

"She's here to do whatever we need," Devon interjected. "And since we're going to the restaurant for the taping of my show, we'd better get busy with our lunch."

Marie rolled her eyes at him, but held her tongue. Thelma, who was the oldest of the women, tapped Marie on the shoulder. "I hope you have another pair of shoes. It gets pretty messy and wet in here."

"I'm sure I'll be fine," Marie replied as she glanced down at her four-inch heels. Thelma shrugged and headed over to her work space. Devon waved for Marie.

Sighing, she crossed over to him. "Yes?"

"I need you to get the seasoning tray, the pots, and . . ." He glanced down at her feet. "You're not going to make it in those shoes."

"Well, what am I supposed to do? These are the only shoes I have with me."

It didn't take long for Marie to find out that four-inch heels on a slippery kitchen floor were a bad idea. She'd slipped when she put the basket of vegetables in the middle of the counter. She'd turned her right ankle when Devon told her to get the knives.

"Are you all right?" he asked her when she limped over to him with the silverware. He wiped his hands on his soiled apron, then scooped Marie up in his arms in one quick motion. "Excuse me, ladies," he said to his students as he carried Marie out of the kitchen.

"I can walk," Marie said quietly as she felt her heart beating like a steel drum.

"I just want to make sure," he said as he sat her on an ottoman in the lobby. "Hold your leg out."

"You're a doctor now?" she asked, but did what she was told.

"I've nursed many ankles of women wearing ridiculous shoes in my kitchen," he replied as he gently squeezed her ankle, searching for a knot. "You're going to have to get sensible shoes while working here. I think you should be fine for the rest of the day, since we're about to head to the restaurant."

"So, you keep your women in heels in your kitchen while you cook at home? Because OSHA would shut you down if you did that in the restaurant," Marie said. "That's pretty sexist."

"First of all, when I cook for a woman, she doesn't enter the kitchen," he said. "I just happen to work with hardheaded women like yourself. Tomorrow, wear flats."

"Do I look like I own a pair of flats?" she quipped. As Devon gave her a slow once-over and offered her a sly smile, Marie felt a heated explosion between her thighs that made her look away from his brown eyes.

"Yeah, you don't wear flats," he said. "You're probably five foot nothing and just too afraid to let people see the real you."

"What's that supposed to mean?" she asked with one sculpted eyebrow raised.

"Just what I said. Who comes to do community service in high heels, expensive clothes, and a fresh hairdo? No one needs to be impressed by how you look."

Marie folded her arms across her chest and glared at him, feelings of desire for this man waning slightly. "A cook, a doctor, and a dime-store psychologist. Is there anything that you don't do?"

Devon shook his head from side to side. "You know what I don't do: deal with diva attitudes," he said. "Since you can walk, why don't you head across the street and see if the van is ready?" He turned and went to the kitchen, and Marie felt as if she'd been dismissed by her principal. Men didn't treat her this way. They were oftentimes in awe of her and leapt to do her bidding. Who did Devon Harris think he was?

Chapter 7

When Devon and his crew arrived at Hometown Delights, he smiled at the excitement bubbling through the ladies from My Sister's Keeper. Even Bria was showing signs of enthusiasm, despite trying to keep her face neutral.

"Hey, Devon," his sous-chef, Daniella King, said when she greeted him at the door. "Are these the ladies I'm taking care of today?"

"Yes," he said, then pointed to Marie. "She's going to be your assistant for the taping."

Marie rolled her eyes, but didn't say a word as Daniella crossed over to her and extended her hand. "Hi, I'm Daniella."

"Marie Charles," she replied with a limp handshake.

Daniella gave her a questioning look. "All right," she said. "Well, let's get busy. Chef is going to have a great show. So many people have been trying to get in here."

Devon hoped Marie and Daniella would be able to handle the seating arrangements because he needed to focus on his cooking. "All right, guys," he said. "I'm going to leave you to it."

He rushed down the hall to change into his chef's jacket

and get cleaned up for the demonstration. As he headed for the kitchen to get his utensils, Serena stopped him.

"Devon, is that Marie Charles in the audience out there?" she asked.

He sighed and nodded. "That's her. She's working with me at My Sister's Keeper."

"Get the hell out of here," Serena exclaimed. "And here I thought all she could do was party. Wait a minute, you mean she's doing her court-ordered community service at the shelter."

"Yeah, look, we can talk about that later. You got your front-row seat, right?"

She nodded. "And you better not say a word about my cooking on your show, or I am going to throw grits at you."

"As long as they aren't hot, bring it on," he quipped. "You probably can't even cook grits."

Serena shrugged, pouted, then sauntered down the hall while Devon laughed at her. The show's director ran over to him. "Devon, five minutes!" Monique exclaimed. "It's pretty crowded out there. This is going to be great. Like Emeril's old shows."

"Hopefully better," Devon said. "I don't have a catch-phrase."

"Good, because I wanted to 'bam' him after hearing it a million times; now let's move," Monique said as she placed her hand on Devon's back and led him to the front of the restaurant. As soon as the audience saw him, they erupted in applause.

Monique gave him the signal to start the show, and he smiled at his adoring public. "Thank you for being here today on *Dining with Devon*. I'm your chef, Devon Harris," he said, full of energy. "Today, we're going to combine two of my favorite things, fish and shrimp."

* * *

Marie watched Devon intently, not because she was interested in what he was cooking or his explanation of the different flavors he was mixing up for his marinade. She was just captivated by his passion. If he was this passionate about cooking, what would he be like with a woman? She watched as he rolled a filet of tilapia in bread crumbs, paying attention to his fingers as they stroked the fish. How would her breasts feel as he brushed his thumbs against her taut nipples the way he did the fish? Would he use his tongue along with his fingers to make her cry out in pleasure?

Shay broke into Marie's wanton thoughts when she pinched her on the arm. "Are you all right over there with all of that moaning?" she whispered. "Hungry much?"

"Well," Marie said, "I did skip breakfast."

"Shh," Bria admonished Marie and Shay. "Some of us are trying to learn something."

Marie threw her hands up and turned her attention back to Devon's big hands. Shay leaned into Marie and whispered, "You don't care about Devon's cooking, do you? I see how you're looking at him."

"What? No," Marie said quietly. "I'm going to try this recipe."

"Whatever."

Bria turned around and glared at Shay, who rolled her eyes in response. Marie crossed her legs and stroked her ankle, remembering how Devon had touched her after she'd twisted her ankle in the kitchen at the shelter. *Stop it,* she thought. *The only reason you're looking at this man like this is because it's been so long since you've actually had some satisfaction in the bedroom.*

William didn't know how to do anything remotely satis-factory.

"All right," Devon said, his silky voice causing Marie to snap her head up and lock eyes with him. "I need a volunteer because this dish is so easy, even the most novice cook can make it." He pointed at Serena, and Marie felt a slight twinge of jealousy, despite the fact that she knew Serena and Devon worked together. She also knew Serena was married since she'd followed Emerson Bradford's trial for the attempted murder of Serena, but she wanted to be up there with him. Close enough to inhale his masculine scent and feel those magic fingers dancing across her hand as she rolled the fish like Serena was doing.

"Now, Serena," Devon said. "Was that so hard?"

"You know, I don't like you right now," she quipped.

Devon laughed. "Serena is a newlywed and one of the owners of the restaurant, so she doesn't do much of this in the kitchen," he said as he directed her to drop the fish in the pan. "Your husband will thank me when he comes home to a hot meal."

"You're lucky we're on TV," she replied as she dropped a second piece of fish in the pan. Marie crossed and uncrossed her legs as Devon squeezed a lemon over the shrimp he had simmering in another pan. As he spoke about the flavor that would come from adding the juice, she watched his lips, taking note of how full they were. When he picked up a piece of shrimp with a fork and took it into his mouth, Marie closed her eyes and imagined what it would feel like to have his lips closed around hers.

The director signaled for a break, and it couldn't have come fast enough for Marie, who bolted from her seat and went outside to catch her breath. She paced back and forth in the parking lot, ignoring the pain in her ankle as she struggled to bring her hormones under control. *He's just a man and it's his job to be charming when he's on TV,* she thought as she continued to pace.

"Hey," Shay said as she walked outside with a cigarette in her hand. "Are you all right?"

"Yes, just needed some air," Marie said. "You know those things are bad for you."

Shay lit up anyway and shrugged. "There are a lot of things that are bad for me. Those shoes, as sharp as they are, will kill your knees one day."

Marie looked down at her feet and nodded. "Touché. May I ask you a question?"

Shay blew a plume of smoke upward. "Sure."

"I'm not trying to be disrespectful when I say this, but how did you end up in the shelter?"

Shay flicked the ashes from her cigarette and looked at Marie. "Well," she said, "I married the wrong man. When he decided to leave me, it seemed as if everything started going downhill from there. When we were married, he was the primary provider, I worked for First Union. Then they merged with Wachovia and my job was no longer needed. I was laid off, living in a house with a mortgage I couldn't afford on my own."

"Wow. So, what did you do?" Marie asked.

"I moved out, got a job at another bank, and then all hell broke loose in the industry," Shay said as she shook her head. Cocking her head to the side, she looked at Marie. "Not the story you expected, huh? Thought I was a former crack head or something?"

Marie didn't want to say yes, but that had been what she'd been thinking. "I just . . ."

"It's all right, a lot of people hear 'homeless' and think drugs, prostitution, and forget that anyone could find themselves in my shoes at any time. Nothing is promised."

Marie nodded. "You're right," she said. "Nothing is promised. Your family couldn't help you?"

Shay snorted and took a deep drag of her cigarette. "My family and I haven't spoken in over fifteen years. Even if I had reached out to them for help, they wouldn't have helped me. My father is a pastor, and he didn't approve of my lifestyle."

"Your lifestyle?"

"He didn't approve of my husband, nor the fact that I had an abortion," Shay revealed. "When he threw me out, I told myself that I would never ask him to help me with anything."

"But . . ."

Shay threw her hand up. "I wish things had turned out differently for me. I wish that I had a home and supportive family, but I'm getting back on my feet and making my own way. I'm learning how to be a chef from one of the most world-renowned chefs around. Things are not as bad as they could be."

"I think it's amazing you can find something positive in your situation," Marie said.

Shay laughed. "I guess you think having to volunteer at the shelter is pretty difficult. Probably the worst thing that ever happened to you."

"Well," she said with a shrug.

"You're lucky and I hope you know that. So many times, we take life for granted until something happens and makes you look at what's really important. I'm going back inside, you coming?"

"In a minute," Marie said. She watched Shay return inside and thought about life without her father. So many times he should've turned his back on her after antics that she pulled, but he didn't. Maybe it was time for her to change her ways.

Marie walked into the restaurant as the filming of Devon's show wrapped and the audience gave him a standing ovation. She watched him as he shook hands with his fans and took pictures with many of them. Devon's smile made Marie melt, made her think of ways she could make him smile. Too bad he simply saw her as a troublemaker.

Devon glanced at Marie, wondering why she was staring at him intently. Figuring that she was pissed off about how long it had taken to complete the filming of the show, he winked at her and continued taking pictures with his fans. *Was that a smile he saw on her face?* he wondered when he glanced at her. Marie was pretty when she smiled. Hell, she was pretty when she scowled, but that attitude of hers. He noticed that she and Shay were talking and smiling at each other. That was interesting. Maybe Marie wasn't as bad as he had originally thought. Shay didn't take well to strangers, but she and Marie were talking as if they were old friends.

"Devon," Alicia said as she nudged him in his ribs. "Are you listening to me?"

"What?" he replied. Alicia followed his gaze to where Marie was standing. She laughed quietly.

"So, what's that all about?" Alicia asked.

"Just watching how she interacts with the ladies from My Sister's Keeper," he said. "Stop trying to read into things."

"I saw how you were looking at Marie Charles, and I'm sure that it had nothing to do with the ladies you work with. You're starting to like her," Alicia teased.

"No, I'm not," he said. "I'm just impressed that she's getting along with the ladies."

"And how are you two getting along?" she asked.

"Today is our first day working together," he replied. "So, I can't answer that. But whatever you're thinking, stop it."

"OK," Alicia said. "If that's how you're playing it."

"I have to get the ladies back to My Sister's Keeper. Do you have some information for me about the fund-raiser?"

Alicia reached into her purse and handed him an invitation. "I'm going to send these to some of the businesses around the city. People who probably won't show up but will make a donation; they're going out this week."

Devon hugged Alicia excitedly. "That's great. I can't wait for this event to happen and see how much money we can raise for these women."

"I'm glad you're excited about this, but I still think you want something extra with Marie. I know that look."

"What look?"

Alicia folded her arms across her chest. "The same look you gave Kandace in college before you asked her out for the first time."

"Whatever," he said as he took his chef's jacket off and draped it across his arm. "I'm going to change and check on the kitchen staff."

"And I'm going to talk to Marie," Alicia said, then walked away.

"Don't do that," he called out. But Alicia ignored him and crossed over to Marie. Devon stopped in his tracks and shook his head as he watched Alicia place her hand on Marie's shoulder to get her attention.

"Hi, Marie. I'm Alicia Michaels, one of the owners of Hometown Delights."

Marie, who'd been watching the conversation between

Alicia and Devon, gave her a cool once-over before extending her hand to her. "Nice to meet you."

"Same here. I've heard a lot about you, but we've never met," she said. "And we do a lot of the same things."

"Excuse me?" Marie asked, convinced that Alicia and Devon had something other than a business relationship. "What do you mean by that?"

"You run M&A Events, right? I'm handling marketing for the restaurant while Kandace Crawford is out," Alicia said, raising her eyebrow at Marie's defensive tone.

"Oh, right," she said. "I guess marketing this place is easy with Devon on board with you guys."

"He does make a lot of people forget some of the less appetizing things that have happened here," Alicia said honestly.

"There have been some nasty events here," she said.

Alicia nodded. "Hopefully, that's all in the past."

"You and Devon seem close," Marie said, struggling to keep her voice cool.

"Yes, we've known each other for years," she replied. "So, how are you enjoying working with him?"

Marie tried to hide her smile, but Alicia saw it. "Today is my first day working with Devon, but I'm sure it will be interesting."

Alicia smiled. "I bet it will be. I hope you'll come by for dinner one day," she said. "I'm sure you'll get a seat at the chef's table."

"I will do that," Marie replied.

Devon crossed over to them, hoping that Alicia wasn't asking Marie the same questions that she'd asked him.

"Excuse me," Devon said. "Marie, can you get the ladies together so that I can give them a tour of the kitchen?"

"Sure," she said with a tight smile as she noticed the

glances he and Alicia exchanged. Was there something going on between them? As she gathered the women together, Marie watched Alicia and Devon talking. She was convinced that they were sleeping together. But when he jogged over to her, smiling as he placed his hand on her shoulder, and said, "Thanks, Marie. You've been a big help today," all she could think about was how much she'd love to sleep with him.

Chapter 8

After Devon showed the women from My Sister's Keeper his actual work environment, he allowed them to help with some of the prep work for dinner, which they loved. When he saw Marie leaning against the wall, watching with a slight smile on her lips, he crossed over to her. "Not the excitement that you're used to, huh?" he asked quietly.

"Nope, but it's amazing how excited the ladies are about cooking. How long have you been working with My Sister's Keeper?" she asked.

"About six months," he said.

"They've taken a liking to you and obviously have learned a lot from your lessons," Marie said. "That says a lot about you."

"What does it say?"

"That you're actually a man who does something to help other people just because. I thought you might have said something about them being in the audience and your volunteering with the shelter during the taping, and you didn't. If you were one of my clients, I might have suggested that you do that."

"I'm not in the business of exploiting people, I told you that."

"And," she said, "I didn't believe you. People don't usually prove me wrong."

Devon took a slight bow. "Glad that I could," he said with a laugh. "We're going to head back to the shelter, but your time is up. So, if you want to head home . . ."

"No," she said. "I need to talk to Shay about something before I leave."

Devon nodded and then walked over to the women, telling them that they were getting ready to wrap things up. Just like the professionals, the women washed their equipment, placed the clean knives in their proper places, and headed for the van. Marie walked behind them slowly, her feet throbbing and her ankle hurting even more. Devon noticed her slow gait. "Hey," he called out. "Are you all right?"

"My feet and my ankle need some serious rest," she replied. Devon scooped her up in his arms, and once again her heartbeat increased tenfold.

"Those shoes are going to be the death of a generation of women." He laughed. Marie instinctively leaned her head on his shoulder, all the while thinking, *What in hell am I doing?*

Devon sat Marie on the front row of the van and then took the seat beside her as the driver climbed behind the wheel and started the van. "Let me take a look at your ankle," he said, reaching out for her leg.

Marie held her leg out to him, and he noticed that her ankle was swelling. "I think you need to go to the hospital," he said. "After we drop the ladies off, I'm taking you to the hospital for an X-ray."

"No, I'm fine," she said, thinking that she needed to get to her meeting with Adriana about the calls that she was supposed to make. But when Devon touched her ankle and a ripple of pain tore through her body, she began to warm to the idea of going to the hospital. "All right," she said. "Damn, that hurts."

"I hope it isn't broken and that you've learned a lesson."

"A lesson?"

"Yes, sensible shoes," he admonished. Marie couldn't help but watch his lips and wonder what it would be like to have them pressed against hers.

"Is everything all right up here?" Shay asked when she saw Devon holding Marie's ankle.

"No, she twisted her ankle and it's swelling," Devon said. Shay looked at her ankle and nodded.

"That might just be broken," Shay said, her voice filled with concern. "Marie, how do you feel?"

"It only hurts when I walk or when it's touched," Marie replied.

"If you'd said something, I would've given you some ice to put on your ankle during the taping," Devon said. "I'm going to take her to the hospital after we drop you guys off."

Shay nodded and then winked at Marie. "Hope you feel better," she said.

"Thanks," Marie replied. When Shay returned to her seat, Marie pulled out her cell phone and called Adriana to tell her that she wasn't going to make it in today. When she pulled the phone out of her purse, it tumbled to the floor of the van, and Devon leaned down and picked up the phone, his fingers brushing across her thigh as he retrieved the phone. Tingles vibrated through her body and made her heart beat like a Congo drum. He handed her the phone and smiled. Marie held the phone, forgetting why she'd been reaching for it to begin with.

"Thanks," she said quietly.

"No problem," he said, brushing his hand across her knee and resting it there. Marie inhaled sharply and closed her eyes. "Are you all right?" Devon asked.

"Yes," she replied, opening her eyes in time to see that the van had arrived at My Sister's Keeper.

Devon told Marie to sit tight in the van when it came to a stop. He and the ladies hopped out of the van. Marie watched him jog over to his car. She waited nervously, her body still tingling from his accidental touch. Since she was alone, she was able to think, and finally, she remembered that she was supposed to call Adriana. "Where are you?" her friend asked instead of saying hello. "I thought you would've been here hours ago."

"Something came up," she replied. "Or rather, went down."

"Ugh, Marie, do I really want to hear this?" Adriana groaned.

"While I was at the shelter, I twisted my ankle. Now it's swelling and Devon is taking me to the hospital."

"Hmm, is this something you did on purpose?"

"Hell no! I scuffed my Jimmy Choos. Now, I may do a lot of things for attention, ruining shoes is not one of them."

"I'm surprised you didn't call nine-one-one when you saw the scuff marks, and have medics rush you to Neiman Marcus," Adriana said with a laugh.

"Glad you find this amusing," Marie said as she glanced out the window and watched the classic red Mustang pull up beside the van. "Look, I have to go."

"Marie, I hope your ankle and, more importantly, your shoes will be all right," Adriana said. "Call me when you leave the hospital and I'll bring you something from Dish and we can talk about what you missed today. That is, if you don't get a special meal from Devon Harris."

"Mmm-hmm," Marie said absentmindedly as Devon opened the door and scooped her into his arms. She hung up the phone and wrapped her arms around his neck.

"And before you say that you could walk," he said, "just know that it's a risk I don't think you should take."

"As much as my ankle is throbbing, I'm not going to argue at all," she said as he sat her in the passenger seat of his car. "I will say one thing: I never took you for a Ford man."

"Come on," Devon said as he slipped behind the steering wheel. "This car is more than a Ford; this is a classic. Feel that leather, soft and supple, just like a woman's cheek."

Marie stroked the seat despite herself and then she burst into laughter. "What is it with men comparing cars to women all the time?"

"Because," Devon said, "nothing drives us crazier than a beautiful woman or a fast car."

"Is that so?"

"Don't tell anyone I told you that. I broke all kinds of man code revealing that bit of information."

Marie stretched her leg out and smiled. "What's in it for me to keep this a secret? Do you know how many women would love to have that information? So, what happens when you see a beautiful woman driving a fast car?"

"That," he said as he turned onto Trade Street, "I'm not telling you."

"No fair," she quipped. "You tell me a secret, I'll share one."

"Maybe another time," Devon replied as he pulled into the emergency room driveway of Presbyterian Hospital. He hopped out of the car, crossed over to the passenger side, and lifted Marie from the car. She started to protest, to tell him that she could walk the short distance to the emergency room entrance, but she just relished feeling his arms holding her.

They entered the emergency room and a nurse rushed over to them with a wheelchair. "What happened?" she asked, looking from Marie to Devon. "Aren't you Devon Harris?"

"Yes," he said. "Miss Charles twisted her ankle and it's swelling."

The nurse nodded and wheeled Marie to triage. "Let's get some paperwork filled out and then a doctor will see you," she said to Marie while smiling at Devon. "So, how did you twist your ankle?"

Marie twisted her head to the side. "Are you talking to me or him?" she snapped.

The nurse looked down at Marie. "Sorry," she said. "Anyway, how did this happen?"

"I slipped in the kitchen," she said.

Devon pointed to her feet. "Wearing those shoes," he said.

The nurse looked at Marie's Jimmy Choos. "Nice. But definitely not shoes you should wear in the kitchen."

"I know that now," Marie mumbled, and Devon stroked her shoulder.

The nurse handed Marie an admission form and a pen, then turned her attention to Devon. "I watch your show every day. You look a lot better in person. I love Hometown Delights," she said.

Marie cleared her throat and held the clipboard out to the nurse, who was starstruck beyond belief. "Excuse me," Marie exclaimed. "I'm done."

The nurse tore her eyes away from Devon and gave Marie a perfunctory smile. "All right," she said. "A doctor will be with you shortly." Devon gripped the back of Marie's wheelchair and pushed her out into the waiting area.

"Does that happen a lot?" Marie asked once they were out of the nurse's earshot.

"What?"

"Women fawning all over you? You know why you're every woman's dream?" she asked. "The way you guys feel about women and fast cars, that's how we women feel about men who cook and do dishes."

Devon laughed, thinking how many times he'd heard that. "I hope you don't think that counts as your secret."

"Why doesn't it?"

"You think I haven't heard that before?"

Marie shrugged. "Maybe not," she said. "But it is a secret, so it should count."

"Nope."

She pouted for a second and then smiled at him. "You know, we could be in here for hours. You don't have to stay here. I'm sure you have something better to do."

"If I did, I'd be doing it," he said. "I can't let you get hurt on the first day. We're going to need you at the shelter."

Marie nodded, secretly wishing that Devon was there with her because he was simply concerned about her injury. But why would she expect him to have genuine feelings about her, especially after the rocky start they had?

Devon watched Marie as she sat in silence. He wondered if he had been wrong about her being a wannabe diva. Then again, she was in pain, and injury changed everyone's attitude. Still, he was able to drink in every detail about the ebony beauty now. Her skin reminded him of his favorite brand of chocolate, Domori Puertofino. Her kisses were rich and sweet like the chocolate he used in his famous *gâteau d'amoureux*, or lovers' cake. He created the decadent cake while in Paris studying with famed Parisian chocolatier Michel Chaudun, who had taught him how to use all kinds of chocolate, especially dark chocolate. Paris had been on his mind a lot lately. Ever since his agent told him that there may be a chance for him to return to the city he loved because the Food Network in France was looking to expand their original programming. Until there was a concrete offer, he wasn't going to say anything to the ladies at Hometown Delights.

"Is everything all right over there?" she asked. "You're mighty quiet."

"Was thinking about something," he said, looking directly into her dark eyes.

"Are you sharing?"

"Well," he began, "you seem like a really nice girl. So, how is it that you end up in so much trouble?"

Marie bristled momentarily, wondering if he was trying to pass judgment on her. No, she wasn't a sugary-sweet woman who needed saving. Better yet, she didn't want to believe that's who she was. Marie's antics were over the top and—according to her father—ridiculous. But she was simply trying to break out of Richard's shadow, something he didn't understand. Maybe that was why she dated jerks like William, jumped in the fountain in the nude, and partied like a rock star. There was no maybe about it. That's exactly why she did what she did. As she focused her thoughtful gaze on Devon, she simply shrugged. "I just go about doing things differently," she said. "Not everyone agrees with what I do."

"Parents?" he asked, fully understanding where she was coming from.

"Father," she said. "My dad doesn't think what I do is a real job, and he definitely doesn't like how I grab attention and headlines." Marie laughed hollowly. "But if you don't make a big splash, you just get ignored."

"That's not true. And you don't need that kind of attention."

Marie cocked her head to the side. "I'm not trying to be rude, but why do you think Hometown Delights is full every night? Two reasons: you and the bad press."

"I'd like to think that the food and the service have more to do with our success than the unfortunate incidents that took place at the restaurant," Devon said as he folded his arms across his chest.

"Well, Alicia invited me for dinner, so I'll have to give you my assessment after I find out if I can walk without pain," she said.

"Wait a minute, Charlotte's it girl has never been to Hometown Delights? Now that doesn't seem right," he quipped. "Let me know when you plan to come, and I'll roll out the chef's table for you."

"Wow, that's nice of you," she said. "I think I owe you an apology."

"You think?"

Marie shrugged and nodded. "I have to admit, I wasn't very open to working with you and My Sister's Keeper when we met yesterday. And I thought you were doing this because you had some secret motive behind it, but watching you today, I see I was wrong."

Devon smirked and shook his head. "There is a reason those ladies are important to me," he said.

"Really?"

He nodded and sighed. Before he could say anything else, the nurse called Marie's name and Devon wheeled her over to the examination room. "Maybe I'll tell you about it over dinner one day," he whispered.

She turned around and smiled, secretly hoping that day came sooner rather than later.

* * *

Two hours later, Marie found out that she had a high ankle sprain, nothing super serious, but she would have to put a brake on wearing heels. That meant she had to go shoe shopping, because Marie didn't own a shoe with a heel under three inches high. The nurse practitioner wrapped her ankle in a tight Ace bandage and handed her a pair of crutches.

"You're lucky it's not broken," the nurse had said as she wrapped Marie's wounded ankle. "Why in the world would you think that you could work in a kitchen with these ridiculously high shoes on?"

"Well, I didn't have any real intentions of working," Marie had replied. When she'd been wheeled back into the waiting room, her shoes stuffed into her Coach satchel and crutches resting on her shoulder, Devon rose to his feet and crossed over to her.

"You didn't break it, did you?" he asked as he took her crutches from her shoulder and helped her out of the chair.

"No, thank goodness," she said. "But I did learn one thing."

"What's that?" Devon asked.

"I'm going to have to do some serious shoe shopping," she said. "Especially if someone is going to be working me so hard in the kitchen."

"Yes," the nurse said. "Because these shoes are not for working; please remind her of that when she gets dressed tomorrow."

"I would if . . . OK," Devon said, rather than explaining his complex situation with Marie. "We'll make sure that she does the right thing tomorrow."

Marie nodded and gripped the crutches, but once again, Devon scooped her up in his arms and carried her out to the car. "There's no way you can walk on crutches and that sky-high shoe," he said when she cast a questioning look at him.

"But I'm going to have to learn how to use the crutches, and I have to get into my condo," she said.

"Tomorrow," he said. "Tonight, you have me."

Marie shivered, wishing that she could have him—naked, deep inside her, and making her scream with pleasure. But how did she know that it would be good? She looked down at the sizable hands holding her and thought about how he kneaded the bread on the one show she'd watched. Would he handle her body that way? Touch her softly and firmly at the same time?

"Thank you," she said when she found her voice. "But I'm sure you have something else you could be doing this evening."

"I thought we'd been over this already," he said as he walked over to his car.

"I don't want to hold you up from anything or anyone."

"Smooth," he said. "If you have something to ask me, then just ask."

"All right," she replied. "What's up with you and Alicia?"

"What? Me and Alicia are old friends," he said. "There is absolutely nothing going on with us. Why would you think so?"

She shrugged, happy but cautious about what was going on with the two of them. They seemed very close, and she wasn't sure that there wasn't more to the story that he wasn't telling. "You two seemed as if you were very close and I was just wondering."

"I used to date her best friend," he said. "And you know how you women are about things like that."

"So, you do want to date her?" Marie asked, or rather,

stated. "I could tell by the way you two were joking around that there was history there or maybe something more."

"Whatever," he said with a laugh. "Alicia is like that annoying little sister from *What's Happening!!*"

"I wish I had siblings," she said. "Maybe my father wouldn't need me to do the right thing all the time."

"So, you want siblings so that you could be the official black sheep of the family? What would your mother think about that?"

Marie sucked her bottom lip in. She hadn't thought about her mother in years, hadn't thought about what her mother would think about some of the things that she'd done. She knew for sure that she would not approve of many—none—of them. Marie simply looked at him and remained silent.

They rode in an uncomfortable silence to Marie's uptown home. She glanced at him as he pulled into the parking garage. "Thank you for bringing me home, but I think I got it from here."

"And I told you already, I'm taking care of you this evening. Or at least getting you in the door."

"You really don't have to do that. All I have to do is elevate my leg, ice it, and wear sensible shoes. That shouldn't be too hard for me to take care of alone," she said. "Besides, I've taken enough of your time this evening.

Devon placed his car in park and hopped out. He crossed over to the passenger side of the car and opened the door. He took Marie into his arms. Their eyes locked momentarily, and a rush of heated desire rippled through them both. And they knew it as another beat passed and they were still standing there locked in a stare that said more than words could at that moment. "You should put me down," she said, her voice barely above a whisper. "At some point, I'm going to have to learn how to use my crutches, unless you're going to carry me around until I don't need them."

"No, I'm not going to do that, but your shoes and your crutches aren't going to work, and when you traverse this parking lot with one shoe on and the other inside your purse, you're going to say, 'Devon Harris could've helped me inside, damn it.'"

Marie laughed as Devon leaned into her and their lips touched briefly, gently, sending a jolt of electric yearning coursing through her system. When Devon devoured her lips, holding her tightly against his chest, Marie wanted to scream out, YES. His kiss had been everything she'd dreamed of and more.

Her lips were like honey, sweet and warm. The longer he kissed her, the more he wanted to rip her clothes off and take her right there. But this was wrong. It wasn't as if he and Marie had met at a club or a social gathering where they could embark on something special and romantic. He was supervising her community service. He was in a position of power over her. One more minute, then he'd pull back. Just another sixty seconds of the hottest and wettest kiss he'd had in months, and he would stop. It took every ounce of self-control in every cell of his body for Devon to break the kiss.

"This. Is. Wrong," he said, yet he didn't put her down. "I have to get you inside and leave."

"What?" she asked breathlessly. "Devon . . ."

He placed his finger to her lips. When Marie flicked her tongue across the pad of his fingertip, he realized just what a mistake that was. "Don't do that," he groaned, snatching his finger away. "We can't do this."

"Why not? That kiss was not one-sided," she said.

"But in the morning, I will still be the person in charge of your community service. This isn't right."

"Put me down," she demanded. "I don't know what kind of game you're playing or if you just get off on women throwing themselves at you, but . . ."

"Listen, I accept responsibility for that kiss, but I told you I was going to get you home safely and that's what I intend to do."

"Put me down," she said as she pounded her hand against his chest. When she saw that he wasn't going to comply with her demands, she stopped pounding and pouted. Devon couldn't help but laugh because she was so sexy when she poked her full lips out like that. Lips he could *never* taste again, or at least not until her community service was complete.

As they stepped on the elevator, Devon looked down at her and asked, "What floor?"

"Seven," she said.

Devon pressed the button and smiled at her as the car rose. "I hope things aren't going to be awkward between us tomorrow."

"I'm not the one with the problem," she said. "How could you kiss me like that and just drop that load of bull about this being wrong?"

"You kissed me, I simply responded. Lost control, and I should've kept my head about me."

The doors to the elevator opened and Devon stepped off. "You know what," she said as she reached into her purse and pulled out her keys. "I think you should lose your head again."

Devon took the keys from her hand and unlocked the door, then walked into her place. He crossed over to the sofa and sat her down. "All right," he said. "Is there anything else I can do for you before I leave?"

Marie propped her ankle on the coffee table and folded her arms across her chest. Did he really ask her could he do anything else for her? He could rip her clothes off and make love to her right there on the sofa. He could run his hands all over her body until she felt as if she would explode from the inside out. Sighing, she said, "No. Just leave the crutches where I can get to them."

"All right," he said as he leaned them against the sofa. "I guess I'll see you tomorrow?"

"Bright and early, right?" she said sarcastically.

"Have a good night, Marie," Devon said, then turned and headed out the door.

Chapter 9

Marie sat on her sofa for about an hour after Devon left, reliving the kiss and the rejection that followed. With her eyes closed, Marie tilted her head back, imagining that Devon had changed his mind and was kissing her again, hotter and wetter than in the parking garage. She could feel his hot hands roaming her body, slowly and tenderly. Before she knew it, she was slipping her hand inside her pants, wishing it was Devon's hand spreading her thighs.

"Oh, no," she snapped, opening her eyes and returning to reality. She was alone in her uptown condo. Leaning over, she reached for her crutches and struggled to stand. She needed to get in the kitchen and fix herself a glass of the coldest water she could find. As she slipped her crutches underneath her arms, Marie's cell phone rang. "Damn it," she muttered as she turned and hobbled back to the sofa as quickly as her crutches would allow. When she reached for her purse, the phone had stopped ringing. Easing onto the edge of the sofa, she checked the missed call and was surprised to see that it was her father.

Immediately, she called him back. "Hi, Daddy," she said when he answered.

"Good evening, Marie. How was your first day at the shelter?"

"How did you . . . never mind, I'm sure your connections in the legal world are how you found out about my start date."

"Well?" he asked. "Did you show up on time?"

"I did," she said. "And I think I knocked eight hours off my sentence today."

"I hope you're taking this seriously," Richard said. "If you don't do what you're supposed to do, then you could find yourself behind bars."

"I understand, Dad," she said. "Look, I have to go. I had an accident at the shelter."

"What happened?" Richard asked, his voice filled with fatherly concern.

"Oh, I twisted my ankle."

"I'm coming over," he said. Before Marie could protest, her father had disconnected the call. She couldn't help but smile; even when he was trying to be tough on her, she was still Daddy's little girl.

Devon drove around aimlessly for about forty-five minutes after leaving Marie's place. He finally ended up at the restaurant. He figured working on a new recipe or something would take his mind off the enigma of Marie Charles. Maybe if he worked with chicken and spices he could erase the sweetness of her kiss from his mind. As soon as he walked through the back door of Hometown Delights, he saw that he would have a distraction.

"Kandace," he said. "What are you doing here?"

A very pregnant and glowing Kandace Crawford turned around and smiled at Devon. "Hey, buddy," she replied. "I came by to meet the girls. Solomon is announcing plans for a Crawford resort in Ballentyne tomorrow, and I couldn't pass up a chance to come to Charlotte."

Devon looked down at his watch; dinner service was over, but he knew his friends would probably want something to eat. "Who's here?"

"Jade's in the office on the phone and Alicia's closing out the bar. Serena's allegedly coming over, but we probably won't see her until breakfast." Kandace laughed and then rubbed her stomach. "Where have you been?"

"That's a long story," he said as he motioned for her to follow him into the kitchen. Before Devon started whipping up something for them to eat, he inspected the cleaning that his staff had done. Excellent job, he surmised.

"Hello," Kandace said. "Did you hear me?"

"What?"

"Tell me the story."

Devon smiled as he looked at Kandace's swollen belly. She rested her hands on her stomach and tilted her head to the side. "You act like you've never seen a pregnant woman before," Kandace joked.

"I've never seen a pregnant Kandace before," he replied. "But anyway. I'm just leaving the hospital. Marie Charles, who is working at My Sister's Keeper with me, twisted her ankle, and when we left the taping today, her ankle was swelling, we thought it was broken."

"This isn't a long story, this is a boring story," Kandace quipped.

Jade appeared in the doorway. "What's going on in here?" she asked, looking from Devon to Kandace.

Kandace tilted her head toward Devon. "He's boring me with a story that's hiding the truth."

"Is this about Marie Charles?" Jade asked.

Devon threw his hands up and shook his head. "And I was going to cook for you nosy heifers."

"A new recipe?" Kandace asked. "Oh, this is serious."

"Alicia said she saw sparks," Jade said.

Devon leaned against the counter and folded his arms. "Alicia didn't see a damned thing," he snapped. Jade and Kandace exchanged a knowing look.

"He had to take her to the hospital," Kandace told Jade.

"And then what happened?" Jade asked as she and Kandace focused their stare on him while he crossed over to the freezer. Devon opened the door and pulled out a package of chicken breasts.

"Well," he said, "I took her home and we kissed."

"I knew it," Alicia exclaimed from the doorway. "This is about Marie Charles, right?"

Devon slammed the meat on the counter. "Do y'all want to eat?"

"She's trouble," Alicia said. "Be careful."

"Did you think she was trouble when you invited her to dinner here?" he asked as he walked over to the spice rack.

Alicia shrugged. "Marie is a walking headline, that's why I invited her for dinner. Marketing one-oh-one. Photographers follow her like moths to a flame."

Kandace raised her hand as if she were in class. "Who is Marie Charles?"

Alicia crossed over to Kandace and placed her hand on her friend's shoulder. "Charlotte's chocolate Paris Hilton. Her father is an attorney, Richard Charles. Ask Kenya about him. He's like the reincarnation of Johnnie Cochran."

"That I did not know," Devon said as he set the spices on the counter. "I wonder why he didn't get her out of . . ."

"Out of what?" Kandace asked.

"While you were in New York, Miss Marie got a DUI charge and has to do community service with Devon at the shelter," Alicia said. "But when they were here earlier today, I know what I saw."

Devon groaned and shook his head. "Here we go," he said.

Jade turned to Alicia. "I thought it was just me," she said to her friend. "But when you and Devon were talking at the end of the taping, she looked as if she wanted to claw your eyes out."

"Why would you say something that stupid?" Devon snapped, then he dropped his head. "How about all of you get out of my kitchen. Go in the office and talk about me there. If you want to stand around, then all of you can help cook." He pointed at Kandace. "Pregnant women can work, too."

"Whatever," Kandace said. "And how are you trying to tell us what to do?"

Devon cocked his head to the side and laughed out loud. "Y'all are a trip, haven't changed since college, just got older."

"Then you know we're not moving until you tell us what's going on with you and Marie," Jade said.

Devon began seasoning the chicken and kept his eyes focused on the meat as he said, "I could like her, under different circumstances. She's different when the cameras aren't around her."

"Oh, snap," Alicia said. "Are you out of your mind? Weren't you lamenting about not being able to find a good woman the other day?"

"And why do you think Marie isn't a good woman? I saw a different side of her today. She was nice to the women at My Sister's Keeper and quickly dropped that diva attitude that she's known for. But it's not as if anything can come from it."

"Why not?" Jade and Kandace asked in concert.

Devon crossed over to the sink and washed his hands, then grabbed a pan for the chicken. "Because, I supervise her community service," he said as he turned the stove on. "I'm sure there are rules against that."

"She's not going to be doing community service forever," Jade said.

"Which means she might not be on her good behavior forever," Alicia said.

"What will getting to know this woman hurt?" Kandace asked.

Devon coated the bottom of the pan with olive oil and pondered Kandace's question. What would getting to know Marie better hurt? Maybe his work at the shelter, maybe his sanity, maybe his heart? There was one thing he knew about her and that was going to stay on his mind longer than it was going to take to cook this almond chicken dish. As the chicken sizzled and his friends bantered back and forth about whatever they were talking about, all he could think about was Marie's kiss: the softness of her lips and the sweetness of her tongue. He wanted more. Needed more, and he couldn't have it, which made the tightness in his loins unbearable.

"Shit," he muttered as he nearly burnt his hand on the side of the pan.

"Are you all right over there?" Alicia asked.

"Fine," he said. "Just broke my number-one rule."

"What's that?"

"Cooking while distracted," he replied.

"You know," Kandace said. "You never answered my question."

Devon sprinkled a half cup of almonds over the chicken as well as his secret blend of spices, then flipped the breasts over and sprinkled more almonds and spices.

"What question was that?" he asked, fully aware of the question.

"Now, you're just playing silly," she replied. "About this Marie Charles lady, why can't you get to know her? Devon, you deserve to be happy."

Jade and Alicia cast a suspicious glance Kandace's way. "I mean," Kandace continued, "I think you've grown and will treat the next woman in your life the way she should be treated. She's going to be a lucky woman."

Devon smiled and shook his head. "I honestly never thought I would hear those words come from you."

"I never thought I would say them, either," she said. "I thought I wanted you to be lonely for the rest of your life, but everyone deserves a second chance."

As Devon continued making the chicken and preparing the jasmine rice to accompany the dish, he wondered if he and Marie could find that second chance together.

An hour later, Devon was setting plates of almond chicken over jasmine rice, steamed vegetables with Devon's secret blend of herbs and spices, and piping hot crescent rolls on the bar in the back of the restaurant for the women to sample.

"Just like old times," he said as he watched them eat. "I cook, y'all eat."

"Better than old times," Jade said. "The cooking has improved tremendously."

"Even if you could always out cook us," Kandace said as she broke a roll in half and slathered it with warm honey butter. "So, have you fed Marie Charles yet?"

"I can take the food away, too," he said as he took a piece of chicken breast from the platter. Devon savored the nuttiness and richness of the chicken. This was good, a menu-ready dish, he decided. "How about we make this a dinner special next week?"

"Sure," Alicia said. "What about that New Orleans chicken dish you make; can we make that a dinner special tomorrow? When we did inventory, there was a lot of chicken that might go to waste."

Devon squeezed Alicia's shoulder and smiled. "My favorite bean counter. We'll make it a lunch special."

"I know where Solomon and I will be for lunch," Kandace said, then took another bite of her chicken.

Devon smiled. "When are you due?"

"Less than a month away," she said, then rubbed her belly. "We decided that my baby is going to be born here." Kandace turned to her friends. "I couldn't bear having my baby without you guys here."

"Aww," Jade said as she dropped her fork and hugged Kandace. "I was ready to load James and Jaden up for a trip to New York."

"Well, I was impressed with the facility at Presbyterian, where you and Kenya gave birth. So, I thought it would be best that we had the baby here, especially since construction on a new Crawford resort will be starting soon."

"Do you know if you're having a girl or a boy?" Alicia asked.

"I'm praying for a girl," Kandace said. "The world is not ready for another Solomon Crawford."

"Amen," Devon muttered, causing the women to focus a glance in his direction. He threw his hand up. "Hey, you said it, I just agreed."

"I wish you and my husband would grill this beef between the two of you, serve it on some yeast rolls and get rid of it," Kandace said with a delicate shake of her head.

"I'm not the one with the beef. That's all on your hubby," he replied. "I can understand why he'd think you'd leave him for someone as devastatingly handsome as myself, but I messed that up a long time ago." Devon winked at her. "If it isn't obvious that we've moved on, I'm going to have to question your husband's confidence."

"Please," Alicia said. "That's the one thing the world knows Solomon Crawford isn't lacking."

Kandace rubbed her stomach and smiled brightly. "He's not lacking in anything."

"And on that note, I'm going to clean up the kitchen and go home," Devon said, then headed for the kitchen. Sometimes when he was with Alicia, Kandace, Serena, and Jade, he felt as if he was the fifth girlfriend in their circle. Amazing that they had remained friends after the nasty breakup he and Kandace had nearly a decade ago. He could understand why Solomon would have a problem with the two of them working together. But Devon wasn't the type of man to go after a woman who could never belong to him. His desire for Kandace had waned long ago. But he couldn't ignore his growing need for Marie. Her lips, their kiss, and the feel of her breasts pressed against his chest were burned into his brain like a tattoo. Just how in the hell was he supposed to work with her now when all he could think about was that amazing kiss and those dangerous curves?

Marie popped two anti-inflammatory pills, then washed them down with the glass of Simply Apple juice her father had poured for her. "Just like the old days," Richard said fondly as he handed Marie a peanut butter and banana sandwich, sliced in half with the crust cut off. Marie couldn't help but smile as she took the plate from her father's hand. He'd been making her favorite sandwich the same way since she came home crying because Joey

Porter had called her ugly and pulled her hair when she was in the fifth grade.

"Thank you, Daddy," she replied. "I'm glad you came over tonight."

"So, how did this happen again?" he asked as he took a seat on the chaise across from the sofa, where Marie was stretched out.

"I wore the wrong shoes to My Sister's Keeper and slipped."

"Was the floor wet? Did they have a sign up?"

Marie took a bite of her sandwich and threw her hand up. "It was my fault," she said after swallowing. "I'd hoped that my community service would've been less service and more sitting."

Richard shook his head. "If you're working in an unsafe environment . . ."

"Daddy," she said. "I was the one who wore Jimmy Choo heels when I should've expected to do some work. But Devon took good care of me."

"Devon? Who is he?"

"The chef who's supervising my community service," she said, struggling to keep her voice even. Somehow, Richard seemed to see what Marie was trying to hide.

"I hope you know getting involved with this man while you're doing community service with him is a mistake."

Marie sighed and took another bite of her sandwich. If only she could explain to her father that after one scorching kiss, she didn't give a damn if it was a mistake; she simply wanted to feel his lips against hers again.

Richard rose to his feet and smiled. "Since I see that you're all right and you've eaten, I'm going to go. I have court in the morning."

"I'd walk you to the door," she said, then pointed to her ankle. "But, you know."

He crossed over to his daughter and kissed her on the forehead. "Marie, please take this community service seriously and remember that Devon is in a position of power over you. You cannot and should not cross the line with him."

"Yes, sir," she said and offered him a mock salute. Richard shook his head, wondering why he even wasted his breath. He knew Marie would do what she always did: anything she wanted. He just wished his daughter would do a little more growing up.

Chapter 10

The next morning, Marie woke up to find that the swelling in her ankle had subsided slightly. Smiling, she limped out of bed, showered, and searched for the flattest pair of shoes she had. She ended up slipping into a pair of two-year-old, barely worn Converse All Stars. The shoes were specially made for her during that period of time when everyone in the world thought Converse sneakers were the coolest thing in the world. She slipped into the silver, purple, pink, and green shoes and realized why she hadn't worn them to the Chuck Taylor party that her marketing company had hosted—she was short. Today, however, Marie was glad she hadn't thrown the shoes away. She could move around her bedroom, albeit very slowly, without the crutches, but she wondered if she would be able to work in the shelter without them. As she called her father's car service to come and pick her up, she decided to take one of her crutches with her, hoping and praying that trying to walk with it would give her something else to think about. Something other than the taste of Devon's mouth. Slipping the crutch underneath her left arm, Marie headed for the kitchen. She figured that she'd better eat breakfast before heading into work. Sadly, all she had to eat in the kitchen was a bagel, since she normally ate breakfast out. As she brewed a cup of coffee in her Keurig machine, Marie promised herself to buy some eggs at the supermarket later. Marie dropped a sesame seed bagel into the toaster and leaned against the counter, wondering if Devon did more than just cook in the kitchen. Would he take her on the counter, using chocolate and sugar as he licked her until she shivered with anticipation and desire? Would he wrap her legs around his waist as he thrust into her, touching her most sensitive spot while she screamed his name?

"Stop thinking about that man," she muttered as she snapped the pod in place. "He plays by the rules."

Just as her bagel popped up in the toaster, her cell phone rang. "Hello?"

"Marie, it's Devon," he said, his voice thick and deep, causing her knees to quiver.

"Hi," she said. Then she wondered why he was calling her.

"I just wanted to let you know that I called your probation officer and informed him of your accident, so if you can't make it in today, it won't count against you."

Disappointment snaked through her body, though she did appreciate his thoughtfulness. "I plan to come in to the shelter today, I'm actually waiting for the car service," she said.

"How's the ankle?"

"It's still sore, but the swelling has gone down some."

"That's good to hear. And you have flat shoes to wear today?" he asked.

Marie laughed. "I do."

"Why don't I come and pick you up? I'll even bring you breakfast," he said.

There was so much more she wanted him to bring her, she thought as she looked at the clock on the wall. If she was going to accept his ride, which she was, then she needed to call the car service and cancel. "I need to call my driver," she said as she tossed her half-burnt bagel in the trash. "Thanks for the ride. I guess I'll have some coffee ready for you."

"Don't worry about it; I'm not a big coffee drinker. I'll see you in about ten minutes."

Marie smiled brightly. "All right." She ended the call and quickly phoned the car service, letting them know that she didn't need to be picked up after all. Moving as quickly as she could, Marie went back into her bedroom to make sure her outfit—black leggings and a white tank top tunic—and her hair were impeccable. As she slathered lip gloss on her lips, she heard the door buzzer go off. Now she wanted to slap herself for not having an intercom installed in her bedroom so that she could tell the doorman to send Devon up. She hobbled to the front door and pressed the Talk button on the machine. "Yes?"

"Mr. Devon Harris is downstairs," the doorman said. "And you have a package."

She heard Devon say he would bring the package to her, if that was all right. "Please send him up and he can bring the package," Marie said, trying to keep the excitement out of her voice. But why was she so excited to see forbidden fruit? Because she knew she couldn't have it and it made her want him even more. Just like when she was a little girl and begged for a pony.

She opened the door and offered Devon a slight smile as he walked in and handed her a box from a florist. "Where do you want me to put breakfast?" he asked after saying hello.

"The coffee table is fine. Thanks for this," she said. "This will be the first time I get to taste the food of the illustrious Devon Harris."

Devon laughed as his eyes roamed Marie's body before setting the bag of breakfast treats on her coffee table. He brought warm croissants with peach preserves, salmon cakes, and grits with cheddar cheese and baked apple slices covered in cinnamon.

"That's a lot of food," she said as she looked at the arrangement on her table. "You eat like this every morning?"

"I'm thinking of doing breakfast on Saturdays and Sundays at Hometown Delights, so I made some samples for the ladies of what we could offer. It's hard to cook for one person," he said. "Especially when you're used to feeding masses."

"Oh," she said, feeling a bit disappointed. Marie had thought this breakfast had been something special just for her. She needed to purge those thoughts from her mind. Devon was just a nice guy. Something she wasn't used to, considering her dating history and her asshole of an ex-fiancé.

"What did they think of it?" she asked.

"You're going to be the first to sample it," Devon said as she sat on the sofa. "Where are your plates?"

"The cabinet above the sink," she said, then attempted to stand. "I could get . . ."

"Keep your seat," he replied as he took off toward the kitchen. When Devon left the room, Marie felt as if she could breathe normally again. She hadn't even realized that she'd been holding her breath, acting as if she was just cool with him being there and feeding her. If this was supposed to make her want him less, chill her hormones to him, it wasn't working.

Devon knew he was playing with fire as he walked into Marie's kitchen. She had a ride to the shelter, she had enough money to buy her own damned breakfast, and she was so cute in those sneakers. He reached up into the cabinet and grabbed two plates. Setting them on the counter,

Devon walked to the entrance of the kitchen and asked, "Do you want some juice or should I fix this coffee in the brewer for you?"

"I can . . . coffee and juice," she said with a smile that made Devon's heart flip like an Olympic gymnast.

"Gotcha," he said. "What kind of juice do you have in the refrigerator?" Devon turned toward the stainless steel ice box, wondering if she actually had food in there or if she just got the top-of-the-line refrigerator because it matched her décor.

"There's some blueberry juice and orange juice. You can just mix them for me," she called out.

Devon shook his head as he opened the door and pulled out the bottles of juice. He mixed them as she'd asked, then grabbed the coffee mug from the counter that Marie had obviously put there for her morning shot of caffeine. "How do you take your coffee?" Devon asked.

"Cream, four sugars," she replied.

"That's a lot of sugar."

"What can I say? I'm extra sweet," she quipped. He knew one thing was certain: She did have the sweetest kiss he'd ever tasted. He was sure that it didn't come from the four sugars in her coffee, though. After fixing the juice and coffee, Devon gathered the mug, the plates, and the glass of juice, then headed into the living room to feed Marie.

She'd gotten a head start on eating, he discovered when he entered the living room and she was biting into a croissant dripping with preserves. As he watched her lips close around the fresh bread, Devon felt a tightness in his crotch. Then, as she licked the peach preserves from her lips, he wanted to feel those lips again. Needed them pressed against his.

This is wrong, he thought as he crossed over to her. "Here you go," he said as he handed her the juice and set the coffee and plates on the table in front of her. When he noticed a bit of peach on her chin, Devon wiped it away with his thumb and held her chin. They gazed into each other's eyes; the air sizzled with sensuality and unspoken desire. Marie tilted her head slightly and brushed her lips against his. Devon captured her lips, savoring her unique sweetness and the tang of the peach preserves. He'd wanted to kiss her since the moment he walked into her penthouse, and it was a delicious treat this morning.

Marie pressed her hand against his chest. "You're going to have to stop teasing me, Devon," she said in a husky whisper.

"Teasing you?" he replied. "I'm teasing myself."

"How so? I can give you just what you want," she replied, then slowly stroked his cheek. Devon's erection nearly burst through his zipper as he took two steps back from her.

"We can't," he said. "This isn't right."

"No one has to know. We want each other, and I don't know if this community service is going to work with me thinking about you naked every time I walk in the door. Besides, if it's horrible, we don't have to worry about it again."

Devon folded his arms across his chest and cocked his head to the side. "It won't be horrible," he said defiantly.

"Then stop talking and prove it to me."

He shook his head and smirked coolly. "In five hundred hours, I'd be happy to. Marie, I don't want to take advantage of you, and you're not going to do the same to me."

If she could've leapt to her feet, she would've gotten in his face and slapped him as hard as she could. "Why do think I'm going to take advantage of you?"

"I'm just saying," he said. "I don't want it to look as if you're getting special treatment because . . ."

"Thanks for the breakfast," she said. "But why don't you go. I'll get to My Sister's Keeper on my own." Her comely face was contorted with an angry scowl, and Devon couldn't turn away from her.

"Marie, let's be real for a second. I don't know you, only what I've read about you in the papers and seen on TV. If I'm wrong about the image you've created for yourself, then prove it to me."

"I don't have to prove a damned thing to you."

"You're right, you don't. But I'm not trying to play games or . . ."

"Or what?" she snapped. "Take the stick out of your ass and do something that you want to do?" Marie slowly rose from her seat on the sofa. She tottered over to Devon and tilted her head. "Sorry that I'm not one of your fans falling at your feet and being sugary sweet. That's not who I am and that's why you want me."

"I want you because sometimes you're sweet and very sexy. Right now, you're acting like the spoiled brat I read about in the news. Big turn off," he said, his voice cool, but as he stared into her eyes, his body was anything but.

She sucked her bottom lip in. Did he just say that to her? Marie wasn't used to a man talking to her like that. She gave orders and he did what she said. Was Devon worth the headache? Yes, he was, she surmised after giving him a cool once-over that tugged at the irrational anger that she'd built up. Devon was right, she had worked hard to build her party-girl reputation. She'd given very provocative quotes to the press, pulled stunts that did make her look as if she would do whatever she wanted to get ahead. She couldn't blame Devon for being apprehensive about going there with her. Now her father's warning about her need for any and all press made sense.

"Listen," she said after taking a cooling and calming

breath. "I can take a hint, and you don't want to cross this imaginary line you've drawn. But for the record, if we do cross that line, I understand that it would have nothing to do with my community service."

Devon placed his hand on her shoulder and smiled at her. "Glad we have an understanding," he said. She glanced at his hand on her shoulder and promised herself that she would not come on to him again. But his touch sent sizzles down her spine and she felt a hot pool of moisture forming in her panties as he stroked her shoulder.

"Do you want to finish your breakfast before we go?" he asked. "I'm actually kind of hungry."

Marie nodded. "All right, let's eat and then go to work."

Despite promises he'd made to himself to keep his hands to himself, Devon picked Marie up and sat her on the sofa. "I don't want you to hurt yourself; we have a lot of work to do at My Sister's Keeper today."

Once she was sitting down, Marie gave him a salute. "Yes, sir," she said, then grabbed another croissant. Devon eased onto the seat beside Marie and filled their plates with the food, and they ate in an uncomfortable silence as they stole glances at one another.

"This is good," Marie said as she spooned preserves in her grits.

"Thanks," he said, then laughed. "I've seen people put a lot of things in grits, but never peach preserves."

"I told you, I like sweet things."

"I see," he replied as he polished off a salmon cake. Marie held her fork out to him.

"Try it."

Devon allowed her to feed him her concoction, and surprisingly, it was tasty. The buttery grits and the sweet peach gave his taste buds a surprise. It reminded him of the woman feeding him. Spicy, sweet, and sticky.

"That is good," he said.

Marie nodded and took another bite of her grits before offering Devon some more. As his lips closed around the fork, she tried not to think of his lips closing like that around her nipple or between her legs, sucking her pearl until she released her desire.

"I guess we'd better wrap this up and head to the shelter," Devon said, breaking into Marie's thoughts.

"Right," she said as he began gathering their plates. While he was in the kitchen, she placed the leftovers in the boxes Devon had brought them over in.

"Ready?" Devon asked. He glanced at the table and saw the food boxed up and smiled. "Thanks."

"No problem," she said as she slowly rose from the table while Devon placed the food in his thermal bag.

"Would you come to Hometown Delights for a breakfast spread like that?" he asked as he strapped his bag across his shoulder.

"I would, if you served breakfast after twelve P.M.," she quipped. Devon walked around the coffee table and leaned into Marie, offering his shoulder so that she could gain her balance. The way she gripped his shoulder made Devon want to strip her bare and take her right there on the sofa. He wanted to feel the bite of her nails in his skin as he thrust into her heated pool of desire.

He turned away from those bewitching eyes and delicious lips, pretending he had to cough.

"Are you all right?" she asked, leaning closer to Devon. Her supple breast brushed against his forearm, and Devon faked another cough.

"Dry throat," he said. "I'm good."

Marie looked at the white florist box Devon had brought in when he'd arrived. "Do you mind if I sneak a peek before we leave? And you can grab some juice for your dry throat."

Devon nodded. "We have time for that," he said as he led her over to the bar. Marie leaned against one of the stools as Devon headed into the kitchen to get a fast drink. As he reached for a glass, Marie shrieked as if she'd seen a mouse or worse. Forgetting the juice he didn't need anyway, Devon rushed over to her. "Are you all right?" he asked as he watched her toss a dozen long-stemmed red and white roses across the room. The petals rained down like a floral snowstorm.

"That sorry son of a bitch!" she groaned. "Roses? Roses are supposed to make up for what he did?"

Devon folded his arms across his chest, hiding his laugh because he knew when she calmed down, this was not going to be pretty to clean up. *Women and their emotional outbursts. Who does she think she's hurting?* He crossed over to her as she beat another innocent rose to death.

"Marie," he said. "You do realize that you're going to have to clean this up—on crutches."

She faced him with a wild look in her eyes. "You don't understand, William had some nerve to send me these roses after he humiliated me!"

"And this does what to him?"

"You know what?" she said, then sighed deeply. "You're right, and I really don't like you."

Devon took the rose stems from her hands and smiled. "You'll learn to love me."

That's what I'm afraid of, she thought as they headed out the door.

Chapter 11

When Devon and Marie arrived at My Sister's Keeper, he gave her an assignment that she could sit down and complete while he taught his cooking class. Marie didn't mind writing a few press releases about the restaurant's fund-raiser for the shelter, even though she had initially thought he was trying to exploit her. Had she not been so hardheaded, she might not be sitting there with a twisted ankle. Marie crinkled her nose as the computer froze up on her again. "They really need to upgrade these systems," she muttered as she pressed Control, Alt, Delete again. She waited for the computer to reboot and turned toward the kitchen, watching Devon as he slowly chopped some vegetables. The women watched him closely, soaking up the lesson he was teaching. Marie focused on his strong arms, because he'd shed his chef's jacket as if it was hot in the enclosure. His arms reminded her of cut ebony wood, strong enough to hold her until the world stopped spinning. She bounced her foot and chewed her bottom lip as she was lost in a fantasy of being laid across that counter and made love to.

"Excuse me. Excuse me," Bria said, breaking into Marie's thoughts.

Marie turned and faced the girl and smiled. "Yes?"

Bria glanced down at Marie's feet. "Those shoes are hot," she said. "But anyway, are you done with the press release?"

Marie shook her head. "This computer keeps freezing up on me."

"It does that a lot," she said. "Have you been saving your work?"

Marie nodded and noticed that Bria was still looking at her shoes. "What size do you wear?" she asked her.

"Oh, umm, size eight," she replied quietly.

Marie nodded and untied her shoe, then removed it from her foot. "Try it on; I rarely, meaning never, wear these. If they fit, you're welcome to them."

Bria put the shoe on and smiled brightly when she tied it up tightly. "This is a hot shoe. Why don't you like it?"

Marie shrugged. "I guess it was made for you and not me."

"And you're really going to give me these?" Bria held her foot out and shifted it from side to side. There was one thing that Marie knew, and that's how a new pair of shoes made a woman feel.

"Sure, you can have them," Marie said. "As a matter of fact, if you lead me to a computer that works, we can go shopping next week."

Bria cocked her head to the side. "Why are you being so nice to me? Yesterday, you were acting like a . . ."

"Raging bitch?" Marie finished.

"Well," Bria replied, "kind of. It was obvious that you didn't want to be here."

"Have you ever gotten away with everything and then finally had to take your lumps? It's never easy, but since I have to be here, I want to help."

Bria didn't reply, she just pointed to another computer. "This one works better," she said after a moment of silence.

"Bria," Marie said, "where did you go?"

The young woman leaned over and untied the shoe, then handed it to Marie. "People always say they want to help, but it only seems to make things worse."

"Well, I've never said that I would help you before and . . ."

"Oh, please," Bria said. "I Googled you last night; I'm sure you don't want to help me at all. What will it do for your party image?"

"Look," Marie said. "I'm not going to sit here and pretend that I've changed overnight. I still like to party and have a good time, but that has nothing to do with you and me in this moment."

"Whatever," Bria said. "I'm going to the store." Before Marie could put her shoe on and go after her, Devon was heading in her direction.

"What's going on out here?" he asked as he saw Bria tear out the door.

Marie shook her head and shrugged. "We were talking, she liked my shoes, and . . ."

"You got into an argument with her about shoes?"

"Are you going to let me finish?" Marie snapped. "I told her she could have the shoes and that we could go shopping next week because I wanted to help her, and she just flipped a switch."

Devon squeezed the bridge of his nose. "I'm sorry," he said. "Bria is really hard to get a read on and . . ."

"Go to hell," Marie snapped as she slowly rose to her feet. "I was trying to talk to her and do something nice for the girl because she was helping me with the computer, and you assume that I'm arguing about some shoes that I'm only wearing because I twisted my ankle?"

"I made a mistake," he said. "I overreacted because Bria has been having a hard time."

Marie took a calming breath; it wasn't as if she'd given him any reason to believe that she wouldn't fly off the handle after the scene he'd witnessed with the roses. "All right," she said. "Maybe you should go after her and make sure she's all right."

"Are we OK? I don't want to keep arguing with you. We have a long time to work together."

Marie nodded, but kept silent. She didn't want to argue either. Devon headed out the door and she banged her hand against the computer keyboard, then started typing the press release—again.

Devon crossed the shelter's parking lot and caught up with Bria as she made it to the corner store. "Bria," he said. "Are you all right?"

"I really wish people would stop asking me that. I need cigarettes, OK. There is nothing wrong with me."

"Listen," Devon said, "people are concerned about you because we care."

"Sounds like the same load of crap she offered in there," Bria said, nodding toward the shelter. "I don't need help, I simply need a home."

"And that's why you're here, but even if you get a job, if you have something in your past that you're running from, it is going to come back and hurt you in the long run."

"I–I . . . Just leave me alone, OK?"

"I will, for now. But you know that it's required for you to do the career training, and you're missing class right now," Devon said, his brows furrowed in confusion, disappointment, and anger. "Who is he, Bria? Who are you running from?"

She stopped cold, as if Devon's words cut through her soul. "What?"

"I know the signs," he said quietly, closing the space between them and placing his hand on her shoulder. "My mother ran from an abusive man."

"I'm not running," she said, then dropped her head. "I'm scared."

He nodded. "You need to talk to someone. There's help for you, but you can't run all your life."

"But . . . What if he finds me? Who's going to protect me then?" she asked as she began to cry. Devon wrapped his arms around her as she sobbed and her body trembled.

"No one is going to hurt you," he said. "But you should take advantage of the counseling services here. What he did to you is not your fault."

"You said your mother ran?"

"Yes, but it didn't help her. She didn't get away from my father completely, she was diagnosed with cancer, and because we only ran, when she needed treatment, she had to go back."

"I don't want to go back. I can't."

"You don't have to. Come with me," Devon said as he took her hand in his. They walked inside, and Marie shot a quizzical look his way as Devon and Bria dashed down the hall. Marie saw Shay crossing over to her and could hear that she was calling her name, but Marie's mind was walking down the hall. She wondered if Bria would be all right. Had Devon been able to talk to her and let her know that people actually did give a damn about her?

"Marie! Did you hear me?" Shay asked. Then she followed Marie's gaze. "I see you're just as worried about that girl as everybody else around here."

"I hope Devon can help her with whatever demons

she's dealing with," Marie said. "But, that doesn't mean I should ignore you. I'm sorry. What were you saying?"

"I got a copy of the press release off the printer and I wanted to suggest some changes," she said, handing Marie the page with notes in the margin. "The first thing is, we want the media to come here and do the interviews, because this is a fund-raiser for the shelter."

"I thought about that," Marie said. "But what about ladies who don't want people to know that they're here?"

Shay stroked her chin. "All right, I didn't think about that. But we're going to be included in the interviews to let people know we're not sitting back just doing nothing, right?"

"Of course," Marie said. "I tell you what, why don't we schedule a day when the media comes to the restaurant and all of you who have been working so hard on this can be interviewed."

Shay tilted her head to the side and looked at Marie. "You've done this before, huh?"

"My business is getting in the news," Marie replied with a wink. "That and shopping."

"So, how do I get a job with you?"

"We will have to talk about it," Marie said. "But you do know your press release writing."

"We're not just homeless dummies. Before I lost everything, I worked in the banking industry and for a public relations company for a while, too. But the money dried up and there was nothing else I could do."

Marie nodded, knowing that the economy caused a lot of qualified people to lose their jobs, but she had no idea how hard times really were. Shay was highly qualified at what she did, but the job market was extremely limited. Marie made a mental note to see if she and Adriana could help Shay find a job. She wished that she could hire her on the spot, but with the business that they'd lost due to her arrest, she wasn't sure if she could.

"Enough of my sob story," Shay said, noting Marie's silence. "So, when are you going to set up this press conference?"

"I will get back to you tomorrow with a date," she replied as she pulled her cell phone out of her purse. "Let me call my partner and see if we can get something set up."

As she dialed Adriana's number, Devon came down the hall with a somber look on his face. Marie quickly hung up the phone and turned to him. "Is everything all right?" she asked.

"I got to go and dismiss class. Do you need a ride home?" he asked quietly.

"If you need to stay, I can make other arrangements," Marie said. "Is Bria OK?"

Devon nodded and instinctively kissed Marie on the forehead. "She will be and I don't have to stay. We were almost done with the lesson and I want to talk to you about what you did today."

Marie felt as if she was melting from his lips gracing her forehead, but she knew that kiss meant nothing. Right?

Devon wanted to kick himself as he stood there looking at Marie. Why couldn't he keep his lips to himself when he was around her? Kissing her made him want to taste the most intimate parts of her essence. But he couldn't fall for her or give in to his lustful needs and desires. Then again, would it be so bad if he did? She made it clear this morning that she wasn't pretending to want to head between the sheets for special treatment at the shelter. She'd even went above and beyond with the way she reached out to Bria. Still, Devon was leery, wondering what could be going on behind those beguiling eyes and who Marie Charles really was.

Marie ran her hand down his forearm and smiled sweetly at him. Devon returned her smile and then quickly returned to the kitchen.

"All right, ladies," he said to the remaining students. "We're going to have to cut class short today. Here's what I need you to do: Finish with the chopping of the onions, oregano, and peppers. Shay is going to be in charge for the rest of the day, and when you store these vegetables, keep them sealed tightly. Tomorrow, we're going to make an Italian soup."

"Is everything all right?" Skylar asked.

"Yeah," Devon said, thinking about Bria's meeting with a counselor. He'd finally seen the young girl smile and let down that guard she'd built around herself. He wished that his mother would've found that kind of support and help when she'd needed it.

"All right, people," Shay said. "Let's get chopping." Devon waved to the women, took a deep breath, and headed out the door.

He watched Marie as she stood by the entrance of the shelter, speaking in hushed tones on her BlackBerry. Part of him teemed with jealousy. Was she talking to the guy who'd sent her those roses? Maybe she'd decided to forgive him his trespasses and was making plans to make up with him? Anger like that was attached to love; being friends with women taught him the signs of a woman not over her ex. Devon crossed over to her in time to hear her say, "All right, Adriana, we'll talk about it more when I limp into the office. And yes, I need some flats. Three good pairs. Can you stop laughing?" Marie turned around and caught Devon's stare. "I have to go."

"Didn't mean to interrupt," Devon replied.

She dropped her phone in her oversized leather purse

and smiled. "No problem. I want to talk to you about something," she said as they headed to his car.

"What's that?"

"When Shay and I were going over the press release, she told me that she was a former PR agent."

Devon nodded. "Yeah, that's why she's heading up the publicity for the fund-raiser."

"I'm going to talk to my partner and see if we can offer her a part-time job," she said.

He turned and faced her, feeling the urge to kiss her again. "Really?"

"I don't know how much we can afford to pay her, but I'm going to try and make sure that will help her get back on her feet," Marie said.

"That's really great." His heart warmed intensely, seeing this side of Marie.

"Well, I don't want to get ahead of myself. Since my arrest, we've lost some contracts and I'm not sure where we stand financially."

"I'm impressed that you want to help," he said as he opened the passenger-side door for her. As Marie slid inside, Devon placed his hand on her knee. "Thank you."

"Don't thank me yet," she said as she looked down at his hand. The heat from his hand made her shiver. Their eyes locked, and for a moment, they just sat there, an unspoken sexual tension crackling between them.

"Let's do lunch," he said. "I know an exclusive place where we can talk without interruption."

"Just talk?" she asked, her voice oozing sensuality.

"I think we've moved beyond just talking," he said as he leaned in to her. Marie wrapped her arms around his neck and brushed her lips against his.

"Are you sure?"

"More than anything. What about you?"

Instead of replying, she slowly ran her tongue across his full lips, and Devon shuddered in hot delight before taking her offering into his mouth, relishing the minty taste of her kiss, and dancing his tongue in each corner and crevice of her hot and willing mouth. Reluctantly, he pulled back. Marie looked at him with surprise in her eyes. Was he about to change his mind? Was he about to talk about that imaginary line they weren't supposed to cross? Didn't he realize that after a kiss like that, the line had been crossed and erased?

"Let's go," he said as he tore away from her and headed for the driver's side of the Mustang. Devon started the car, and while stealing glances at Marie, he peeled out of the parking lot.

For about a mile, they rode in silence, then Marie mustered up the voice to ask, "Where are we going?"

"To the most exclusive bed and breakfast in the city," he replied as he turned down Davidson Street.

"How is it that I've never heard of this place?" she asked with her eyebrow raised. "I pride myself on knowing all of the hot spots in the city."

"Like I said," Devon replied as they pulled into the NoDa City View lofts, "exclusive."

She looked up at the new housing complex and smiled. "You live here, huh?"

"Yes. And the food is amazing, if I do say so myself," Devon replied.

"Is that so?"

"You'll find out soon enough," he said as he pulled into a parking spot. Devon hopped out of the car and crossed over to the passenger side of the car before Marie could even remove her seat belt. He opened the door and lifted her from the car. Marie wrapped her arms around his neck and he brushed his lips against hers. "We have a lot of stairs to climb," he said, then winked at her.

"I bet you carry all of your girls up the stairs," she said.

"You would be the first I carried and brought here," he replied. She eyed him suspiciously. There was no way this sexy man was celibate, not with all the thirsty women in Charlotte who would love to link up with a celebrity.

"You don't believe me?" he asked as he climbed the stairs.

"Nope. It sounds like I should be erecting a statue to Saint Devon," she quipped.

Devon shook his head and laughed. "Never said I was a saint, and I have something that's very erect that you can crown."

Marie was surprised at his brash tone, turned on, and ready to see where that crown would go as he unlocked the door to his loft.

Once they entered, he placed Marie on the leather sofa in the middle of the living room. Glancing around the room, she saw another side of Devon, rugged and über masculine. The room was decorated in deep browns and blacks, giving the area a smoldering tint, even with the blinds of the wide bay windows open and the sun slicing through. The soft leather against her legs made her wonder if they could be comfortable making love right in this spot. He straddled her body and lifted her legs, sitting them on the wooden coffee table in front of the sofa.

"Comfortable?" he asked, his voice a husky whisper.

Marie nodded and stared into his eyes as he unbuttoned her shirt. Marie was so glad she decided to wear her favorite red lace bra as he pushed the tunic down her shoulder. Devon stroked her shoulder, moving his hands slowly down her body, causing her to writhe with anticipation. His fingers felt like butterfly wings as they moved down to the waistband of her leggings. With a quick motion, he'd slid them down her hips, his fingers moving against her skin like hummingbird wings. She could barely keep still, trying to move against his touch, but Devon held her in place. "Be still, woman," he ordered. "I've been waiting to see these curves up close." Devon slipped his forefinger under the lace crotch of her panties and sought out her throbbing pearl. She was so hot, so wet, and removing his finger, he brought it to his lips to find out she was so tasty. Marie moaned as he lifted her right leg to pull her pants all the way down. Easing between her legs, Devon rubbed her to a near climax through her lacy red panties before pulling them to the side and covering her sweet wetness with his mouth. Marie tossed her head back in ecstasy as he wrapped his tongue around her pleasure. Her thighs shivered and her body tingled as he expertly licked and sucked her to a loud orgasm. Marie had never screamed so loud as her body went limp. She'd nearly forgotten about her sprained ankle until her left foot slipped from the table and slammed on the floor. "Oww, oww, oww," she howled. Devon grabbed her foot.

"Are you all right?" he asked as he removed her shoe, checking her bandaged ankle. "Should I take you to the hospital?"

"It's all your fault," she said, trying to joke through the pain. "That magical tongue of yours made me forget all about my injury."

Devon told her to stretch out on the sofa, and he grabbed a pillow from the love seat in the corner and put it underneath her foot. "I'll get you an ice pack and some Advil."

Marie blew him a kiss as he headed upstairs. Closing her eyes, she wondered if this was ever going to happen. Maybe her foot slipping had been a sign that she should slow things down with Devon. But now that he'd given her another sample of what he could do to her body, the only thing that would keep her moving slowly would be her bum ankle.

Chapter 12

Devon stood in the kitchen wondering if he needed an ice pack for himself as well. His body wanted to melt with Marie so badly that he ached. And it was an aching that would stop them from doing anything. Her ankle. Grabbing the ice, a glass filled with orange juice, and a bottle of Advil, he headed into the living room. Even though Marie had a look of pain on her face, she looked so beautiful lying on the sofa, adding color and sex appeal to his room with that lacy red bra against her chocolate skin.

"Orange juice and Advil," he said as he tapped two pills into her outstretched hand. Then he handed her the glass before placing the ice pack on her ankle.

"This isn't the day you had planned, huh?" she asked after swallowing her painkiller.

"You know what they say about planning. Besides, I had no idea we'd end up here, together. My plan was to work you at the shelter."

Marie took another sip of juice and nodded. "Right," she said. "So, why did you bring me here?"

"I think that's obvious," Devon replied.

"Yes, but where do we go next?" she asked. "You tried

so hard to deny what we both wanted. Do you feel like you made a mistake crossing that line?"

"No," he said. "I feel like we haven't crossed it enough. But, you have to get on both feet first."

Marie looked down at her ankle. "Right."

Devon leaned down and kissed her slowly, flicking his tongue against hers and making her moan. Her mouth was nearly as delicious as the rest of her. He didn't have a problem admitting that she was becoming his addiction. And Devon had every intention of indulging in it every chance he got. Still, with her in pain, he had to pull back.

"Lunch. I still owe you lunch." Devon handed her the remote to his TV. "I'm going to get cooking and you relax."

"Careful, Mr. Harris," Marie said with a smile. "I could get used to this really quickly."

"Used to what?"

"You pampering me and waiting on me hand and foot."

He winked at her. "Play your cards right and I might make a habit of it."

While Devon was in the kitchen, Marie sat up, quickly dressed and then stretched her arms above her head, lazily resting against the sofa. When was the last time she'd been pampered by a man? Her normal MO was to get what she wanted and move on. Sure, she had been engaged to William, but that relationship had been about two things, shutting Greta up and trying to fit into the sensible pumps her father wanted her to wear. A wife and a mother. Less flamboyant and media hungry. But that wasn't what she wanted for herself. However, she was seeing something new and different, something that was more important than her image as Charlotte's party girl.

Maybe making a fool of myself that night was the best thing that happened to me, she thought as she turned the TV on and flipped the channels mindlessly. When her cell phone rang, it startled her, and Marie nearly tumbled off the sofa when she reached for her purse. Looking at the time on Devon's cable box, she was sure it wasn't Adriana, because it wasn't close to three o'clock. She didn't recognize the number, but answered anyway. "This is Marie Charles."

"Hello, Marie," a voice she wished she wasn't hearing said. "Did you get the roses I sent you?"

"William, why are you calling me?" she snapped.

"I've been thinking about you and missing you. That's why I sent you the flowers."

"Funny, because two weeks ago you were telling me that you and Greta were rekindling your romance. Does she know your broke ass is using her credit cards again?"

"I'm not with Greta anymore. I heard about your incident with the car. I can't believe your father didn't get you out of it."

"Why don't you take a long walk off a short bridge? In case you haven't figured it out, we're done. I don't want to see or hear from your sorry ass, understand?"

"Look, I was confused and I made a mistake. But I still want to marry you and—"

Marie clicked the phone off and dropped it in her bag. William had nerve, but she wasn't going to allow him to mar her lunch with Devon. Whatever made him think he could slink back into her life, he could choke on it. Devon returned to the living room with two plates of strawberry and spinach salads. "The salmon is grilling, so I hope you enjoy the salad, for now."

"It looks great," she replied as she took her salad plate from his hand. "And strawberries are my favorite, though I usually like them dipped in chocolate."

She took a bite of her salad and realized that chocolate wasn't the only way to make her favorite fruit taste great.

"How is it?" he asked as he slowly ate his own salad.

"Delicious," she replied, then licked her lips.

Devon set his plate on the table. "I forgot the wine," he said. "Merlot cool with you?"

Marie nodded, then took another bite of her salad. Devon went into the kitchen, and she smiled, thinking that this was the first time she'd been on a lunch date where there weren't photographers—either because she called them or was tossing a drink in someone's face.

He returned and took his seat on the sofa beside her, then poured the wine for them. "A toast," he said as he held up his glass.

"What are we toasting?" she asked before raising her glass.

"Getting to know the real Marie Charles."

She raised her glass and tapped it against Devon's. "I can drink to that."

Devon took a sip of his wine and then headed back to the kitchen to check on the fish. Marie wished she could go into the kitchen with him, not because she wanted to help him cook; that he didn't need help with. But she wanted to see if he had the kind of counters that could be used in her kitchen fantasy.

Devon lifted the salmon steaks from the pan and placed them on a bed of wild rice, then squeezed a lemon over the fish before topping it off with a sprinkling of his zesty blend of seasonings. After garnishing the plates with a sprig of parsley, he headed into the living room with their lunches. "That looks so good," Marie said as he set the plates on the table.

"I forgot the wine again," he said. "Do you want more?"

"No, I'd better not. The last thing I need to do is show up to the office smelling like wine," she said.

"I have some sweet tea," he said as he turned toward the kitchen.

"Sounds perfect," she said as she picked up her plate and dug into the food. By the time Devon returned with two goblets of tea, half of Marie's salmon steak was gone.

"Delicious," she said in between bites. "This is the best salmon I've ever tasted."

"That's good to hear," he said as he handed her the tea. "I pulled out all the stops for this lunch. Got to impress Charlotte's it girl."

Marie stopped drinking and tilted her head to the side. "I don't think I want to be that girl anymore." She set her fork on the side of her plate and met Devon's quizzical glance. "Look," she said. "I know that I created this image of this party girl. I was trying to do something that would set me apart from my father. And I'm willing to admit that I took it too far."

"You won't get an argument from me. But why the whole party-girl thing? You're obviously more than that; you have a big heart and you're pretty smart."

"And smart women get ignored and pushed aside by the media. I take my shirt off and I'm all over the news and headlining the papers," she said. "Go figure. Maybe the party-girl image was just a way for me to . . ." Marie stopped short of telling Devon about the nagging insecurities that she hid with her bravado and outlandish acts. Marie wanted to be recognized for being more than Richard's daughter.

"You took your shirt off? How did I miss that?" he asked with a laugh.

"If this food wasn't so good, I'd toss a piece of fish at you," she replied. "But, yes, to raise awareness about animal abuse."

Devon stroked his chin, thinking that seeing her topless would make him take notice of a lot of things; well, two things actually, but not animal abuse. "Well," he said, "don't you think that was very over the top?"

Marie nodded as she polished off her salmon. "Charlotte's Mecklenburg Police felt the same way. Me and my friends were taken into custody. But PETA bailed us out and we raised about seven thousand dollars for a no-kill shelter in Gaston County."

"OK," he said. "So, how do you explain the car wreck?"

"Possibly the worst thing that ever happened to me or the best thing," she said.

"Best thing?" he asked with his eyebrow raised.

"I've had to take stock in my life and make some decisions," Marie said as she smiled at him. "This image of me and that I created has taken over who I really am."

"And who are you?" he asked, setting his plate on the table and easing closer to her.

"That's what I'm going to have to rediscover," she replied honestly. She placed her hand on Devon's knee. He leaned in and kissed her cheek.

"If you're serious about it, it won't be hard. Just do what's in your heart and you will be fine."

She leaned her head against his shoulder and hoped that he was telling the truth. As Devon stroked her shoulder, Marie knew one thing for certain: This was how a man was supposed to treat a woman at all times. She and William posed for pictures, never had a real romance. He was a means to an end for her, and she was a step up the social ladder for him. Could Devon offer her something real? Would he want to take her on with all the baggage she came with? Glancing into his warm eyes, she hoped that he would. She was going to be a better person; did that mean she'd be able to fall in love with a better man? A man like Devon?

"Well," he said after a comfortable silence had enveloped them. "I'd better get you to your office and I need to head to the restaurant."

"Thanks for . . . everything."

"You don't have to thank me," he said. "And there is more to come."

"I'm definitely looking forward to that," she replied with a huge smile that melted Devon's heart. Maybe Marie Charles wasn't as much trouble as he initially thought.

Devon released her and took their plates into the kitchen. He could hear her moving around in the living room. Devon couldn't wait to see her in a pair of those killer heels again and nothing else. After washing the dishes, he returned to Marie, who was walking gingerly to test out her ankle.

"You OK?" he asked.

"Not bad. I know this might be asking a lot, but I really want Bria to have these shoes, so . . ."

"You want me to take you to the store to get another pair?"

She nodded. "If you have time. I still have a couple of hours before Adriana and I are scheduled to meet—and I'm not going to take that long." She laughed.

"Let me call my sous-chef and let her know that I'm going to be late. Then we can head to Payless Shoes," he said. Marie studied his face. Was he serious? She said she was willing to change, but there was no way in hell she was going to buy shoes from Payless.

"Umm, what?" she asked.

"They have BOGO, right?" he said, then burst into laughter. "I wish you could see your face right now."

Marie didn't have to see a reflection in the mirror to know that she was giving him a look akin to someone seeing hell frozen over. "I have a personal shoe shopper at Nordstrom."

"Excuse me. I didn't know that actually existed," he said as he dialed the restaurant on his cell phone.

After handling the scheduling at the restaurant and

getting assurances that everything was running fine in the kitchen, Devon drove Marie to SouthPark Mall. "Please tell me why women spend so much time and money on shoes," he asked as they headed into the store. As they passed through the vast shoe department, every sales clerk knew Marie's name.

"This is my Cheers," she joked. "And we mostly buy shoes for men and other women to notice."

"I've heard that before," he said, thinking about the wildly high-heeled shoes Serena wore. "I have to say, under different circumstances, I would've loved to see you walking toward me in those shoes that you twisted your ankle in."

"Really? You noticed them, despite the fact that you had your nose turned up at me as if I was the worst thing you'd ever seen?"

"I was simply wondering, what the hell is she thinking wearing those shoes to work in the kitchen?"

"To be honest, I'd hoped to not do any work. You showed me a thing or two," she said.

Devon shrugged. "I had to," he said. "I'm very serious about the work I do at the shelter."

"Why is it so important to you?" she asked. "And I'm not asking because I think you have some motive behind it, but seeing your relationship with the ladies and how serious you are about it, it makes me wonder why you decided to give so much of yourself."

Devon looked deep into Marie's eyes and wondered how much to tell Marie about what was behind his work at the shelter. He didn't like opening up about his past. In interviews, he'd been known to walk off the set if questions about his father came up. Outside of Kandace, no one knew the extent of what he and his mother had gone through and how helping women who couldn't turn to anyone else for assistance went much deeper for him than simply giving back to the community.

No one knew that it had been nearly a decade since he'd had a conversation with his father.

And despite the fact that he and Marie were getting closer, he wasn't ready to share that with her. Not right now. "Too many people don't stand up for what's right," he finally said. "They wait for someone else to do something and nothing gets accomplished."

"That's true," Marie agreed. "But I think you deserve a medal for giving a damn and doing it from your heart."

"Thanks," he replied. "Maybe this fund-raiser will inspire other people to give a damn, as you so eloquently put it."

Marie smiled and squeezed Devon's hand. "I've always been told that I have a way with words," she kidded.

"Marie Charles, are you wearing sneakers?" a tall ebony man with a blue-black bob and a tailored suit called out. "I'm guessing hell has frozen over." He pushed his perfectly coiffed hair behind his ears, then clasped his hands together as he gave Devon the once-over. "Is this famed chef Devon Harris? *Il est une amélioration énorme au-dessus de votre dernier amoureux.*"

Marie shook her head and Devon smiled, then said, "I'm flattered."

"You speak French?" the man asked, then he covered his mouth with his hand.

"Jorge, I need some flats," Marie said through her laughter.

"Flats? Well, if you say so. But I . . ."

"I sprained my ankle," she said, "This is only a temporary change."

Jorge clasped his hands together. "Thank God, because the new Louboutins are screaming your lovely name."

Marie smiled as Jorge led her and Devon to a private room in the rear of the store. Devon was surprised to see that an area like this existed in the swanky store. There was a velvet sofa, a coffee table with live flowers on it, and mood music playing in the background.

"So, his real name is George, isn't it?" Devon asked when Jorge walked out of the room.

"Leave him alone," Marie said. "He's a lifesaver. So, Jorge, George, or whatever, I love that man."

"I'm starting to feel a little jealous," he said.

"Of Jorge?"

"No, your love of shoes. Will anyone ever live up to that?" he asked with a laugh.

"Hmm," she said, then slipped her finger underneath her chin as if she was thinking about it. Before she could reply, Jorge returned with four boxes of shoes.

"All right, Bella, here's what I think you will like. I've never seen you in a pair of flats so this was hard." Jorge turned to Devon. "Would you like something to drink? Water, chardonnay, whiskey?"

"I'll take a water," Devon said. Jorge then turned to Marie and smiled.

"Bella, your usual?" he asked, then mouthed, "Make sure you keep bringing him around."

Marie narrowed her eyes at Jorge, then said, "I'll have a water, too."

As Jorge left the room, he glanced at Devon's feet. "Size twelve?" he asked.

"Yeah."

"I have something in a brown leather loafer that I think you would love," he said. "I'll be back with the water and the shoes."

"I told you," she said once they were alone. "Jorge is the man." Marie smiled as she thought about the old adage about men with big feet. She really hoped it was true in Devon's case.

Chapter 13

When Devon and Marie left Nordstrom, all he could do was shake his head. Marie had four bags of shoes and he was carrying a pair of brown Ferragamo lace-up boots. He'd never paid three hundred dollars for a pair of shoes or understood what was so important about a pair of shoes, but Jorge and Marie had spent thirty minutes talking him into them. This, he decided, would not become a habit.

"You're quiet over there," she said. "Don't tell me you're having shoe buyer's regret."

"I'm still wrapping my mind around that shoe dissertation you and George gave me about a good pair of shoes," Devon said, then laughed. "I really zoned out when he said a good-fitting pair of shoes is better than sex."

"It's the truth. But please tell me you won't wear those in the kitchen."

"Not at all," he said as he shook his bag. "I'm wearing these when we go dancing."

"Dancing? You dance?"

"I have moves that you will not be able to describe."

Marie chewed her bottom lip and raised her eyebrow. "That could go either way."

"You're going to have to take me up on my offer and find out."

She smiled, thinking that she wanted to see his moves and the dance floor wasn't the proper setting, but she said, "OK. As soon as this ankle of mine is ready to slip into my favorite pair of Ferragamo T-straps."

"That sounds kinky," he joked. "I'm looking forward to it. So, tell me something, do you really believe a pair of shoes is better than sex?"

"If I say yes, will you prove me wrong?"

Devon winked at her. "It will be my duty to prove you wrong." He looked down at his watch. "It's getting late. Where's your office?"

"Off Providence Road."

"OK, I'll drop you off, and what are you doing for dinner?"

"I don't have plans," she said.

"You do now. Why don't you and your partner be my guests at Hometown Delights tonight?"

"All right," she said. "And I'll wear my new shoes."

Devon laughed. "Which pair? You bought so many."

"If you're going to be hanging out with me, you're going to have to develop an appreciation for shoes."

"I have an appreciation for shoes," he said, glancing down at her feet. "It's the shopping for them that I can do without."

She placed her hand on his shoulder, happy to be walking without her crutch just so she could touch him, then she kissed him on the cheek. "You'll get used to it."

"How about I introduce you to my friend Serena. You two have a lot in common already," he said.

A twinge of jealousy attacked her. Why did he keep talking about Serena and was she simply just a friend?

This man is single, and if he hangs out with some other woman, how can I hold that against him? It's not my concern.

"Marie," he said. "You all right?"

"What?"

"I asked you a question," he said. "Your ankle seems to be doing a little better."

"Yes, and I don't like lumbering around on those crutches." Before she said another word, Devon scooped her into his arms. Marie squealed with shock and delight. "What are you doing?"

"The sooner your ankle heels, the sooner I wear these shoes on our date," he quipped as he carried her and all of her shoes to the car.

By the time Marie met Adriana, her mind was gone. All she could think about was her afternoon with Devon. The skillful way he licked and kissed the most precious part of her body, his concern for her injury, and moreover, his indulgence of her shoe shopping. She smiled like a satisfied kid on Christmas afternoon.

"Hello!" Adriana snapped. "Am I talking to myself here? You know, you've been loopy since Mr. Harris dropped you off, and don't think I missed those looks you two were exchanging when he invited me to dinner."

"A dinner you're not going to be able to make," Marie chimed in.

Adriana waved her hand. "Yeah, yeah, whatever. You slept with that man."

"I did no such thing."

"Marie, two things in the world make you act like this: brand-new Louboutins and good sex."

"Add good food to the list, because Devon and I had lunch and looked at Louboutins today. So, yes, in the life of Marie Charles, today was a good day. Oh, remember I said there was something I wanted to talk to you about?"

"I assumed that's what we were doing," Adriana said. Marie pouted and threw her hand up at her friend.

"This is serious. How is our budget looking these days?"

"Well, we've lost a couple of clients, but we're still in the black," she replied. "Why?"

"I want us to bring one of the women from the shelter on."

"To do what?"

"A publicity assistant on a part-time basis, and if business picks up and she does as well as I think she will, then full time," Marie said.

"Are you doing this to impress Devon?" she questioned.

"No," Marie exclaimed. "Shay is actually qualified and I want to help her."

"And that's all this is?"

Marie folded her arms across her chest and glared at her friend, tempted to tell her that if she wanted to hire five new people, she could, since she had a controlling interest in their company. "You know what, why don't I bring Shay over and you can meet her and judge for yourself?"

"When you say it like that, I guess you are doing it for all the right reasons," Adriana said. "But, I have to say that I'm impressed that you want to do this."

Marie could understand her friend's attitude. Her previous charitable acts had been all about getting headlines and making a donation. But she'd also never met anyone like Shay and the other women at My Sister's Keeper. "I think once my community service is over, we should do some more work over there."

"We?"

"Our company. That place is filled with women who could make a difference if given a chance."

Adriana leaned back in her plush leather seat. "Forgive me if I sound harsh or misinformed, but when I hear 'homeless' I think about the man at the gas station begging for a dollar."

"Until a few days ago, I would've been right there with you," Marie said. "But with this economy, the mortgage crisis, and all the job losses, who's homeless has changed."

"I hadn't even thought about that," she said.

"I'll admit that I wouldn't be thinking about it if it weren't for Devon," Marie revealed. "But you'd have to be pretty heartless not to start caring about these women."

"I knew he had a role in this," Adriana replied with a smile. "And I hate to change the subject, but William has been seeking you. He came by here three times today."

"He has a damned nerve."

Adriana shrugged. "Word on the street is that Greta put him out."

"I'm not surprised. Once she figured out that I wasn't torn up about the relationship ending and my life didn't end with my arrest, I imagine the luster of winning that bastard back wore off."

"That sounds right," she replied. "And the client she took from us, Destiny Food, has been calling for you as well."

Marie couldn't help but smile, and while she wanted to call her contact with the company and tell them what part of her body they could attach their lips to, she decided that if they wanted M&A to handle their press, Shay would take the lead.

"I guess I could give them a call," she said. "Go up on the price and let Shay handle the campaign."

"Good idea. But I hope she can handle it," Adriana said. "And, I spoke to the new management at Mez, since one of our new clients will only have their product launch party there."

"Let me guess, they said yes as long as I don't show up."

Adriana nodded and gave Marie the thumbs-up sign. "I figured they wouldn't have a problem with the money Unique Brands is spending on this party."

"Money talks in Charlotte," Marie said.

"Well, at least you're seeing someone who doesn't need your money, now."

Marie smiled. She wouldn't say that she and Devon were seeing each other, but she knew something was developing between them, something real. Or was she expecting too much again?

Devon walked into the kitchen of Hometown Delights with a smile on his face. It startled his sous-chef as she told him about some serious problems they'd been having in the kitchen with the oven and a couple of burners on the stove.

"It's all right," he said to the frazzled chef. "I'll take a look at the burners on the stove and you call the repairman and tell him that he will be fixing the oven for free today." Then Devon patted her on her shoulder in a comforting manner. "It's going to be all right. I'll even do a no-bake dessert to make things easier."

"What's going on with you?" she asked.

Devon glanced down at his watch; three hours until dinner. "Nothing," he replied, "I just don't feel the need to get upset about things that we can fix."

"Who are you and what have you done with Chef Harris?" she asked with her eyebrow raised.

"Who's in the office?" he asked.

"Jade, I think," she replied. Devon nodded and headed out of the kitchen, leaving his sous-chef totally confused.

When Devon arrived at the office, he knocked on the open door when he saw Jade and her husband, James, embracing passionately. "Excuse me," he said.

The couple turned and looked at him. James nodded hello, then kissed his wife's hand. "We'll finish this later—at home."

"We sure will," she replied with a sly smile. Devon smirked as James shook his hand and headed out the door.

"Still acting like newlyweds, huh?"

Jade shrugged and leaned against the desk. "Who wants a boring marriage? What's going on with you?"

"The bigger question is: What's going on with the oven and the stove in the kitchen? Two burners are out and the oven's dead."

"Oh my goodness," Jade said. "I wish your staff felt comfortable talking to me and the other ladies. Lunch was a mess, food came out late and we had no idea why." She tilted her head to the side. "Where were you? At the shelter?"

Devon's smile said more than he wanted it to, and Jade picked up on it immediately. "So, what's her name?" she asked.

"You know what they say about assuming, right?" Devon said, trying to keep a poker face.

"Boy, how long have I known you? Now, what's her name?"

"It's a long story, and I don't have time to tell it. I need you to get me some kitchen equipment that works," Devon said, smirking as he spoke. "The oven has to go."

Jade nodded as she made a note of what Devon had been saying about the oven. Then she looked up at her friend. "It's Marie Charles, isn't it? I can't believe you."

"What?" he asked. "She's nothing like what you read about in the papers, and she's going to be my guest for dinner tonight. Marie and her business partner."

Jade dropped her pen and shook her head. "But aren't you like her supervisor for community service? That has to be wrong and against the rules or something."

"It isn't, and I do hope you're going to hurry home and finish what you and your husband were about to start in here."

Jade offered him a knowing smile. "James and Jaden can have dinner and bath time without me tonight. Especially since Serena and Alicia are coming through for dinner and drinks."

"Don't scare the woman off," Devon warned, knowing that telling them to leave her alone would be akin to beating his head against a brick wall and expecting it to come tumbling down.

"Are you sure this is the kind of woman you don't want to send off running?" Jade asked. "I mean . . ."

"It wasn't too long ago that someone was asking those same questions about you," he said.

"Touché," Jade replied, recalling the rocky relationship that she and her brother-in-law, Maurice, had during the early days of her relationship with James. "I'll be nice, but I can't vouch for the others."

"I'm telling you, you guys are a street gang in stilettos." Devon shook his head and squeezed the bridge of his nose. "Marie and I are just getting to know each other, and I don't need you guys putting your two cents in."

"All right, all right," Jade said. "But we only want what's best for you. I'm not convinced that it's Marie Charles, but if you like it, I love it."

Devon bowed like a Broadway actor. Oh, he liked it, and maybe he liked it a little too much. Was Marie the woman he'd spent the day with or really the wild child that showed up in the newspapers and ended up doing community service?

"Devon," Jade said, breaking into his thoughts. "Did you hear me?"

"No, what?"

"Will replacing the oven cause us to have to shut down?"

"No," he said. "As long as it's done at least four hours before lunch."

"All right, I'll make some calls and we'll get it taken care of tomorrow. Will you be here to supervise?"

He nodded. "Now, let me go make a no-bake chocolate dessert."

"Make sure you save me some. I think my husband deserves some chocolate tonight."

"I'm not touching that one," he said as he threw up the peace sign and headed for the kitchen. Devon decided that he'd do a special dinner for Marie: his New Orleans chicken with tomato and onion pilaf, a crisp spinach and strawberry salad, and a goddess chocolate and rum pudding. This would be the perfect meal for her, and Devon couldn't help but laugh as he thought about the last time he'd made the goddess pudding. He'd made it for Monique, a pastry chef he'd met in Paris, and she'd loved it so much that she'd smoothed it across his chest and licked it off. Sex and food had been his life when he'd been a student in Paris as he tried to get over Kandace and rid himself of the guilt he'd felt because of what he'd done and how much like his father he'd become.

Maybe that's why he wanted to do things right with Marie. He wanted to make sure whatever they were doing was because they both wanted it. One thing was for sure, he thought as he cracked two eggs into a mixing bowl. He wanted Marie for Marie and nothing else. He just hoped she felt the same way.

Chapter 14

Marie smoothed gloss across her lips as she took another look at her image in the mirror. Hair curled and hanging in loose tendrils, eyes smoky and mysterious, ears adorned with silver and diamond hoops. She felt flawless and overdressed. *It's just dinner,* she told herself as she closed her tube of gloss. *But dinner with Devon.*

Marie knew with him, she didn't have to do that attention-seeking thing she was known for. As a matter of fact, she probably wouldn't see much of Devon anyway. She'd been to many restaurant openings as the guest of a chef. Sure, your table is in the middle of the restaurant and everyone sees you, but it's not as if the chef joins you for dinner.

She pulled a pomegranate makeup remover wipe from the box and scrubbed her face clean. The face that looked back at her seemed ten years younger and fresher. "No wonder Daddy called it war paint," she whispered as she smoothed a light coat of gloss on her lips, then headed into her bedroom to grab her shoes. Dressed in a pair of snakeskin designer leggings and a pink and silver tunic, Marie wished she could wear her taupe peep-toe Louboutins. But there was no way she could walk in those shoes with her ankle still giving her problems. She'd settle for her Tory Burch ballerina flats; that way she could walk without carrying that annoying crutch. As she reached for her phone to call a car service, it rang.

She shook her head as she recognized the number belonged to William. Speaking to him was the last thing she needed. He was history, the past, and she was looking toward a future with a man who didn't have an agenda. Granted, she'd picked William for her own agenda, but it became clear that he'd been enjoying her limelight a little too much and had no intentions of actually marrying her as they'd agreed to. He'd been enjoying using Marie's connections to get into Charlotte's hottest night spots and get up close and personal with some of the other party girls. There'd been rumors of his infidelity, but Marie hadn't cared because there hadn't been real proof of him sleeping around. Other than the fact that they'd stopped having sex about a month after they'd started.

William had proven to be as selfish in bed as he'd been in every other aspect of his life and Marie couldn't be so bothered. But she hadn't planned on William embarrassing her at her own event.

Not that getting arrested is ever a good thing, but if it weren't for William's disrespectful display at Mez, I wouldn't have met Devon. I can't believe that punk actually did something that helped me, she thought as she hit the Ignore button on her phone. That would be the best thing she could do for and to William. After calling the car service, Marie gave herself another inspection in the mirror. Simple outfit, cute hair, flat shoes; this was a Marie Charles no one would expect to see.

* * *

Jade laughed as she watched Devon prepare a plate. It looked as if he was making a meal for the president of the United States or the Queen of England. He turned to his friend and scowled at her. "What?"

"She's not here yet. You don't hear the clicks of cameras, do you?" Jade quipped.

"Whatever. I don't have many people sitting at the chef's table, so I'm trying to make this special," he said, though the truth of the matter was, he wanted it special because it was Marie.

"Alicia and Serena aren't going to come through tonight, so you can relax and enjoy feeding your new . . . What are you and Marie doing?"

Before he could respond to her, there was a loud crash from the freezer, prompting Devon and Jade to rush back to see what was going on. "This is all we need tonight," he muttered, thinking about how behind the kitchen had gotten while waiting for the repairman to fix the burners on the stove and offer a temporary solution to the oven issue.

"I hope it's nothing," Jade said as he opened the freezer. Luckily, their fears were unfounded as the crash had come from cartons of angus steaks stacked too high.

"Who did this?" Devon bellowed. "First of all, there's a chart, right here on the damned door, detailing how to stack food in the freezer."

Jade jumped, surprised to see the *Hell's Kitchen* side of Devon. "Chef," one of the kitchen expeditors said, "that's my fault. Things got busy and I just . . ."

Devon stepped in the young man's face and glared at him. "Don't let it happen again. We have rules in the kitchen for a reason."

"Yes, Chef," he replied.

Devon shook his head and turned back to Jade. "The

kitchen isn't for the fainthearted," he told her. "Don't look at me like that."

"I've never seen this side of you," she replied. "Then again, I don't spend much time in the kitchen."

"And you shouldn't because you look like you want to cry right now," he said as he walked Jade out into the hallway.

"You're mean!" She laughed as they walked into the dining room. Devon's heart nearly stopped when he saw Marie being led to her table. She was breathtaking with her clean face and fashionable outfit. Even without high heels, her legs were amazing, and that round bottom of hers made his mouth water. He waited before approaching the table, wondering where her business partner was, since he had invited them both. A few moments passed and he realized that Marie was alone. A slow smile, which didn't go unnoticed by Jade, spread across his face.

"Well, well," she said. "The evil chef smiles. I'm going to greet your guest." Devon touched her arm.

"Let me do that," he said. "Then you can interrupt us."

Jade rolled her eyes and stepped aside. Devon crossed over to Marie, drinking in her image again before saying, "I'm glad you could make it."

She smiled at him, her lips glimmering under the dim lights. "I couldn't think of anywhere else I wanted to be."

"Will Adriana be joining you?" he asked.

"Umm, she sends along her regrets," Marie replied. "I guess I'll be dining alone tonight."

"Not necessarily," he replied as he pushed a stray curl behind her ear. "I'll be happy to join you for the main course."

Marie blushed as his finger brushed across her cheek. How she wished he was the main course. Even in his chef's jacket, pants with a smattering of food and oil, and a pair of sneakers that looked about three years old, Devon Harris was a sexy man. Lust-worthy, even. But Marie wanted and hoped that the vibe between them was something deeper; something that could blossom and grow.

"Ready for the first course?" he asked as he pulled her chair out.

"Sure," she replied once she was seated. Devon stood behind her, and she felt electric currents ripple through her body as he described the salad that he'd made for her and the wine that would accompany it. He could've told her that he was going to feed her bread and water; it wouldn't have mattered.

"Sounds good," she said.

"It'll be right out," Devon said as he took her hand and placed a sweet kiss on her palm. Marie could've melted in her seat.

"I can't wait."

Devon winked at her and headed to the kitchen. Marie hugged herself tightly and smiled. She didn't notice Jade when she approached the table.

"Hello," Jade said, breaking into Marie's thoughts of Devon. "I'm Jade Goings, one of the owners. Welcome to Hometown Delights."

"Thank you," Marie said as she and Jade shook hands.

"Mind if I sit for a moment?" she asked.

"Not at all. This place is a pleasant surprise," Marie said as Jade took her seat.

"Oh, this is your first visit for dinner? Now, how could Charlotte's it girl not come here?"

Marie shuttered inwardly; she now hated that moniker. "Well," she said.

Jade held her hand up. "I know, there were a lot of bad things that happened here. I get it."

"Had I known the food was so great, I would've come a lot sooner."

Jade smiled and nodded. "I'm sure. Marie, I don't know you and I don't want to prejudge you, but we're like a family here."

"OK," Marie said, wondering where this conversation was going.

"I just hope that your interest in Devon, who is a lot like a brother to me, is genuine," she said. "Because if it isn't . . ."

"Listen," Marie said, cutting her off. "Devon and I are just getting to know each other, and I really feel as if he's someone I want to get to know and see where it goes."

"And this has nothing to do with the fact that he supervises your court-ordered community service?"

Marie folded her arms across her chest and glared at Jade, wondering if this big-sister act was hiding something more. "Why do you care? Last time I checked, Devon's a grown man, and if he thought I was using him, I wouldn't be here."

Jade shrugged. "Maybe, maybe not. We all know what to do to blind a man to the truth."

"For someone who claims to know and love Devon like a brother, you have a low opinion of him," Marie retorted.

"I just want you to prove me wrong," Jade said. "And I don't want to see Devon hurt."

"I don't intend to hurt him," she said. "What about him hurting me? Can you have this same conversation with him, or are you simply judging me because of what you've read?"

"That's all I know about you," Jade said. "And you did a good job of crafting your image. Maybe Devon has met the real you, maybe you're still the party girl, but trying to clean up your image by hooking up with Devon?"

Marie tilted her head as she watched Jade question her. On the one hand, she was pissed off. Who did this woman think she was? But on the other hand, she admired the friendship that she and Devon seemed to have. Still, Jade needed to mind her own business and get away from her table so that she could enjoy her meal with Devon.

"Are you done?" Marie asked.

"Excuse me?" Jade asked, taken aback by her bluntness.

"Devon invited me as his guest, and I know you're his friend and you have his best interest at heart, but I don't intend to be grilled by you all night."

"Then why don't we meet for coffee?" Jade suggested.

Marie reached into her purse and handed Jade a business card. "Please call me," she said, then offered her a plastic smile while hoping she'd leave.

"I will," Jade replied. "Enjoy your dinner." As Jade left, a waiter walked over to the table with the first course of dinner.

"Thank you," Marie said when he set the salad, filled with succulent strawberries, in front of her.

"Chef Harris said he will be over in a few moments to check on you," the waiter said. Marie smiled her thanks and dug into the salad. When she was half done, Marie wondered, where was Devon?

When Devon's cell phone rang, he figured that it was important or one of his producers calling about next week's show. But when he saw the 404 area code, he knew he should've ignored the call. Yet, he answered anyway.

"Yeah?"

"Well, hello to you, too, Son," Devon Sr. said. "I've been trying to reach you for a month."

"What do you want? I'm a little busy," he replied.

"It's been a while since we've had a conversation."

"And?"

"Junior, we really need to sit down and have a conversation. How long has it been? Ten years?"

"Not long enough," Devon snapped. "I knew I shouldn't have answered the phone. I'm busy."

"I'm dying."

"Why don't you tell it to someone who cares." Devon clicked his phone off and leaned against the wall to catch his breath. He didn't have time to deal with his father and whatever drama he was dealing with. Still, if his father was really dying, could he simply ignore it?

"Chef, your guest is getting restless," the waiter said.

"I'm going to take her main course out," Devon said, pushing his father's voice deep down into his subconscious. As he plated Marie's dinner—New Orleans chicken with tomato and onion pilaf, with crisp steamed vegetables—and wiped the plate, Devon decided to focus on Marie and ignore his father as he had been doing for the last decade.

By the time he locked eyes with her as he approached the table, he'd forgotten about his short conversation with his father. "I heard you were waiting for this," Devon said as he set the plate in front of her.

"Looks delicious," she replied.

"Yes, you do."

Marie blushed as Devon sat down. "Are you enjoying your dinner so far?" he asked. Marie nodded as she cut into the juicy chicken breast.

"Everything has been great, but now that you're here, it can't do anything but get better."

"You mean Jade didn't ruin the evening for me?"

Marie laughed as she popped a piece of chicken in her mouth. The flavor exploded in her mouth and she shivered in delight. "If she had, you'd certainly make up for it with this chicken."

The waiter walked over to the table and set a plate in front of Devon. "Thank you," he said to the waiter. Then Devon turned back to Marie, watching her enjoy her meal. As her lips closed around the fork, he wanted nothing more than to have those lips pressed against his. Tonight, he would have Marie or he would explode. "Make sure you save room for dessert," he said. "I made something especially with you in mind."

"And what would that be?"

"You will see, and I hope you love it," Devon said before digging into his food. The New Orleans chicken, which wasn't on the menu every night, was one of his favorite dishes. It reminded him of the kind of women he always fell for: spicy, exciting, and savory.

"This is the best chicken I've ever tasted," Marie gushed as she polished off the last of her chicken.

"Are you ready for dessert?" Devon asked as he finished half of his chicken. If he could've gotten away with it—at that moment—he would've simply scooped Marie up and taken her home. He would slowly and carefully peel those skintight pants off her and have her sweet womanhood for his dessert. The way she tasted, he wouldn't need the chocolate dessert he'd created.

Devon waved for the waiter and told him to bring the dessert out. "Here's the extra special dish I made with you in mind."

"I'm going to have to hit the gym so hard after this dinner and dessert," she said as she reached across the table and stroked his hand. "Is it chocolate?"

He winked at her and lifted her hand to his lips. "Would dessert be dessert if it wasn't? You know, when I made this, I thought about you."

Before she could say, "Really?" the waiter walked out with the chocolate goddess—a creamy chocolate mousse nestled in a sweet torte crust drizzled with caramel and surrounded by dark chocolate curls. Marie couldn't wait to taste it as the waiter set it in the middle of the table. Devon reached into the pocket of his chef's jacket and pulled out a silver fork. "When a goddess eats the chocolate goddess, she has to be fed," Devon said as he dipped the fork into the dessert. Marie leaned forward and allowed Devon to feed her. The flavor of the dessert just exploded in her mouth, and she moaned as if she'd just reached her sexual peak. Devon smiled at her. Marie had her eyes closed and her head tossed back in delight.

"Oh my goodness. This is the best torte ever." Devon offered her another forkful.

"You know, this would taste even better inside my loft," he whispered, deciding that dinner service would be just fine without him.

"I totally agree," she replied.

Devon waved for the waiter and instructed him to wrap up the dessert, and then he rose from his seat, crossed over to Marie, and pulled her chair out, then linked arms with her. "Let's go, madame."

Marie smiled and followed his lead. The waiter met them at the door and handed Devon the dessert. As they exited the restaurant, a camera flash went off in their faces. Marie was used to being stalked by the local paparazzo, but Devon certainly was not. He threw his hand up and turned to the photographer. "Get the hell out of here," he exclaimed.

"So, are you two a couple? Aren't you Devon Harris, the Food Network star?"

He glared at the cocoa-skinned man with a dyed blond

Afro and big sticker on the side of his camera that said *Queen City After Dark*.

"Ignore him," Marie said as she tugged on his arm. "This is my personal stalker, Giancarlo Alverez."

Devon shook his head. Despite this interruption, he was going to take her back to his place and they were going to enjoy their dessert. Once they were in the car, he turned to Marie and smiled. "You get that a lot, huh?"

"*Queen City After Dark* is a blog that tries to be a local *TMZ*, and I'm a favorite target."

"So, that means we're going to have to spend a lot of nights in, huh?"

Marie smiled brightly. She liked that Devon was talking about a future with her. She definitely wanted a future with him. "That works for me," she said.

"Good, because I'm about to show you how much fun it can be to spend a night in," he said.

Chapter 15

When they reached Devon's loft, Marie was happy for the quiet and the darkness. The moment he opened the door, Marie pulled his keys from his hand and tossed them across the room. Then she pressed her body against his. "Can I tell you that I've wanted to do this since you fed me that delicious dessert?" she said, then brushed her lips against his.

"That's why I fed it to you," he said, then ran his tongue across her lips. Marie moaned as Devon slipped his hand between her thighs and stroked her through her leggings. "These have to come off. I want to feel your heat."

"Take them off me," she moaned, her heart beating in overdrive as she stepped out of her shoes. Devon slowly eased the leggings down her hips, kissing each inch of exposed skin while squeezing her ample bottom. Once the leggings were off, Devon lifted Marie into his arms and carried her upstairs to his bedroom. He laid her on the bed and drank in her sensual image against his black bedding. With her hair fanned out on the pillow, she reminded him of something both erotic and angelic. Devon's desire grew against his zipper. His plan had been to feed her the goddess in bed, but it was time for him to have his chocolate desire.

He snatched his chef's jacket off, tossed it aside, and eased onto the bed, spreading Marie's legs apart. He could feel the heat radiating from her body as he pushed the flimsy lace crotch of her thong to the side. "Umm," she moaned as he slipped his finger between her wet folds of flesh. Devon pulled his finger out and brought it to his lips.

"Tastes good," he said as he licked her essence from his finger. "I want more." He dove between her legs, lapping her sweetness and kissing her deeply. His tongue danced around her clitoris, making her desire rain down like a thunderstorm in the middle of a Carolina summer. Marie's moans and screams boomed like a trumpet and urged Devon on. He sucked harder, kissed deeper, and grew harder. By Marie's second climax, he knew he had to lose his pants and melt with her. Pulling back, he stripped out of his pants and boxers in one quick motion. Marie rolled over and crawled to the edge of the bed where Devon stood.

"Can I get a taste of chocolate, too?" she asked as she reached out and stroked his penis. He didn't think that it was possible for him to get harder, but the moment her lips touched the tip of his throbbing erection, it happened. Marie gripped the base of him as she licked him like the rich dessert he'd fed her earlier. Devon quivered as he felt the explosion inside him building, but Marie would not take her lips off him. Then he looked down and saw her hand between her legs, touching and pleasing herself. It was all he could do to stay upright. Finally, she pulled back, just moments before he was about to climax. Devon reached over to his nightstand and grabbed a condom. Marie took it from his hands and rolled it down his erection, then he joined her on the bed.

Devon pulled Marie against his chest and lifted her shirt above her head and tossed it aside. He wrapped her legs around his waist as he brought her lips to his and kissed her slowly, his tongue tangoing against hers as their bodies melted together. They rocked in the center of the bed, finding each other's rhythm. Marie liked it when Devon thrust forward and touched her most sensitive spot. Devon loved how she squeezed tightly against him as if she were milking the desire from him.

She reveled in the way his palms felt against her breasts, stroking and kneading them like she imagined he did with the dough he baked. But more than anything else, she loved the lick of his tongue against her nipples as they ground against each other. Devon took Marie's pleasure seriously, something she'd never experienced with another man. While he made her body feel sensations she'd only read about in steamy novels, she went hoarse from calling out his name and screaming her pleasure.

Devon tried to hold back the burning desire to spill himself inside her, simply because he wanted to prolong her bliss. But the deeper she drew him into her wetness and the more she called his name, then licked and sucked his neck, the more powerless he became to his own climax. He tumbled backward on the bed and Marie collapsed against his chest. Their bodies were still connected and sweat covered them like a damp satin sheet. "Umm," Marie moaned, kissing the center of his chest. "Wow."

He brought his finger to her lips and smiled. "And just think, you haven't even finished your dessert yet." Neither of them felt as if they could move, but when Marie shifted against Devon, he felt one part of his body move and so did she.

Straddling his hips, she returned his smile with a sultry grin and rode him slow. "Dessert can wait."

He gripped her ample hips and groaned passionately. "Oh, yes, baby. The whole world can wait."

Finally spent from their lovemaking, Devon and Marie lay in the bed, polishing off the chocolate goddess. "Well," she asked as she took the last bite of the dessert. "I hate to say it, but you're going to have a lot of questions to answer in the morning."

"I know how to say 'no comment.' And I hope you will do the same," he replied.

"I never kiss and tell," she retorted. "And I never expected to wind up lying here with you."

"Really?"

Marie propped up on her elbows, and as much as Devon tried to be a gentleman and look into her eyes, all he could focus on were those cocoa brown breasts. His mouth watered and his loins began to rise again. Obviously, she realized he wasn't paying attention because she pinched his shoulder. "Hello," Marie joked. "Eyes up here. It's not as if you haven't seen them before."

"I just like looking at them. But you were saying, beautiful?"

Marie smiled, hiding her inner gushiness at the fact that Devon was just as sweet now as he was before they made love. "When we met, you gave me all kinds of hell."

"You don't think you deserved it?" Devon asked. "I believe you accused me of using a charity for ratings. That was a little hard to take, especially from someone I didn't know."

"OK, maybe I deserved a little bit of your attitude, but it wasn't as if I knew anything about you either," she said, then stroked his cheek. "You know I had to Google you to see what you looked like."

"Yeah, but you weren't very impressed, huh?" he ribbed.

"I was, until you opened your mouth. You were so mean to me."

Devon rolled closer to her and brushed his lips across her shoulder. "How many ways can I make it up to you?" he asked.

"Umm, you can start with breakfast in bed, served by you completely naked," she said.

"That's easy," he said. "I guess you're not the high-maintenance woman that we've all read about in the papers, huh?"

"Only seventy percent of my press has been true. The rest was for fun and attention. But I'm starting to see the error in that."

Devon stroked her smooth hip. "How so?"

"It's obvious your girl Jade believes what she reads," Marie said quietly, recalling the contentious conversation she and Jade Goings shared. "What's the deal with you guys?"

"What do you mean?"

"Are you simply just friends and coworkers or is there a history there? I know some exes remain . . ."

"Whoa, whoa, Jade is like the annoying little sister I never wanted. Ex, no. That's Kandace."

"Right. She married the mogul. What did you do to her?"

Devon ran his fingers through Marie's silky tresses. "What do most men do to ruin relationships? I cheated."

Marie turned her head and looked directly into his eyes. "You? I would've never thought that."

Devon laughed sardonically. "I'm no saint."

"I can't tell."

"You should've known me ten years ago," he said. "But, that was then and this is now."

Marie nestled against his broad chest and looked up at him. "Imperfect souls, the two of us," she said, then kissed his collarbone. "Maybe that's why we clashed and connected."

"I like that."

"And I like you," she said. "I like you a lot more than I thought I would."

"Well, it goes without saying that I like you. The bare Marie Charles is amazing," Devon said, then kissed her cheek. "But if you want naked breakfast in bed, then we'd better get some sleep."

She reached between his legs and stroked his flaccid penis. Immediately, Devon's body reacted to Marie's expert touch. "Sleep is so overrated," she said as she reached for a condom and straddled his body.

The next morning, Devon woke up to the chiming of his BlackBerry. The fact that he had Marie's warm body wrapped up in his arms made him want to ignore the ringing. Because, seriously, someone was calling him at five forty in the morning? Voice mail could handle whomever was on the other end of that call, he decided as he held Marie a little tighter. Before he could drift off to sleep, the phone rang again. Marie stirred in his arms and opened her eyes. "That must be you," she said, her voice thick with sleep. "Everyone who knows me, knows better than to call me this time of morning."

"Yeah," he grumbled as he released her and scrambled for his phone on the floor. Picking up the device and looking at the number, he groaned. It was his father—again. There were three missed calls from the Atlanta number.

"What?" Devon snapped when he answered the phone.

"We need to talk, Son," Devon Sr. said, then began coughing uncontrollably. "I'd like to see you and mend fences."

"It's a little late for that," he said. "And do you know what time it is?"

"Well, the last time we talked, you hung up on me. Devon, Son, I know I wasn't the best father. I wasn't there for you and your mother, but I want . . ."

"Don't mention her. You're not fit to talk about her," Devon spat. Though Marie wasn't sure who he was talking to, the venom Devon hurled into the phone made her shudder. How could the man who'd made love to her so tenderly and so passionately be so cruel and cold? She pulled the sheet back and headed into the bathroom. Even behind the closed door, she could hear Devon's voice booming.

"If you're going to die, have your people e-mail me a copy of your obit. I don't want to meet with you. I've gone ten years without talking to you and would be happy to go another ten. Evil like yours doesn't die. You're like a roach, I'm sure you will outlast a nuclear holocaust."

Marie jumped when she heard what sounded like Devon's phone bouncing off the wall. She dashed out of the bathroom and crossed over to Devon, who was kneeling near the foot of the bed.

"I'm afraid to ask what that was all about," she said in a timid voice.

"Then don't," he said coldly as he rose to his feet. "I'm going to start on breakfast. You can go back to sleep if you'd like."

"No," Marie said. "You don't get to sound all angry and psychotic on the phone and then offer to cook me breakfast and send me to bed with a pat on my ass."

Devon dropped his head, and his shoulders sagged as if he had the weight of the world resting on them. It was times like this when he missed Kandace because he was able to open up to her about his contentious relationship with Devon Sr. and she understood the issues he had with his father. Could he open up to Marie in that way?

He faced her and stroked her tussled hair. "That was my father," Devon said. "As you can tell, we don't get along."

"You were talking to your dad like that?" she asked, then brought her hand to her mouth.

"That bastard is lucky I spoke to him at all," Devon boomed. "Listen, I don't expect you to understand my relationship with Devon Sr. You grew up with a decent man for a father. I wasn't so lucky."

She shrugged, but her face showed how vexed she was. Marie, though she gave her father headaches with her past behavior, was extremely close to him and couldn't imagine speaking to him in such a vicious manner. As much as she wanted to ask him what caused such a volcanic rift between him and his father, the look on Devon's face said he wasn't ready to share.

He reached out and touched her cheek. "It's a long story," he said. "And as bad as that conversation sounded . . ."

"You don't have to explain anything to me if you don't want to."

Devon sighed, sounding relieved to Marie, and smiled. "Is it too early for breakfast?"

"It is early," she said as she eased back on to the bed. "But, I'm not the one who has to do the cooking." She winked at him and pulled the sheet up to her chin. "I'll be waiting."

Devon crawled back into bed and straddled Marie's covered body. "Well, Miss Charles," he said, "I don't want to start cooking, in the kitchen, just this second when your lips look so kissable right now." Devon captured her lips and kissed her sweetly, passionately, and apologetically. She melted against him, now wishing she'd never pulled that sheet up so far. When he broke the kiss, Devon stroked her cheek. "Listen," he said. "That conversation with me and my father has a lot of history behind it and I don't like to talk about it. He's not a good man, hasn't been the kind of father that you're used to."

"All right, but he's still your father."

Devon leapt off the bed. "He's my sperm donor," he snapped. "Devon Sr. was never a father to me, nor a husband to my mother. He was a monster who hid behind his jump shot. The man people saw on TV and hugging little kids at the Ronald McDonald hospitals wasn't the man who came home to me and my mother. He was abusive, and if my mother hadn't had access to his money, she would've been just like many of the women at My Sister's Keeper. You asked me why I do what I do there, and it's because I see my mother in all of them. Especially Bria. I know what these women are facing and how no one gives a damn about them until they're a purple ribbon on the police department's domestic violence Christmas tree."

Tears sprang into Marie's eyes, and her heart broke for him. It all made sense, his fierce loyalty to the women at the shelter, the way he'd run after Bria, and his anger when he'd thought Marie had done something to the young girl. "Devon," she whispered.

He pressed his finger against his lips and shook his head. "I'm going to get breakfast started."

Marie hopped out of the bed and grabbed his elbow. "You like to drop bombs and walk away," she said. "Devon, you need to make peace with your father."

"This is something I don't want to talk about right now," he said.

"The anger inside you, you can't keep hiding that behind your work at the shelter," Marie said.

"And what makes you the expert? You stay in the papers acting out because you had everything handed to you. You have no idea what's going on inside me or what it was like growing up . . ."

"Forget breakfast; why not just take me home," she said. "I'm not going to be your wh—"

"Marie, look," Devon said, throwing his hands up. "This doesn't have anything to do with us and what we're building here. It's basically none of your business."

She shook her head from side to side. "Maybe you're right. I guess if I'm just someone you're only sleeping with, I shouldn't give a damn about what's going on in your life. Should I call a cab or do you plan to take me home?"

Sighing, Devon felt like he should say something, but what? Why were they even having this disagreement? "I'll call you a cab," he said, wanting to avoid further conflict.

She narrowed her eyes at him and reached for her clothes. "To hell with you, Devon. I should've known this was a mistake."

Chapter 16

Later that afternoon, Devon's mood went from bad to worse following his argument with Marie and her unscheduled cab ride home. He'd called her three times, but she hadn't bothered to answer the phone. Since it was Saturday, he knew he wouldn't see her at the shelter. He wondered, would he see her at all outside of their arranged relationship through the state? But as soon as he'd put Marie on the back burner and started to focus on the dinner at Hometown Delights, his cell phone started buzzing in his pocket and Alicia burst into the kitchen.

"Devon, what in the hell is going on? The dining room is crawling with reporters looking for you and Miss Party Girl Marie Charles," she said as he glanced at the text messages coming through on his phone.

"Damn it," he groaned as he saw the picture his producer forwarded to him. The blogger who saw them leaving last night had posted the picture under the headline CHARLOTTE'S NEW IT COUPLE?

Alicia looked over his shoulder and burst out laughing. "Are you kidding me? I knew it."

"Knew what?"

"That there was more going on with you and Marie

Charles than you were saying," Alicia said, then smacked Devon on the shoulder. "What are you going to tell the reporters?"

"There's nothing to tell because we're not a couple, and even if we were, I wouldn't talk about it in the press."

"But that's how she gets down. From what I understand, she lets the photographers know her every move so . . ."

"Alicia, shut up," he barked. "You don't know her; you know what you've read about her."

She leaned back, shocked by his tone and his defense of Marie. If they weren't a couple now, she knew they would be soon. Devon was fiercely protective of people he cared about. "Do you want me to get rid of the reporters?" she asked.

"Yes. And I'm going to take off. I need to talk to Marie about this."

"So," Alicia said, "there is something more here, huh?"

"Mind your business—for a change."

"Whatever," she said, then headed into the dining room to clear away the reporters. Devon turned to his sous-chef and put her in charge for dinner service. The menu was simple enough for her to handle, and since he didn't plan to be at Marie's place long, he'd be back to prepare something for dessert if he felt like it.

Marie stepped out of the town car and walked into My Sister's Keeper because she needed to do something worthwhile to get her mind off Devon and their fight. She'd already rearranged her closet, loaded up some clothes that she wanted to donate to the shelter, changed her bed sheets, moved the bed three times, and gotten together some shoes to donate as well. Marie had even tried her hand at cooking herself something for lunch, which turned out to be a steaming, burnt pile of couscous and half-baked chicken. She'd ended up tossing it out and ordering Chinese from her favorite restaurant.

After eating, she decided that staying inside wasn't going to do anything but drive her nuts. Adriana was out of town with a client and Marie wasn't in the mood to party anyway.

Somehow, going to the shelter seemed like the right thing to do. When she walked in with two big suitcases and a rollaway bag filled with shoes, Elaine Harper looked at her with a puzzled face.

"Marie, what are you doing here on a Saturday?" she asked as she walked from behind the reception desk.

"Well," she said. "I did some cleaning and decided that I wanted to donate some clothes and shoes to the ladies here."

"All of this?" Elaine asked.

"Yes, and all of the clothes are clean and the shoes are mostly new," Marie said. Elaine pulled Marie into her arms and hugged her tightly.

"This is so amazing of you, although, I'm not sure how many of the ladies will be able to wear these outfits. Would you mind if we sold them in our store, the things that the ladies can't use?"

"That's fine," Marie said. "Do you need any help around here today?"

"Well," she said. "Saturday is usually a free day for the ladies. Some of them work at our store for credit so that they can shop later. A few have real jobs that help with their savings so that they can get back on their feet."

"How's Bria doing?" Marie asked.

Elaine nodded. "Better. She's in the kitchen. We have

different chores we take care of around here. Maybe Bria might need some help in the kitchen."

"I will go and check," Marie said with a smile, remembering that she had to give Bria those shoes she wanted. She reached into the bag with the shoes and pulled out the sneakers, then bounded into the kitchen. Bria turned around quickly when she heard the door open.

"It's just me," Marie said, then held up the bag. "I brought you these shoes."

"Are you serious?" Bria said as she dried her hands and crossed over to Marie. "Wow, thank you."

"I'm a woman of my word, at least I try to be," she replied as she handed over the shoes.

"These shoes are amazing. Are you sure you want to give them up?" Bria asked as she examined the sneakers.

"Trust me, I'm not a sneaker chick," Marie joked. "So, what are you doing in here?"

"Just finished cleaning up the breakfast dishes, and then I was going to go chill in my room and read a book," she replied. Marie noticed that Bria seemed a lot calmer than normal, relaxed and acting her age. One thing she was sure of was that spending a beautiful afternoon reading was not something she wanted to do.

"Since you're finished in here, what do you say to a little retail therapy? You have this fund-raiser coming up at Devon's restaurant and you've been through a lot."

Bria ran her fingers through her cropped hair and smiled. "You know, yesterday when you were here and I took off, you and Mr. Devon showed me that people do care about you. Just one session with my counselor has helped me. I kept so much bottled up and I needed to release it."

"Sounds like a reason to shop to me," Marie said. "Do you have to sign out or anything?"

"I just have to be back by six," Bria said.

Marie looked at her watch, it was six after three. "Then we'd better get a move on. The car is outside."

When Devon pulled in to the parking garage attached to Marie's building, he wondered how he was supposed to handle this, not just the picture and the story, but the awkward way they'd left things that morning. Part of him wondered if she didn't have a Google alert that had already told her what the blogs said. Hell, Devon knew he wasn't there to simply tell her the press was sniffing around. He wanted to know if he still had a chance to be a part of her life. To explain the anger he felt toward his father and let her know that Devon Sr. was a nonfactor in their lives. Would she listen? Was he ready to tell the whole story? His thoughts raced back and forth as he headed up to Marie's place on the elevator. When the car stopped on Marie's floor, Devon saw a guy knocking on her door, and a tidal wave of jealousy washed over him. Who was this clown and why was he at his woman's door. *My woman? What am I thinking? How do I know she wants anything else to do with me?* The man, who had a notepad in his hand, turned to Devon and smiled. "Mr. Harris, are the rumors true? Are you and Marie Charles dating?" he fired.

"Who are you and why would I answer your rude questions?" Devon snapped.

"Wilson Luther, pop culture writer for the *Charlotte Observer*," he said, then extended his free hand to Devon. Devon ignored it and glared at him. Had Marie called him? How did he know where she lived? "So, are you dating Charlotte's it girl?"

"No comment."

"She's not home," he said. "I've been knocking on her door for about an hour."

Devon shook his head and started to ask the reporter a few questions of his own—specifically, how he got past security—but he didn't want anything he said to be quoted in the story. Instead, he simply walked away, pulling his cell phone from his pocket to call Marie. Just as he started to dial, the phone rang. It was his father, again. Marie's voice echoed in his head. *You have to make peace with your father.* He answered the call. "Hello?"

"Son," Devon Sr. said. "I'm hoping we can have a civil conversation."

"What do you want?" he asked, looking over his shoulder to ensure the reporter wasn't on his heels.

"I want to see you, before it's too late," he said. "I know you won't come to Atlanta, but I'd like to come to Charlotte. Maybe even have dinner at your restaurant."

Devon snorted as he pressed the button for the elevator. "What's killing you?" he asked as he waited for the car.

"Iron overload in my body. The doctors call it hemochromatosis. I've been undergoing treatment for the last two years and there's nothing left for them to do."

"Umm," Devon said, not knowing exactly what to say to his father or if he should show sympathy for his father when all his life, all his father had ever done was cause pain and make his life hell. But he couldn't make himself say a word.

"This is a very rare disorder and disease. I'm guessing that this is the Lord's way of making me pay for the mistakes that I've made. Especially when it comes to you and . . ."

"So, what do you want from me? I hope you don't think this talk of Jesus and forgiveness is supposed to make me forget the hell you put me and my mother through. Or how, when you finally accepted that I wasn't going to be your little clone, you wanted to give me a send-off to Paris."

"I thought I was doing what was right for you. I didn't think Kandace was right for you, and obviously, my theory was right. She's a fortune hunter, which is probably why she married Solomon Crawford."

"This is why I don't talk to you," Devon snapped. "Kandace has never been after my money or anyone else's."

"I was trying to protect you the best way that I knew how," he said.

"You've never known how to protect anyone other than yourself," Devon snapped.

"I'll be in Charlotte next week and I hope that we can get together," Devon Sr. said.

"Maybe," he said. "But I don't see how that's a good idea, since even though you're on the brink of death, you're still an asshole." Devon clicked off his cell phone and stepped into the elevator.

Marie and Bria walked across the parking lot to the awaiting car, trying to figure out where they would eat dinner before heading back to My Sister's Keeper. Bria held her Nordstrom bags tightly and smiled. "I haven't shopped like this since my mother died."

"How old were you when you lost your mom?" Marie asked as she shifted her purse to her left hand.

"Fifteen. Feels like yesterday," she said wistfully.

Marie placed her hand on Bria's shoulder. "I know how you feel. I lost my mom, too. I was ten when she died. I always wonder what life would've been like if she was still here."

Bria nodded. "We were so close, since it was just the two of us. When she died, I went to live with my aunt Michelle.

Had I known she just looked at me as a paycheck, I would've done something else. I know my life would've been different."

"Where was you father?" Marie asked.

Bria shrugged. "Never met him."

Marie's heart broke as Bria told her that while she lived with her aunt in Charlotte, she met Patrick Hargro—the man she was now running from. Patrick had been the person Bria had turned to when being with her aunt had become unbearable. At first, he'd been sweet, loving, and supportive. A lonely and naïve Bria had fallen hard and fast for Patrick. But the moment she'd moved in with him, he'd changed into a monster. The beatings began shortly after she'd moved in. Then there had been the incident that forced her to leave. Patrick had decided to pass her around to his friends as a living, breathing sex toy. She'd run away and lived on the street for about three months, hiding from Patrick and the men he associated with. Then she'd found out about My Sister's Keeper and decided to stay there.

"He told me that I would never be free of him," Bria said quietly. "In six months, my trust kicks in and I'll be able to take care of myself."

"What are you going to do then?" Marie asked. Bria didn't reply, she simply stopped walking and dropped her bags at her feet. Marie turned to her and saw a look of sheer terror on her face.

"Bria?" Marie asked as she followed the girl's stare. A man was running in their direction.

"Patrick," Bria breathed. Marie pushed Bria toward the car.

"Go get in the car," Marie said.

"Yo, bitch!" Patrick yelled. "I knew I'd find your ass." He charged toward Marie and Bria. Marie reached in her purse and grabbed her container of pepper spray and flushed Patrick's face with the hot spray. He mumbled more profanities and reached out to grab Marie. With her good foot, Marie kicked Patrick in the center of his family jewels. He moaned like a wounded dog. "You like hitting women?" she spat. "Well, I hit back!" She kicked him again, even harder. He reached blindly for Marie's other ankle, but before he could grab her, the burly driver rushed over to them and clutched Patrick's neck. "Miss Charles, I called nine-one-one."

Marie nodded and ran to the car to check on Bria. When she opened the door, she found Bria huddled in the backseat, trembling like a baby bird separated from its mother. Marie climbed into the car and wrapped her arms around her. "It's all right. He's going to jail. The driver called nine-one-one, and when the police get here, we'll just give them a statement."

"I'm scared, Marie," she said, then began sobbing uncontrollably. "I wanted him to think I was gone. I wanted him to believe that I was gone or dead. He's going to come after me."

Marie was about to assure Bria that she was going to be safe when she saw two cops marching toward the town car with Patrick in tow. But he wasn't handcuffed as he walked with the officers.

"That's her," Patrick said and pointed at Marie. "That bitch pepper-sprayed me and attacked me."

Marie positioned herself in front of Bria, who had seemed to stop breathing. "I was protecting myself and my friend," she exclaimed.

"She was trying to rob me," he lied. Even the two officers didn't believe that tale as they focused on Patrick.

"Rob you of what? You ass! This man is a pimp and he was trying to assault me. Was I wrong to defend myself?"

Bria gripped Marie's shoulder tightly. "Why is he here? I thought you said he was going to jail."

"Ma'am," one of the officers said to Bria. "Is everything all right?"

"Tell them," Marie said as she looked at Bria. What she didn't see was how Patrick had locked his eyes with Bria and the fear that it inspired.

"Ma'am?" the officer asked again. "Is everything all right?"

Bria closed her eyes. "No," she said.

"Did he hurt you?" the officer asked as his partner pulled Patrick back from the car.

"Not today, but he-he has."

Marie waved for her driver and the officer ordered her to step out of the car. "But, why?" she asked.

"We're going to have to take you in for questioning," he said.

"What? Questioning? So, you're telling me you're taking the word of this lowlife abuser over mine?" she demanded. "Do I need a lawyer?"

"Look, lady, no one is being charged right now. We just need to get to the bottom of this."

"What about her?" she exclaimed as she pointed to Bria. "If you're taking me in, I hope you're arresting that bastard."

The other officer motioned for his partner, momentarily leaving the trio alone. "You say a word against me," Patrick growled through clenched teeth, "bitch, I'll kill you."

Bria wound herself into a tight ball and moaned, and then Marie leapt from the car and stood toe-to-toe with Patrick. She had him by about two inches and it made sense why he abused women. He had the Napoleon complex and needed to control something. "Say another word and I will kick your ass again!"

"Nobody's scared of you!" He inched closer to Marie and she coldcocked him, knocking him out. She felt good about herself for about two seconds, then she realized she had just committed assault in front of two police officers. Damn!

Chapter 17

All day, Devon waited to hear from Marie. He'd called, he'd texted, and he'd gone by her place two more times since he saw the reporter knocking at her door. Nothing. Was she mad? Had she found a party to attend? Pissed off at the world, especially his father, he decided to run his kitchen tonight. That way he would have to focus on something else, the one thing that always calmed him down when he felt like this—food.

The moment he walked into the restaurant, Serena and Alicia whisked him into the office. "Your girl is all over the news today," Serena said. Alicia nodded.

"What are you two talking about? I know about the 'it' couple thing," Devon said. "Why is the media pumping that up? No real news happened today?"

Alicia turned the desktop screen around. "Oh, this is deeper than that blog post," she said. Devon scanned the computer screen, reading the headline: CHARLOTTE SOCIALITE FACES ASSAULT CHARGE.

"What in the hell was she thinking?" he mumbled as he read the story.

Already on probation for a DWI charge earlier this year,

Marie Charles is in trouble again. Charles was involved in an altercation outside of Southpark Mall.

Patrick Hargro, a convicted felon, and Charles were arguing in the parking lot and Hargro said she pepper-sprayed him and tried to rob him.

Devon shook his head. "Robbery? What kind of . . ."

Alicia pointed to another paragraph.

Police were simply going to take Charles, Hargro, and an unidentified woman in for questioning. But when the officers ran Hargro's name, it was discovered that he had an outstanding warrant. However, before they could put him in handcuffs, the officers at the scene said Charles assaulted Hargro and was taken into custody. She's being held in the Mecklenburg County Jail.

"I can't believe this!" Devon exclaimed. "She's on probation; does she realize what this could mean for her?"

Serena and Alicia exchanged knowing glances. "Why is it so important to you?" Serena asked. "I guess this morning's story was true."

Devon glared at his friends, then turned back to the computer screen. "What the hell," he exclaimed when he caught a glimpse of Bria in the photo. Dashing out of the office, he headed to his car and sped to My Sister's Keeper to find out what in the hell was going on. Why was Bria with Marie? And who was that man she assaulted? When he arrived at the shelter, a frantic Elaine met him at the door.

"Oh my God, Devon, have you heard?" she said.

He nodded. "Is Bria all right?"

"She's great and trying to get Marie out of jail."

"What?"

Elaine twisted her oversized onyx ring on her index finger as she began to tell Devon what Bria said to her when she returned to the shelter. "Marie took her shopping after helping her in the kitchen earlier this afternoon. They were walking to the car and Bria said she saw the guy that she'd been running from."

"What? Is she all right?" Devon asked.

"She's inspired," Elaine said. "Bria said for the first time she saw what a little punk that man was, since Marie kicked his behind with one good foot and then knocked him out."

Devon smiled despite himself. "Where is Bria?"

"She went to the police station with Dana Toliver, her counselor, to file charges against that monster and tell them that he had been abusing her for years. This is a big step for her and we have Marie to thank for this. I just hope this doesn't get her into more trouble."

"I'm going to the police station and see if I can find out what's going on," Devon said, then turned toward the door.

"Devon," Elaine said. "Marie was really trying to do a good thing. She brought in clothes and shoes for the ladies. She claims that she cleaned out her closet, but many of these items still had price tags on them. She's not the party girl that I thought she was. So, if there is anything I can do to help her, please let me know."

Devon nodded and headed out. He had no idea what he was supposed to do. This wasn't *Law & Order;* he couldn't just march into the police station and demand to see Marie. He wondered if she had contacted her father. All Devon could do was wait.

Marie folded her arms and glared at the officer who'd been questioning her. She hadn't opted to call her father because she hadn't wanted to hear a lecture. This was big-time trouble and she recognized that. But was she supposed to allow Patrick to terrorize Bria? Why had those stupid cops brought that man over there? His claim of robbery was laughable and they should've known that.

"Miss Charles, did Hargro threaten you in any way?"

"I told you that one time he threatened Bria. Said he was going to kill us and he's the reason she's homeless now. He rushed toward us and I protected us. Didn't those officers on the scene tell you how afraid she was?"

"But what does that have to do with you?"

Marie cocked her head to the side and was about to tell the officer that he could take a long walk off a short bridge when the door opened. "Not another word, Marie," her father boomed. "Have you Mirandized my client?"

"She didn't ask for an attorney," the officer said.

Richard looked at his daughter and shook his head. "Well, I'm here now and this interrogation is over."

"Mr. Charles," the officer said. "I'm trying not to charge your daughter. Hargro isn't the kind of man we want on the street, but my hands are tied."

"So, if Marie hasn't been charged, why is she still here?" Richard asked and then motioned for Marie to stand up. "We're leaving."

"We'll call if there are further questions," the officer said and allowed the duo to leave. Marie was in awe, but also waiting for the next shoe to drop.

She and Richard headed out of the interrogation room in silence, but he placed his arm around his daughter's shoulders protectively. As they crossed into the lobby of the police department, Richard asked, "Why didn't you call me?"

"Because, I thought that I had done the right thing by trying to keep that creep away from Bria. Daddy, had you seen her face and how scared she was," Marie said with tears welling up in her eyes.

"Who is Bria?"

"One of the women from the shelter. She's barely eighteen and she has had it rough. Am I going to go to jail?"

"Not if I can help it," Richard said. "This isn't one of your stunts, I see that. But Marie, do you realize the danger you put yourself in?"

She was about to tell her father that she wasn't thinking about that when she saw Devon walk in the door. Richard looked from him to his daughter and shook his head.

"Marie," Devon said as he crossed over to her, then took her hand in his. "Are you all right?"

"Yes, I'm fine. I think Bria's here, too," she replied. Devon turned to her father and extended his hand.

"Mr. Charles," he said as the older man shook his hand. "I'm Devon Harris."

"I know who you are," Richard replied, not revealing that he was impressed that Devon had acknowledged him, something none of Marie's other male friends had ever done. Still, he wasn't sure that Marie and Devon should've had anything more than what the state had arranged. But Richard wasn't blind. He could see this man cared for his daughter. Cared for her in a way he'd never seen in the eyes of other suitors.

"So, Marie, are you all right?" Devon asked, turning his attention back to her. "What happened?"

Marie leaned against Devon's chest and he hugged her tightly as he felt her warm tears seep through his shirt. "It's all right," he whispered. "Is Bria OK?"

She nodded. "I never meant for any of this to happen. I just wanted to give her a chance to get out of the shelter and be a normal teenager."

Devon kissed the top of her head. "But do you realize how dangerous what you did was?"

"Now, you sound like my father," she replied as she wiped her eyes.

"Is that such a bad thing?" Richard asked, growing a little more impressed with Devon as he spoke.

"I guess not," she replied, smiling at Devon and her father.

"I'm sure your father was just as worried, even more so than I was," Devon said. Marie leaned in closer to him and nodded, forgetting, until he cleared his throat, that her father was still there. Turning to him, Marie asked, "So, what happens next?"

"We wait and hope that the district attorney has the good sense not to file these bogus charges against you."

Devon wiped away moisture from Marie's cheek. "It's going to be fine. Your dad and I are going to make sure of that."

Marie felt the tingle of security course through her body. Devon and her father were standing by her like guardian hawks, and she honestly felt like gold. Moments later, Bria and her counselor approached them. Marie broke her embrace with Devon and crossed over to Bria, wrapping her arms around her. "Are you all right?"

"Yes, now that I know that monster is off the streets, and I'm going to do everything I can to make sure it stays that way. You taught me something when you stood up to him."

"I just don't want you to be afraid anymore," Marie said.

Devon spoke with Bria's counselor briefly and then crossed over to the women. Bria smiled brightly when she saw Devon. "I'm so glad I listened to you and talked to someone about what was going on and what I was running from." He smiled and gave her a brotherly hug.

"I told you that you'd get through it," he said.

"I just didn't believe it."

Marie smiled at them, happy that Bria had finally stood

up to her tormenter. She knew what that meant to Devon as well. She was sure that he saw his mother's struggle through Bria's life. But Marie knew things wouldn't get easy for her right away. Bria needed money, and it seemed as if her aunt was holding the purse strings to her trust fund. As Devon and Bria talked, she walked over to her father to see if there was something more they could do to help her.

Smiling at Bria, Devon was about to tell her that she would be able to do so many more things now that she'd faced her fears, when his cell phone rang. He pulled the phone from his pocket and groaned inwardly as he saw the 404 area code. "Excuse me," he said to Bria and her counselor, "I have to take this." He dashed outside and answered the call. "Yeah?"

"Is this Mr. Devon Harris Jr.?" an unknown female voice asked.

"Who is this?"

"My name is Clara English, I'm an admitting nurse at Carolinas Medical Center. Your father was rushed here from Charlotte Douglas International Airport. His condition is very grave. Your number was listed in his cell phone, and I thought it would be best if I called you."

"All right," Devon said. "And what do you want me to do about it?" He wondered why his father was in town, since he'd said he wouldn't be in Charlotte until next week.

"Well, I, um, figured that you would want to know the condition of your father," she said, her voice brimming with surprise.

Devon sighed, realizing that he needed to check on his father—especially if he was going to let go of the issues that had plagued their relationship. "Where do I need to go?"

The nurse gave him the particulars about his father's

admittance to the hospital and that he was in the ICU and was nonresponsive.

"I'll be there shortly," he said, then disconnected the call. He turned toward the lobby and saw Bria, Marie, and Richard engaged in an intense-looking conversation. He wondered if he should tell them that he was leaving, yet another part of him wondered, what were they talking about that was so intense? Walking into the police department, he wondered why Bria was crying.

"What's going on?" he asked.

"This is the best day of my life," Bria exclaimed through her tears. Marie wrapped her arms around Devon with a big smile on her face.

"My dad is going to help Bria get back on her feet," Marie said.

"That's great," Devon replied. "I have to head out. My . . . . A family member is in the hospital and I need to . . ."

"Oh, no," Bria said, bringing her hand to her mouth.

Marie looked up at him and saw a flicker of sadness and weariness in his eyes. "Want some company?" she asked. Richard started to voice his objection and tell Marie that she needed to focus on her own issues and problems. But he wasn't blind to what was going on between his daughter and the chef.

"Yes," he replied.

Marie caught her father's gaze and recognized that look of "be careful" on his face. Crossing over to him, she kissed him on the cheek and whispered in his ear, "I know he's different. I'm going to be careful."

"All right. At least I know he has your best interests at heart."

Marie turned her head, looking over her shoulder at Devon, "You're right about that."

She gave her father a hasty hug and kiss, then headed out the door with Devon. Once they had settled in his car, Marie turned to Devon and asked, "Is it your father?"

He nodded. "We had decided to meet and talk, and I guess he fell ill on the plane. I got a call from the hospital."

"I guess that was a pretty surprising call to receive. Are you OK?"

Devon shrugged. "I honestly started to ignore the call," he said. "Then, I thought about something you said. I do have to make peace with my father and release the anger."

"Are you ready to do that now?"

"I don't know. It's really hard to muster up enough emotions to care," he said. "And I don't understand why the nurse would call from his cell phone."

Marie grimaced and wished she could say something that wouldn't start another disagreement. Devon glanced at her and said, "I know this isn't how you and your father get along or interact, but . . ."

"It's all right," she said. "I'm glad you actually decided to see him. Maybe this is a step in the right direction for the two of you to come to peace before he dies."

"I'm hoping that's where we're going," he said quietly. But he honestly didn't know where he and his father were going, and he couldn't be sure that the relationship could be repaired. Did he even want to repair the explosive fault between them?

He'd give it a try, especially if this could be the last time he saw his father alive.

Once they arrived at the hospital, Marie squeezed his hand and kissed him on the cheek. "I'm here for you, no matter what."

Devon leaned over the car seat and kissed her cheek. "Thank you."

They got out of the car and headed to the emergency

room entrance. Nothing could've prepared Devon for what he saw when he walked in. His father, who he'd expected to find near death, was holding court with a group of nurses and orderlies. Momentarily, he studied his father, looking for any similarities between them. When he didn't find any, Devon wondered if his dad hated his mother because their only son looked more like her than him. Anger filled his body as past hurt and pain came to mind.

"What in the hell is going on?" Devon demanded as he stalked over to his father. Marie thought he was going to slug him from the angry scowl that darkened his face like a thunder cloud.

"Son," Devon Sr. said, throwing his hand up. "After our last conversation, I wasn't sure that you would meet me. I had to do something."

"So, you create this bullshit-ass story about you being near death, lure me to the hospital, and expect that we're going to have a reunion, and I'd just forgive you for the hell that you put me and my mother through?" Devon's voice boomed with years of anger, disgust, and pain.

"Do you really want to do this here?" Devon Sr. asked, looking at the shock on the faces of the people who'd been eating out of the palm of his hand moments earlier. Devon glanced around the room and smirked.

"What? You don't want your adoring public to know you used to beat your wife and cheated on her with any and every groupie that showed you a little leg?"

Marie pulled on Devon's arm, trying to urge him to stop his public rant. One thing she knew, it wouldn't take long for someone to pull out a cell phone with a video camera or call the media so that this private fight would become a public headline. "Come on," she whispered. "Let's go."

Devon Sr. looked at Marie and scowled. "Who brought a

groupie to the hospital, Son? You want to hate me because you know we're just alike. Only, I know what to do with a groupie after getting out of bed with her. You profess to love them."

Marie felt Devon's arm clench as if he was about to punch his father, and she wasn't sure that she would stop him. Because that man did just call her a groupie! Didn't he know who she was?

"Excuse me," Marie exclaimed. "You obviously don't know who I am, because if you did, you'd speak to me and not about me as if I'm not here."

"This has nothing to do with you," Devon Sr. said, barely giving Marie a second look. "This is between me and my son. Why don't you run along?"

"Why don't you go to hell?" Devon growled. "Nothing has changed about you. You're still the same selfish, self-righteous son of a bitch you've been all of my life. I want nothing to do with you. And if you are dying, I hope it happens sooner rather than later. You stood by my mother's death bed with a camera crew, hoping to cement your image as the perfect husband losing his first love when you and I knew you didn't give a damn about my mother. You didn't care about me once I decided to step out of your shadow, and now, here you are. Whatever you want, whatever wooden God fooled you to think I'd have anything more than disgust in my being for you, forget it. You're dead to me. Make sure your assistant sends me an obituary."

Devon stormed out of the emergency room with Marie on his heels. "Slow down," she exclaimed as her ankle began to throb a bit. Devon turned around, slowing his gait and reaching for her hand. "I'm sorry you had to witness that," he said in a quiet voice. "Maybe now you understand why I don't want anything to do with that bastard."

She nodded and took his hand. Devon enveloped Marie in a tight embrace and kissed her forehead. "You know what I need to do," he said. "I need to get in the kitchen or I'm going to go in there and do something horrible to that man."

"Do you want to be alone?" she asked.

"Actually," he said, "I don't. Do you think you can stand being around me?"

She smiled sweetly and nodded. "I could always be in jail," she quipped.

He kissed her again and smiled. "That's true," he replied. "It has been a hell of a day."

"That's one way to put it. I guess that means we have a better night to look forward to."

Devon smiled. "I can't wait to see what a better night looks like." The couple hopped in the car and headed to his loft in NoDa. As they drove along, passing through the quiet Myers Park neighborhood where Marie spent a pampered childhood, she thought about Bria's and Devon's upbringings and felt thankful, and everything her father had been saying about her wasting her talent trying to make a public spectacle of herself hit her like a ton of concrete.

I have been wasting my life, she thought. Glancing at Devon's clenched jaw and ashen knuckles, she knew that he would've appreciated what she'd always considered boring. Devon caught her gaze and smiled. "What's going through that pretty head of yours?"

"I should be asking you that. You look pretty pissed," she said.

"That's the effect my father has on me and people who don't keep their lips pressed to his ass. I'm sorry he disrespected you."

Marie fanned her hand as if she was swatting away annoying gnats. "I don't care what he thinks. Me, a groupie. That's laughable. Have you two ever gotten along?"

Devon tried to remember a time when he didn't think his father was a monster. His mind went back to a game of basketball he and Devon Sr. played when he was about eight years old. His father had taken the time to explain the rules of the game, had taught him how to finger roll and box out another player. After their game, Devon Sr. had taken his son to Baskin Robbins on Peachtree Street. However, the trip to the ice cream shop had been marred when a woman walked up to Devon Sr. and kissed him in a way Devon had only seen his mother and father embrace. Two days later, he and his mother had taken off on one of their adventure trips, heading to Nashville.

"No, never," Devon said once he pulled into a parking spot at his loft.

"Wow," she said in a near whisper.

"Don't feel bad," he said as they stepped out of the car. "He taught me everything I needed to know about how to be a real man."

Marie furrowed her brows, totally confused by Devon's statement. He laughed and stroked her forearm. "I just do the opposite of everything that loser did," he said, then scooped her up in his arms and spun her around. "Let's put this day behind us."

He dashed up the stairs to his door with Marie in his arms, ignoring the vibrating phone in his pocket. He was sure it was his father, and the last thing he wanted to do was hear that man's voice again. Devon set Marie down in front of the door as he unlocked it. Once they were inside, Marie's phone rang. They sighed and decided if they answered their phones now, they could ignore them for the rest of the night.

While Marie talked to her father, letting him know that

she was all right and hanging out with Devon, Devon called the restaurant back—happy that the missed called had been from Hometown Delights and not his father.

"What's going on?" he asked when Alicia answered the phone.

"Your father just left here," she said in an exasperated tone. "And he made a scene when Kandace and Solomon came in. I had to step in between your dad and Solomon because I thought they were going to come to blows. What in the hell is going on?"

"He's supposed to be dying, but obviously that's a lie. He concocted some story about being rushed to the hospital after flying in. I get to the hospital and he's being his usual self. Charming those who don't know him."

"Wow," Alicia said. "I'd never seen him in action until tonight. He called Kandace a fortune hunter and told Solomon that he'd come off better marrying a common street hooker."

"And I imagine that's when the altercation got started?" Devon said.

"You got it. Man, this is just what we need, more bad publicity," Alicia said. "I'm looking forward to going to Atlanta for the Atlanta University Center reunion because this is getting to be too much."

"Don't worry about my father, I'll take care of him. Just not tonight," he said as he watched Marie walk into the kitchen with a sultry smile on her face.

"I guess Marie was the groupie your father had referred to. Tell her I said hello if you two decide to come up for air at some point," Alicia teased.

"Good-bye, Alicia," he said, then ended the call. Next, Devon shut his phone off and tossed it on the kitchen table. "Now, you have my undivided attention."

"I like the sound of that," she said. "Is everything all

right at the restaurant?" Devon brought his finger to her supple lips and shook his head. "The problems will be there tomorrow. Right now, it's all about me, you, and some dinner."

She grinned, thinking that she was hungry, but the dish she wanted the most was standing in front of her. The energy between them sizzled like a skirt steak on an open flame. They needed the closeness as they reached out for each other. When their lips met, the kiss was more than passion; it was like a cool glass of wine washing away the pressure and stress they'd been dealing with all day. When Devon touched her, Marie felt comforted first, then her body heated up like smoldering fire. She melted against his broad chest and sighed as their lips parted. Marie stared into his eyes, seeing a mix of everything etched in his face—want, need, desire, and a bit of melancholy. She wanted to take the hurt away. Wanted to make Devon feel nothing but bliss. He brushed his finger across her cheek. "You are so beautiful," he whispered.

"I want you," she intoned. "I need you."

He didn't respond with words. Instead, Devon lifted Marie up and sat her on the counter, kissing her with a hot need that made her quiver as his hands roamed her body, causing her desire to flow like a rushing river between her thighs. Devon slipped his hand inside her pants, savoring her liquid heat.

"Mmm, baby, you're ready for me, huh?" he said in a near growl. Marie nodded, as she couldn't speak with his hand stroking her mound of femininity back and forth. He slipped his index finger between her wet folds of flesh, seeking her throbbing pearl. When her breathing became shallow and her breasts heaved up and down, Devon knew he'd found it.

Marie's knees quivered as Devon made small circles

inside her, making her wetter, hotter, and even more ready to feel him inside her. She called out his name, her voice hoarse with want for him. "Need. You."

"You got me," he replied as he pulled her leggings off. Spreading her legs apart, Devon smiled at the flimsy lace panties she wore. Not only were they soaked with her desire, but they didn't stand in the way of him getting to her essence as he brought his lips to her heat. With his tongue, he lapped and licked her thighs. Marie's sweetness only made him want more of her. *Thank God for flimsy panties,* he thought as he pushed the lace crotch to the side and buried his lips inside her, his tongue dancing with her throbbing bud until she exploded, frosting his face with her juices. If Marie thought he was done because he stepped back and admired the sated look on her face, she was wrong.

Devon crossed over to the refrigerator and pulled out a can of whipped cream, a bowl of strawberries, and an unlabeled jar that looked as if it was filled with chocolate sauce. She shivered with anticipation as he set the ingredients on the edge of the counter. "What's all of this?" she asked.

"You may not be hungry, but I always want dessert," he said, then pulled her top off. The demi bra she wore barely contained her cleavage, and Devon was not even mad about it. In fact, he salivated at the thought of licking chocolate from her bosom. "Lay down," he commanded softly. Marie glanced at the wide counter, then followed Devon's command. He ran his hand down the center of her chest, then kissed her erect nipples, eliciting moans from her before he reached for a juicy strawberry. Devon brushed the fruit across her lips and then fed it to her. Juice dripped down her chin, and Devon kissed it away, savoring the sweetness of the berry and the saltiness of her skin. As his tongue glided down the column of her neck, Devon reached for another berry. He rubbed it slowly and methodically across her breasts as her body writhed underneath his touch. Devon brought the berry to his lips and bit into it, then he fed it to Marie. The strawberry painted her lips dark pink, making them look like luscious candy.

Devon opened the jar of chocolate sauce and dipped his index finger in it. Then he traced her full lips with his finger, and Marie licked the chocolate from his finger as he made a second pass over her mouth. When Devon felt the heat of her breath on his finger, every nerve in his body tingled and his erection nearly burst through the zipper of his slacks. She circled her tongue around the tip of his finger, and Devon felt his erection throb with want. Sensing a shift in power, Marie decided that she wanted to lavish Devon with the sweet torture he'd been inflicting on her. She sat up and swung her legs down from the counter and wrapped them around his waist.

Pulling him against her body, she tugged at his shirt and pulled it over his head. Then she reached for the jar of chocolate and dipped two fingers inside of it. She spread it across his chest, paying extra attention to his nipples. "My turn for dessert," she said, then licked the chocolate from his body, making Devon's legs feel like rubber. He unzipped his slacks, and Marie skillfully used her thighs to inch his pants down his waist. She reached for more chocolate, drawing a line down his abs to where his pants started. Casting her eyes upward, she said, "Those have to come off."

Unclamping her thighs from his waist, she watched as he made quick work of removing his pants and gray boxer briefs. His erection stood up like a magic wand ready to put her deeper under his spell. Getting more chocolate from the jar, Marie slinked off the counter's edge, dropping to her knees in front of Devon. She slathered the chocolate down the length of his erection, licking her lips in anticipation of tasting him. Devon stroked her hair as she inched closer and closer to him. The wet heat from her mouth sent his body into overdrive, as she closed her lips around him. Sucking, licking, moaning, and sucking some more, Marie took him to the brink of climax. One thing was for sure, playtime was over. He had to bury himself inside her and feel her walls closing in on his hardness. He wanted to be one with her. *Now and forever,* a voice in the back of his head clearly said. Marie was his, and he was beginning to think about forever with her. Was it too soon for that kind of thinking? Had he lost his damned mind?

Marie pulled back, noting the silence and pensive look on Devon's face. "What's wrong?"

"Nothing's wrong, nothing at all," he said as he kneeled down and scooped her into his arms. "Time for the main course."

Dashing up the stairs, Devon took a left turn at the bathroom. He sat Marie on the edge of the tub and then turned the water on. "Though I love you sweet and sticky," he said, "I want you in the shower."

Marie smiled and tested the water with her hand. It was warm, but from the looks she and Devon exchanged, it wouldn't take long to bring it to a boil. Devon reached over on the sink and grabbed a bar of soap, then he and Marie stepped into the shower. He backed her against the marble wall and lifted her leg. Then he rubbed her thighs down with the soap, an exotic scent called dragon's blood. She trembled as his hands snaked up her thigh and came to a rest around her waist. As the water beat down on them, Devon captured her lips in a thirsty and sensual kiss that nearly knocked her off balance. She wrapped her soapy leg around his waist and drew him into her needy body. They meshed together. Devon pumping into her with power, making her call out his name as she dug her nails into his shoulder. "Yes!" Marie exclaimed as she felt his raw passion. "Devon, love me."

"Aww, baby, you feel so good. So damned good." He ground against her, gripping her waist tightly as she met him stroke for stroke. He felt her first orgasm and then her second. Just as he was about to reach his own climax, reluctantly, he pulled out. "Damn," he groaned. "I didn't protect us."

Still shuddering from the aftershocks of her multiple orgasms, Marie tried to wrap her mind around what they'd just done. Unprotected sex. She knew that she was disease free, as she'd had a battery of tests just two weeks ago.

But she also realized there were other issues to consider. Namely, an unexpected pregnancy. She'd promised herself time and time again that she was not popping out kids for a man who was not responsible enough to marry her. Looking up at Devon, she wondered if he'd neglected to tell her something. "Should I be worried?"

"Physically, I'm fine. No STDs or anything like that. But what if we created something neither of us is ready for?"

"I am on the pill, though I haven't been taking it regularly. But seriously, that's how you feel about children?"

Sighing, he realized his words sounded harsh, but what kind of father would he really be? Devon had a habit of messing up his relationships, and he wondered if he'd mess up the greatest relationship a person could be blessed with—being a father. He certainly didn't have a role model in that department.

"I wouldn't even know how to be a father," he said. "The last thing I want to do is bring a child into this world and not be man enough to take care of it. I never said I was perfect."

"Wow," she replied, not wanting to further mar the moment. Still she wondered, if they had made a baby in the shower—would he be responsible?

Chapter 18

The next morning, Devon woke up from a restless sleep, despite the fact that Marie spent the night sleeping like an angel beside him. When he'd started tossing and turning, he'd released her and watched her sleep before he'd gotten out of bed and went into the kitchen to clean up and work on a new recipe. After he had decided that his marinade had been too bland and didn't go well with steak, he'd returned to bed. What had been bothering him had nothing to do with the fact that he could've gotten Marie pregnant, but the thoughts that he had about hoping that he did. Despite years of punishing himself for betraying Kandace and the self-imposed exile he'd been living in when it came to serious relationships, he did want a family. That had been clearer since Marie came into his life.

Sitting up in the bed, Devon tried in vain not to wake Marie. Feeling her hand on his shoulder, Devon turned around and kissed her cheek. "Good morning," he said.

"Is it? Because you didn't get much sleep, did you?" she asked, then yawned. "Do you want to talk about it?"

He pulled her down into his lap and stroked her cheek. "You're too good to be true. I keep you up all night, wake you at six A.M., and you want to talk about it." Devon kissed her again, gently nibbling on her bottom lip.

She placed her hand on his chest and pulled back from him. "You know, since you kept a girl up all night, I think you owe me breakfast and lots of coffee."

"It will be my pleasure. As a matter of fact, I've been neglecting my duties at the restaurant, so I'm going to go in and you're coming with me, and you're going to love what I have in store for you."

Marie raised her hand as if she were in a classroom. "I really can't go out in the clothes I got photographed going to jail in."

Devon glanced at the clock on the nightstand. "I can take you home and you can change into something spectacular."

Marie snapped her fingers. "I don't even have to go home. With everything that happened yesterday, I forgot about the shopping that Bria and I did. And I even managed to pick up a little red lacy number that I know you're going to love. Wow me with breakfast and I'll model it for you tonight."

"Consider yourself about to be wowed," he said, then leaned in and kissed her cheek. "Want to join me in the shower?"

She hopped off the bed and gave him a little shake. "You don't have to ask me twice."

Devon followed her into the bathroom and joined her in the shower. It was quite a different scene from last night, even though Devon teased Marie's nipples with his loofah sponge as they washed and prepared to head for the restaurant. As Marie dried off and tried to tame her hair, Devon pulled on a pair of cotton shorts and headed downstairs to his car. Marie told him to bring the Nordstrom bag in and not to peek in the others. He grabbed the bag and shook his head as he glanced at the others. He wouldn't begrudge his wife a shopping spree every now and then. *Wait a damned minute,* he thought. *Marriage is the last thing I need to be thinking about. Like Marie is ready to settle down.*

When he headed upstairs, Devon was greeted at the door by a naked Marie. "You know," she said. "I'm more of a brunch girl."

Devon closed the door, dropped the bag at his feet, and scooped her up in his arms. "I like the sound of that," he said as he scaled the steps and headed to his bedroom. After a quick romp that left them both breathless and wanting more, Devon and Marie pulled themselves out of bed and headed to Hometown Delights. Sundays at the restaurant were a quiet time, and since the economic downturn, they'd moved from serving breakfast to lunch starting at one P.M. Things usually got busy around two thirty when most people left church. Many Sundays, Devon ended up cooking for his friends and their families. Especially during the NFL off season when Carolina Panthers superstar Maurice Goings and his wife, Kenya, joined the party. Those breakfasts were like scenes from *The Big Chill.* He wondered how Marie would fit in with the group, especially since she and Jade had previously had words. Walking downstairs to the car, Marie yawned and tugged at her crude ponytail. "I need coffee," she said.

"That's all you need?" he asked, then wiggled his eyebrows.

"All right, Chef. You're going to end up with a restaurant full of hungry people if I tell you what else I really need." Marie reached into her purse and pulled out her cell phone. When she turned it on, she wasn't surprised that she had several text messages, voice mail messages, and missed calls. Her phone beeped and chimed so much that she nearly regretted turning it on again.

"The whole city must have missed you last night," Devon quipped.

"They should get used to missing me. I've come to a decision about my life," she said succinctly.

"And what's that?" he asked as they climbed in the car.

"I'm giving up this party-girl lifestyle," she said. "Being with those women in the shelter and hearing Bria's story has taught me the lesson that the judge wanted me to learn. If I'm going to make headlines, I want it to be because I did something to help someone else. Better yet, no more headlines. I want to learn to be selfless like this sexy guy I know."

"Who's that bum?" he joked. "I'm glad to hear that, because I don't like to see reporters hounding my woman." *My woman. What am I saying?*

Marie smiled, but tried to temper it. Still, she liked being called Devon's woman. Especially when everyone she usually dated fell into the role of Marie Charles' arm candy. Glancing at Devon, she knew he was more than eye candy or a living accessory. He was the real thing— wasn't he?

When they arrived at the restaurant, Devon wasn't at all surprised to see the parking lot filled with cars—Alicia's and Jade's, and Antonio's truck. "Looks like we're going to have a full house for brunch. Are you ready for this?"

"Guess we're going to find out, huh? You guys are a strange group."

"We put the funk in dysfunctional," he joked as he parked his car.

Marie opened her door and smoothed her peach romper, and for the first time ever, she felt flutters of nerves as she entered a location. This wasn't normal for the showstopper. But Marie was actually worried about the impression she was about to make on Devon's friends. He crossed over to her and took her hand in his and then kissed it. Before they took another step, a car pulled into the parking lot, barreling toward them. Devon positioned himself in front of Marie, then yelled, "It's a parking lot, jackass, not Charlotte Motor Speedway!"

The door swung open and Solomon Crawford emerged from the car, then stalked over to Devon with a very pregnant Kandace waddling behind him, screaming for him to calm down.

"What the hell is wrong with you, Crawford?" Devon hissed as the men faced off. Marie watched with her mouth agape; they were like two raging bulls. It was obvious Solomon and Devon hadn't accepted each other as brothers.

"Where is he?" Solomon bellowed.

Kandace placed her hand on Solomon's arm. "Solomon, please," she pleaded.

Ignoring Solomon's rage, Devon turned to Kandace. "What is this all about?"

She sighed. "Your father."

Devon's shoulders sagged and he shook his head. "What now?"

Solomon glared at Devon, took a deep breath, then said, "Have you seen that stupid blog, Dark Charlotte or something?"

"*Queen City After Dark*," Marie piped in. Solomon eyed her suspiciously and Kandace smiled at her once she recognized who she was.

"Whatever," Solomon snapped. "Your father has disrespected my wife for the last damned time, and now he's put that bullshit out for the world to see."

"So what are you going to do about it? I'm sure Kandace

has tried to tell you that my father and I don't talk, don't associate with each other, and I couldn't really give a damn about him or where he is."

"You may not, but I'm not going to let this shit slide."

"Solomon," Kandace said in an exasperated voice. "Will you just let this go?"

"No. I let it go in the restaurant, but this is too much. Putting those insults out for the world to read about my wife is unacceptable."

"I'm afraid to ask, but what did he say?" Devon asked as he saw Solomon calming down. Marie had pulled the site up on her BlackBerry and read the article. If she had been Solomon, she'd be mad as hell, too. She handed her phone to Devon and his eyes grew to the size of quarters as he read: EXCLUSIVE INTERVIEW WITH FAMED HOOPSTER DEVON HARRIS, SR.

On the hardwood of the NBA, they didn't come tougher than Devon Harris, Sr. In the 1970s and 1980s, playing against Harris usually meant a couple of stitches. These days, the hoops legend has a softer touch, working with various charities in Atlanta, where he makes his home. But there is one battle that Harris knows he isn't going to win. He's been stricken with a deadly disease and he came to Charlotte to make peace with his son, famed chef Devon Harris, Jr. The senior said that he and his son have not spoken in nearly a decade.

"I love my son, but he allows outside influences to alter his decision making. My son could've been better than me on the court, but he started dating this fortune hunter in college, and he allowed her to talk him into this cooking thing."

When asked who his son's ex was, Harris revealed that she's restaurant owner Kandace Crawford, wife of hotel mogul Solomon Crawford. He didn't have kind words for Crawford.

"She's the worst kind of woman. Though she claims to be a businesswoman, she is nothing but a common gold digger. She latched on to my son nearly a decade ago, used whatever connection they have to talk him into basically becoming her fry cook while she went after a bigger wallet," he said.

Calls to Hometown Delights weren't immediately returned.

Devon angrily shoved the BlackBerry back into Marie's hands. "I'm sorry," he said to her when he noticed the startled look on her face. "I ought to sue this blogger and push my father into a shallow ditch!"

"Devon!" Marie and Kandace called out in concert. Solomon smiled and stopped short of offering to drive Devon around to locate the senior Harris.

Throwing his hands up, Devon said, "That man has gone too far. I became a chef to honor my mother. Had he paid any attention to me, he'd know that. Working here has done nothing but bolster my career, and he doesn't see that."

"I've always hated your father," Kandace said bitterly.

"Join the club," Devon said. "The line starts behind me."

"Do you have room for me?" Marie asked. Devon enveloped her in his arms and kissed her cheek.

"You don't even have to ask," he said. Devon caught a glimpse of Solomon, who had a smug smirk on his face.

"You know, Harris," Solomon said. "I've been wrong about you."

Kandace shook her head. "One day my hardheaded husband will start listening to me."

"How were you wrong?" Devon ribbed.

Solomon threw his hands up and shook his head. "I can admit, I was wrong about you holding a torch for my wife. Your father's rant didn't help."

"My father and I are nothing alike," Devon asserted again.

"I used to like that dude, except when he played the Knicks. Now, I see what a bitter asshole he is, and I thought my brother was bad." Kandace popped Solomon on the shoulder.

"Looks like I'm going to have to work extra hard to make sure we don't become our parents," Kandace said.

"Your mom isn't that bad," Devon said as they headed inside. "Sure, she cries a lot, but that's just women."

This time Solomon did slap Devon a high five. "Really?" Marie said with a giggle. "Not all women cry."

"Girl," Kandace said, "don't even bother. I've seen them both cry. One during *The Color Purple* on Broadway."

"Hey," Solomon said. "That was supposed to remain between us."

Kandace winked at her husband, but didn't say another word as they walked into the dining room.

"Well, it's about time," Serena called out when she spotted Devon. "I didn't think we were ever going to eat." She glanced at Marie and then turned to Alicia. "I guess we're supposed to be on our best behavior today."

Antonio stroked his wife's shoulder. "Baby, I don't think you can spell 'best behavior,'" he said, then kissed her hand.

She leaned in and whispered something naughty in his ear and then slipped her hand between his thighs. Antonio laughed heartily and said, "All you did was prove my point."

Devon wrapped his arms around Marie's shoulders. "Let me introduce you to these crazy folks." He started with Serena and Antonio. Then he pointed out James and Jade. Marie smirked at Jade. "Oh, we've met," Jade said as she crossed over to Marie and shook her hand. "We still haven't had that cup of coffee."

"I plan to be around," Marie said. "We have time."

Jade smiled. "I like the sound of that," she said.

"You're Richard Charles' daughter, right?" James inquired.

Marie nodded and braced herself for a comment about her exploits. James surprised her by saying, "I've worked on a housing board with him, and he's always talked about his brilliant daughter. It's nice to finally meet you." He extended his hand to her. She shook it proudly. Marie was surprised her father had described her in glowing terms that way, but he'd always told her that she could do anything she put her mind to.

Devon glanced around the room as Marie spoke with Jade and James. "No Maurice and Kenya today?"

"Kenya and Mo are playing super aunt and uncle this weekend. They have Jaden and Nairobi, and I think they've gone to a petting zoo or something," Jade said. She followed Devon's eyes and noticed he was staring at Marie with a smile on his face. "She's special, huh?"

"That doesn't even begin to describe it," he said. "But I don't know where we're headed, you know."

"What do you mean?"

Devon shrugged and was about to tell Jade about what happened last night, but Serena crossed over to them and handed Jade a champagne flute filled with a mimosa. "Excuse me, but can we get some pancakes or eggs to soak up the alcohol?" she asked. "You can go in the kitchen and we'll be nice to your girlfriend."

"You and the word 'nice' don't even go together.

Hey, Antonio, how do you deal with this one?" Devon called out.

"This *Serena* that you guys keep describing, I've never met her," he said as he walked up to his wife and encircled her waist with his arms and kissed her on the back of her neck. Serena seemed to melt in his arms. "Besides, she's only evil when she's hungry."

"Maybe she ought to learn how to cook," Devon teased. "Fear not, folks, I have a special breakfast dish for you to try this morn—" He looked down at his watch. "Afternoon, rather."

Marie walked over to Devon and whispered, "Should I come and help?" He smiled and then picked up an empty flute from the table. Tapping it, he called for his friends' attention.

Everyone focused on Devon, and even Marie eyed him with questions dancing in her eyes. "Write this down," he said, then pointed at Marie. "Here is the first and only woman who has ever offered to help me in the kitchen."

Alicia and Serena tossed napkins in his direction while the men broke into laughter. "She's a keeper then," James called out. Devon turned and looked at Marie with a smile on his face. *Yes, she is.*

"Well, are you going to take me up on my offer?" she questioned with a broad smile on her lips.

He gave her a quick peck on the cheek and whispered, "You know you and me in the kitchen together is a combination that never leads to food getting cooked."

A slow smile spread across her lips as she nodded in agreement. "And, I'm supposed to be wowed today, anyway," she said. Once Devon headed to the kitchen, Marie took a seat at the table near Kandace and Solomon. It didn't take long for the other women to join them and for Solomon to head to the bar with the other husbands.

Alicia handed Marie a mimosa and gave Kandace orange juice in a champagne flute. "Since you can't have the real thing, you can look the part," she said.

Kandace rubbed her belly. "Just a few more weeks. Solomon is hoping for a boy."

Serena swallowed a gulp of her drink and shook her head. "You know I love Solomon, but God is going to pay him back for his womanizing past. That's my goddaughter right there."

Jade nodded. "And God help us if He decides to pay you back with a daughter, as well, Serena."

"Oh shut up, Jade," Serena replied before they all started laughing. Alicia turned to Marie.

"They really are as crazy as you think," she said.

"I always wondered what having sisters would be like. I'm guessing a lot like this," she replied.

"We also have a brother," Kandace said.

"So," Serena started, "what are your intentions with him?"

Marie nodded, knowing this was coming. "I really care about him and admire the man that he is."

The women looked around the table as if her words were unexpected. "Devon is special and you have to forgive us if it seems we're a little in awe of you two being together," Alicia said diplomatically.

"In other words," Serena said, "we've read your press and we don't want to see you taking Devon down tabloid road."

"His father does a great job of that," Kandace commented snidely.

Marie nodded. "What is with that man? You know he had the nerve to call me a groupie?"

"He hasn't changed a bit. I got called that, too," Kandace said. "Now, 'fortune hunter' is new."

Serena tapped her fingers against the bottom of her champagne flute. "What was it that he called us, Jade?"

"Umm, a trio of harlots?"

Alicia nodded. "He was always such a charmer. Welcome to the club, Marie."

"Looks like I'm in good company, so thanks," she said with a smile as the women clinked their glasses. Marie's gaze fell on Kandace as she stroked her stomach in a way that pregnant women do. In the deep recesses of her mind, she questioned if Devon's anti-parenthood spiel had anything to do with the fact that his first love was carrying another man's baby. *Stop it; he is not harboring some secret desire for this woman. You're starting to sound like Solomon.* Marie took a swig of her drink and tried to focus on the conversation at hand. She loved how the women welcomed her into their fold and didn't say much about her party-girl ways. Looking at them furthered her belief that she had wasted too much time trying to grab cheap headlines rather than using her skills for more positive things.

"So, Marie," Jade said. "Are you excited about the fund-raiser?"

"Yes, the ladies at the shelter have been working really hard on putting this together."

Serena nodded in agreement. "They are an impressive group over there."

"And Devon does such a great job with them," Marie said with a sparkle in her eyes.

"Looks like Devon isn't simply doing a great job at just the shelter," Alicia said with a knowing smile.

"Did I hear my name?" Devon asked from the doorway. In his hands, he held a breakfast quiche with a southwestern flair.

The other men headed over to the table, and James

said, "Man, they have been talking about all of us, more than likely. You know how women are when they get together."

Jade stood up and crossed over to her husband and wrapped her arms around him. "Only good things, baby," she said, then kissed his cheek as Devon set the quiche in the middle of the table.

Antonio wrapped his arms around Serena's waist and kissed her neck. "Don't believe that," he said.

"Is that so, Mr. Billups?" Serena asked. "Why would we have anything bad to say about our wonderful husbands?"

He gently squeezed her bottom. "No reason at all, beautiful."

Devon shook his head as he placed the serving utensils on the table. "All of you are sickening." He pointed at Serena with a plate. "I don't even recognize you anymore."

She rolled her eyes and fanned her hand. "You'll find out soon enough," she replied, then cast a glance in Marie's direction. Devon shook his head, but when he looked at Marie as she sipped her mimosa, he silently admitted that Serena might be right.

Chapter 19

By the time the group finished eating, the kitchen and waitstaff had begun coming in to start their shifts. Devon headed into the kitchen to give his sous-chef instructions for the lunch and dinner service and to prepare the day's dessert. As he left the dining room, he winked at Marie and blew her a kiss. The smile she returned to him melted his heart. How had he fallen for this woman, a woman like no other he'd ever known, so fast? Maybe that's why he'd allowed himself to be careless enough to make love to her in the shower without a condom. He wanted to brand her as his and be the last man she ever kissed or made love to. But was that what she wanted? Was Marie Charles really ready to give up the lifestyle that she'd become accustomed to? How long would it be before she was bored with just being simply his girlfriend?

"Chef!" Devon turned and looked at his sous-chef, who had obviously been talking to him for a while.

"Yeah?" he asked.

"Where is your mind?" she asked. Devon shook his head and stifled his smile. He had a reputation to keep in the kitchen.

"Dessert," he said. "Today we're doing a chocolate

crème pie as our special, along with the other standards on the menu."

She nodded. "What do you need from me?"

"Get the staff started on the prep work; I'll finish up the filling and the chocolate lining for the pie crusts."

He headed for the corner of the kitchen that had been dubbed the chocolate corner. Devon smiled as he began to mix the chocolate filling for the pie, the deep brown color reminded him of Marie's smooth skin and how amazing it had been to lick sweet chocolate from that body. Devon didn't want Marie to become another casualty of his father and his bitterness. He was going to have to force his father to stop meddling in his life once and for all.

After finishing the pies and placing them in the oven, he told his sous-chef how long the pies needed to bake and then headed into the dining room to find Marie. Alicia, who had been behind the bar serving drinks to a couple of customers, told him that Marie was in the office with Solomon and Kandace.

"Thanks," he said, then headed in that direction. When he entered the office, the three of them were laughing and drinking more mimosas—well, plain OJ for Kandace. Devon shook his head and smiled at the irony of the situation.

"Hey," Devon said. "Y'all are having a party and I've been slaving in the kitchen; what's wrong with this picture?"

"There's no party without you," Marie said as she rose from her seat and crossed over to him. She planted a wet kiss on his cheek.

"Is that so?" he asked as he pulled her closer to him. Kandace smiled at the couple, happy that Devon had found someone special to share his love and his life with.

But she was a bit worried that Marie would have to go against Devon Sr.

"Devon," Kandace said. "Close the door for a second, we need to talk."

Solomon shot his wife a perfunctory glance and she placed her hand on his knee. "Don't look at me like that," she said.

Devon closed the door and walked Marie over to the chair where she had been sitting. "What's up?" he asked as Marie perched on his lap.

"If I'm overstepping, any of you can feel free to stop me," she said, looking around at Solomon and Marie. "But, your dad has basically declared war on you through the media, and anyone can see that you and Marie really care about each other."

Devon held up his hand, sensing where Kandace was going. "I will take care of my father. And while I appreciate your concern, you have your own life to worry about."

"That's very true," Solomon said. "My son doesn't need his mom getting stressed out."

"Your daughter's mother is just fine," Kandace shot back. "Devon, we've been down this road . . ."

"I was a lot younger and actually cared what he thought. Those days are over, and Solomon is right: Stressing about something that doesn't concern you isn't good for your baby."

Marie stroked Devon's shoulder. "Honestly," she interjected. "If he wants a media battle, he picked the right person to fight with. I know how to work the press."

Devon shook his head. "I'm not stooping to his level, and I thought you were done with stunts for headlines."

Solomon pointed toward the door. "That's our cue to leave," he said to Kandace. She frowned briefly, but deferred to her husband's suggestion for them to leave.

Once they were alone, Devon tilted his head and looked at Marie, as if to say, "Well?"

"Listen," she said. "I'm not saying go tit for tat with your father in news stories and things of that nature. No stunts, just you finally letting people know about the work you're doing at the shelter. This will take the focus off the nonsense your father is spouting."

Devon shook his head furiously. "I'm not exploiting my work at My Sister's Keeper."

"It's not about exploitation. This will bring more attention to the fund-raiser, which may result in more money for the shelter. In this world of blogs, twenty-four-hour news cycles, and your own celebrity, you can't ignore this."

He wanted to argue and say that she was wrong, but he was sure that Marie was right. After all, she wasn't just a party girl; she did work in public relations. Devon chewed his bottom lip and squeezed the bridge of his nose. "I really hate this."

"What do you hate most?" she asked, treating him as if he were a client. "Because you're going to have to control the story, decide what you will and won't talk about. I can come up with some talking points for you, call some reputable reporters, and . . ."

"Wait, you're not doing anything. I want you as far away from this as possible."

Marie hopped off his lap and stood beside the chair with her hands on her hips. "And why not? This is what I do and I want to help you."

"If you want to help me, just be here for me. I don't want you to work for me, I don't want you close enough for my father to touch you and hurt you."

Marie dropped her defenses, but she still wanted to do more than stand beside him and smile like a politician's wife at a press conference. "Well, are you going to hire a PR staff to help you?"

"Sure," he said. "How about your partner, because I know you're not going to stay out of this."

She closed the space between them and hugged him tightly. "You're a smart man."

"And I always fall for your type," he said. "Hardheaded woman." Devon kissed her softly with a slow burning passion that made her shiver. Her mouth was sweet like the drink she'd been indulging in. The taste of her, coupled with the feel of her hot hands stroking his back, made him hard as a brick. Before they got carried away, Devon pulled back from her. "Let's go back to my place," he said.

"Mine's closer," she replied breathlessly.

"Then that's where we're going." The couple rushed out of the office and dashed out the back door.

Devon was almost reckless in the way he sped out of the parking lot heading to Marie's. His want for her nearly overpowered his common sense, and she didn't help matters by stroking his thigh and licking her lips as they rode. The torture ended quickly as they arrived at her place. They hopped out of the car, and looking around the empty parking deck, Devon decided he wasn't going to wait for a taste of his woman. He pressed her body against a stone column and kissed her with a hot urgency that shook her to the core. A soft moan floated in the air from deep in her throat as he sucked her bottom lip and gripped her waist. Had he had his way, Devon would've ripped her clothes off and buried his hardness inside her right then and there, but the sound of a car alarm interrupted them.

Releasing her mouth, he stared at her flushed face. "We'd better go inside," she breathlessly said. Devon nodded, unable to speak. The couple practically ran to the elevator, and once they were inside, the owner of the car, who'd stopped them from getting too carried away, joined them. He smiled at Marie and nodded a respectful acknowledgment to Devon.

"Nice weather we're having," he said as he pressed the button for his floor.

"Yeah," Devon replied, holding Marie a tad closer to him. She gasped when she felt his erection against her behind and warm breath on her neck. Noting what was going on with the duo, the man didn't say another word. It seemed as if the elevator moved slowly up to the third floor, where the man was going. When the car finally came to a stop and the doors opened, the man tipped his imaginary hat to Devon and Marie. "Be safe," he said before the doors closed. As bad as he wanted to kiss her, touch her in her most sensitive spots, Devon held back for two reasons—cameras and the possibility of another passenger getting on to the elevator. That was publicity neither of them needed. For now, he was content holding her against him, teasing her neck with the tip of his tongue, and feeling her round bottom pressing against his erection. They were driving each other crazy and Devon couldn't wait to be alone—away from electronic eyes—with her.

Finally, they made it to Marie's floor. It took them less than five seconds to rush to the door. Devon took Marie's keys from her hand and made short work of unlocking and opening the door. Once inside, he kissed her the way he'd wanted to in the elevator—a lot of tongue, hot and wet. He slipped his hands between her thighs, stroking her until he could feel and smell her need. The perfume of her sex turned him on like a light switch. Breaking off the kiss, Devon said, "I'm going to make you come right here, before I take your clothes off."

"Oh, really?" Little did he know, it wasn't going to take

much effort to do that because his kiss had nearly brought her to the brink. Devon stroked slow, then fast. Her lips puckered as he extracted more of her desire. She thrust forward, mirroring his hand motion. "Mmm," she moaned. Devon closed his mouth around her neck, licking, sucking, and kissing until her moans reached a fevered pitch.

"Tell me what you're feeling. Talk to me, Marie," he commanded.

"I–I feel good. I'm coming for you."

That was music to Devon's ears as he pulled down her romper, dropped to his knees, and pushed her panties to the side and lapped her sweetness as if he were receiving sustenance from her. Marie's knees went weak as his tongue stroked her throbbing bud. She was going to come again or pass out on the floor.

After getting his fill of her essence, Devon scooped her into his arms, kissing her again, offering her his tongue and a chance to taste herself. Marie shivered as his tongue twirled around hers. Every pore, every nerve, and every fiber of her being was open and standing on end from his touch. The desire to have him between her thighs and touching her in all the right places made her ravenous, sped up her heart beat, and all she could do was squeeze his shoulders. "Need. You," Marie moaned, her words dripping with sex.

Devon bounded up the stairs to Marie's bedroom and laid her on the bed. She snatched her panties off, tossing them aside like an afterthought as Devon unbuckled his belt and pulled his pants off. Marie smiled at the erection poking through the opening of his boxers. Her mouth watered in anticipation as she slid closer to the edge of the bed. Placing her hand against his stomach, she stopped him from joining her on the bed.

"What you did to me downstairs was almost cruel," she

said, bringing her lips closer to his hardness. She gave him a quick lick and then said, "I think it's time for some payback."

Taking the length of him into her mouth, Marie unleashed a torrent of moans from him. As she took him deeper inside, she nearly brought Devon to his knees. She was licking him as if he were a chocolate lollipop, and Devon felt as if he were about to explode. Mustering a minute bit of strength, he pulled back and asked if she had a condom. Marie opened her nightstand drawer and fumbled around for a condom. Once she found one, she handed it to Devon.

He quickly tore the package open and slid the sheath in place, and then climbed into bed. Devon dove between Marie's thighs, joining with her as she clamped her thighs around his waist. "Oh, you feel good. So hot, so wet."

"Love me," she cried, digging her nails into his shoulder as he pumped into her. She rolled her hips like a salsa dancer as they fell into a dance that was part lambda and part stripper routine. Devon nibbled her neck and ground against her, then he rolled over, holding her hips as she mounted him. He gazed at her, transfixed by the look of bliss on her face and the way her breasts jutted upward. This woman was his chocolate addiction, the one he wanted to wake up with every day for the rest of his life. He leaned forward, licking her nipples until she cried out in ecstasy. She tightened herself around his penis and Devon exploded, filling the condom with his ejaculation, and Marie collapsed against his chest.

Devon held her tightly, kissing her neck gently as she shivered like a kitten. She drifted off to sleep, and moments later, he joined her in a restful slumber. Neither of them let go of each other while they slept; their heartbeats seemed to synchronize as they rested.

When they woke up three hours later, Marie was starving. "It's a good thing you're with a chef, huh?" Devon said as he yawned and stretched his hands above his head.

"It is," she said with a smile.

"What do you want to eat? Or the bigger question is, what is in your refrigerator?" Devon asked.

"Umm," she said. "Maybe we need to take a trip to Trader Joe's."

"But before we go," he said, grabbing a hold of Marie and pulling her against his chest. "I want to take a different kind of trip."

She tossed her leg over his hip, giving him direct access to her hot valley of desire. "I definitely want to enjoy this ride."

Chapter 20

Over the next three weeks, Devon and Marie turned their attention to the fund-raiser for My Sister's Keeper. Shay had been working with Marie's company and had saved enough money to pay a security deposit on her apartment. Marie had helped Shay find another part-time job with an advertising agency in South Charlotte that needed an assistant.

Since Marie had virtually disappeared from the headlines and hadn't had any more legal problems, and the district attorney declined to bring charges against her, things had been smooth as silk. She and Devon spend most of their days at the shelter and many nights in bed.

On this Monday, when Marie woke up, she had an appointment with her probation officer. "Do you want me to drive you to the court house?" Devon asked over coffee at Marie's condo. She shook her head as she sipped her coffee and reached for a mango-infused biscuit that Devon had prepared.

"I wish I could simply skip this meeting, but the sooner I go and turn in my hours, the sooner I can get over to the shelter."

Devon crossed over to the sink and dropped his empty

cup in, then he returned to the table and kissed Marie's cheek. "Do you think you can pick up the programs and donation cards from Kinko's before you come in?" He looked down at her feet and shook his head at the four-inch snakeskin heels she wore. "And change your shoes."

Marie stuck her leg out and held her foot out. "These are actually sensible heels. Notice the rounded toe," she said as she waggled her foot back and forth.

Devon grabbed her foot and removed the shoe, massaging her foot, inching up her ankle, spending time around her calf and stopping at her knee. Marie moaned in delight until she glanced at the clock on the stove. "Damn it," she groaned.

"It is getting late," he said before kissing her knee. "And you don't need any trouble with your probation officer."

"He hates me, and I think he's hoping I'm going to mess up."

Devon folded his arms across his chest and shook his head. "You do realize that he doesn't get to deal with convicts like you all day," he said with a wink. "Some of them are actually mean, don't do as they're told, and are probably pretty ugly. Then there's you, sexy, smelling good, and beautiful. It's not you he hates, it's the job."

She stroked his leg and smiled. "You know just what to say to make a girl's day. May I have my shoe back now?"

Devon kneeled down and placed her shoe on her foot. "There you go, Cinderella."

"Why, thank you, Prince Charming," she said in an exaggerated Southern drawl. "Maybe later, you can take them off."

When she stood up, Devon pulled her against his chest and brushed his lips against hers and said, "Maybe the shoes are the only thing I want to see you in at the end of the day."

Marie's phone rang, her signal that the car service was downstairs. Kissing Devon quickly, she grabbed her over-sized purse and headed out the door. She'd packed a pair of flats in the bag because she'd learned her lesson about wearing the wrong shoes in the kitchen.

When she got into the car, Marie released a calm sigh. "Excuse me," she said to the driver when she noticed that they hadn't moved an inch. "What's the problem, I have an appointment."

The driver turned around, revealing himself to be William. "The problem is, you won't return my phone calls."

"Are you kidding me? Where the hell is my driver?" Marie yelled and reached for the door handle. William locked the door.

"Can we talk for just a few minutes?" he pleaded.

"Unlock the door, now! I have nothing to say to you."

"I miss you and we're going to talk," he said. "We're supposed to be planning our life together."

Marie grabbed her BlackBerry. "Open the doors or I will call the police."

William started the car. "That's extreme, don't you think?"

"Move this car, and I swear, I will have your ass arrested for kidnapping."

"Marie, I made a mistake and I want to make up for it. I love you."

She released a thundering laugh and punched the back of his seat. "You are a damned joke. And let's be real, we didn't share love. I needed a husband to shut my father up and you needed my coattails. Now that Greta has kicked you out again, you think you can come crawling back to me?"

"That's over because my heart is with you," he said.

Marie looked at the time on her phone. She had five minutes to get to her meeting with her parole officer; playtime was over as she dialed 911. "Yes, I need the police," she said to the operator. "I'm being kidnapped by a homicidal maniac. His name is William Franklin. I think he killed my driver and he has me locked in a Lincoln Town Car outside of . . ." The door lock clicked. "Never mind, he's letting me go." Marie hopped out of the car and took off running down the street. She hoped that she could make it to the Gold Rush trolley in time. Heads were going to roll at the car company. *I need my driver's license back so I can run William over!* she thought as she reached the trolley stop just as it pulled up. Maybe her morning wouldn't be completely ruined.

Devon washed the breakfast dishes before leaving Marie's place. When he drove by the front of the building, he was surprised to see the town car was still parked out front. Had something happened? Devon slowed the car and pulled up beside that vehicle. Turning his hazards on, he placed the car in park. Dashing to the driver's side, he banged on the window. "Hey, is everything all right?"

The man Devon assumed was the driver rolled the window down and scowled at him. "Who the hell are you?"

"Where's my girlfriend? You should've picked her up thirty minutes ago."

The driver opened the door, nearly knocking Devon over. "What's your problem, partner?" Devon growled.

"First of all, the name's William Franklin. And secondly, Marie is my fiancée, not your girlfriend."

"You're delusional," Devon said. "Everybody knows

Marie came to her senses about what a son of a bitch you are and you two have been over. Now where is she?"

"I'm *delusional?* That would be you, buddy, if you think Marie Charles is going to stay with you and continue on this little I'm-a-saint-now routine. She's a party girl, she likes being seen and talked about. That's why we're perfect for each other. Who the hell are you, anyway? Some nobody her father handpicked for her? Much like the punk I snagged her from in the beginning."

Devon shook his head, wondering what Marie ever saw in this idiot to begin with. Still, he had to know if he'd done something to Marie. "Is she in the car?" he demanded.

"No."

Devon pushed William aside and peered into the backseat. He didn't see any signs of Marie. Turning around, he grabbed William by his shirt and threw him against the open door.

"Where the hell is she?" he asked, putting pressure on William's throat with his elbow.

"Shh–she got out . . . the car," he gasped. Devon tossed him to the ground and glared at him.

"Stay away from her. Understand me?" he hissed, then jogged over to his car. Devon headed to the courthouse, hoping Marie made her meeting and that William hadn't caused her any more trouble. He would've called her, but if she was in a meeting with her probation officer, the last thing he wanted was for the phone to ring and interrupt them. Besides, he did have to deliver his verification report to the probation officer—no time like the present.

After finding a parking spot and walking the block and a half to the courthouse, he was happy to see Marie exiting the building. "Devon," she said when she spotted him. "What are you doing here?"

"Checking up on you. I saw the town car in front of your building as I left and your 'fiancé' was masquerading as the driver. I just wanted to make sure you'd made it to your meeting and see if you were OK."

"Did that idiot really tell you he was my fiancé?" Marie asked as she shook her head. "I was just about to call the car company and give them a big piece of my mind. I can't believe he just got rid of the driver and took over the car like that. What kind of bootleg organization are they running?"

Devon shook his head. "We can take care of that later. Since I'm here, we might as well ride to My Sister's Keeper together. That way you won't have to worry about running into William again."

"Well, this morning hasn't been all bad," she said with a smile. "My probation has been completed early and my driver's license will be reinstated in five days."

"Wow. I guess you impressed the right people with your work."

"That and a letter Elaine wrote on my behalf," she said with a smile.

"So what does this mean for you and volunteering at the shelter now?" he asked.

Marie shrugged. "I don't have to do it anymore. But it doesn't mean that I plan to stop working with you and the ladies. My Sister's Keeper has really grown on me, and I want to make sure things work out for Bria."

Devon hugged her tightly and kissed her forehead. He couldn't have been happier to hear her say that. Part of him thought she would stop working with My Sister's Keeper. But the changes in Marie hadn't been just for show. Now, he could believe it. He took her hand in his and kissed it. Looking in her eyes, Devon knew he loved her more than he thought was possible. Still, he wasn't sure if he should put his cards on the table. Not that William had gotten to him, but he wasn't sure if Marie was ready to settle down. She may have tempered her partying ways, but was she going to get bored?

"What?" she asked when she caught the gleam in his eye.

"Nothing," he replied. "I was just thinking that you and I have some serious celebrating to do. Maybe we should actually go out."

Marie shrugged, thinking that the only party she needed was with her man in the bedroom or on the kitchen counter. Smiling, she said, "I think we should go someplace ultra-exclusive, where we are tops on the guest list and won't be worried about other people. And the food is always great."

"Where is such a place?" he asked, though he knew exactly where she meant.

"In the heart of NoDa. I stay on this guest list," she said with a wink as they got into the car.

"Is that so? Sounds like I need to have a talk with the owner of this establishment," he joked.

"Yeah, I like him a lot. Coolest man on the planet," she replied, then leaned over and kissed him. "Sexy as hell, too."

"Is that so?"

She nodded as he pulled into traffic. Once they arrived at My Sister's Keeper, the first thing Marie did was seek out Elaine so that she could give her a huge hug of thanks.

"Well," Elaine said. "All I did was tell the truth. I hope this doesn't mean we've seen the last of you."

"Oh, no," Marie said. "I'm thinking that my company should add you guys to our company's roster and help you when you need publicity campaigns."

"Wow, Marie, that is so sweet, but I'm sure we wouldn't be able to afford . . ."

Marie cut her off. "Who said anything about charging you? What this shelter does for women should be on the front page of the *Charlotte Observer*, leading the local newscasts, and on the lips of everyone in Charlotte."

Elaine hugged Marie again. "You're too kind, thank you so much."

"Anytime," she replied. "Now, let me get into the kitchen before the boss gets mad at me."

Elaine smiled. "I got a feeling that he's going to be just fine."

Inside the kitchen, Devon was trying to keep his students on task, but they kept asking him questions about his father, Marie, and the upcoming fund-raiser. "Hey, ladies," he said, pointing to the dough in the middle of their workstations. "If we don't knead and stretch, our bread is going to be hard and won't rise."

"We don't care about the bread," Bria said, her voice light and full of life. "When's the wedding?"

"That's right," Shay said. She still participated in Devon's class despite the fact that she didn't live at the shelter anymore. "And I hope you set your dad straight. I read that mess on the blog and I wanted to hunt him down and beat him with my shoe."

Devon laughed and started kneading his dough. "Join the club. But seriously," he said as the door opened and Marie walked in, "we have to get this bread ready for baking." She winked at him and walked over to the full trash cans and began gathering the bags.

"I saw that," Bria called out as she kneaded her dough. "Marie, are you going to tell us when the wedding is?"

She turned around as she tied up the trash bags. "I defer to the chef," she quipped and then made a hasty exit.

All of the women stopped kneading and focused on Devon. "Well?" Shay asked.

He looked down at his watch and smiled. "Don't you have to go to work?"

She looked up at the clock on the wall. "Not for another three hours, which gives me time to question you into submission."

"Not if that yeast doesn't rise," Devon said.

The women settled into the lesson and Devon thought about all of the wedding talk and wondered if his mind should even be going there. Was Marie ready for marriage? Her quip about deferring to him made him wonder if she had simply been trying to take herself off the hook.

Mrs. Devon Harris, Marie thought as she loaded the garbage into the green trash compactor. *Marie Charles-Harris. Oh my God, I'm acting like a damned high school freshman. Just because someone said marriage, I can't simply believe that it's what Devon wants. He's never mentioned it.* She pressed the compression button and tried to think of something other than walking down the aisle in a strapless butter yellow Angel Sanchez–designed dress. Her cell phone rang and she reached into her pocket, hoping it was the car service so that she could give them a sharp piece of her mind. It was an unknown number, but she had an idea who was on the other end of the phone.

"What do you want, clown?" she answered, assuming the caller was William.

"Is that how Richard Charles taught his daughter to answer the phone?" an unknown voice said.

"Who is this?" Marie asked.

"This is Devon Harris, Sr., and we need to have a serious conversation about you and my son," he said.

"Are you serious?" Marie inquired. "Your son doesn't have anything to do with you, so what could we possibly have to talk about?"

"Young lady, I thought you would appreciate what family means; after all, unlike the last trollop my son was involved with, you were raised with class even if you don't display it."

Marie gripped her phone and gritted her teeth. "You're going to give me a lecture on class when you went to one of the sleaziest blogs on the Internet to dish about your son last month?"

"The same blog that made you a star? Was it sleazy then?" Devon Sr. asked.

"I have nothing else to say to you."

"Listen," he said. "I honestly want to make peace with my son before I leave this planet. Maybe I haven't done things in the right way, but he's all I have left."

"And what am I supposed to do about it?" she asked.

"I'd rather not get into it over the phone. But if you could talk my son into coming to Atlanta for a fund-raiser I'm hosting in his mother's memory, we can talk about it."

Marie released a low whistle; after what Devon had told her about his father and the abuse his mother had suffered at the hands of his father, this was going to be an explosive minefield that she wanted to avoid. "Does he know about this?"

"He would if he answered my calls."

"I don't want anything to do with this," she said, then hung up the phone. Marie trembled as she tried to figure out how to tell Devon about the phone call she just received.

Chapter 21

When Marie and Devon headed to Hometown Delights after his class, he noticed that she was very quiet. "Is everything all right?" he asked as he turned into the restaurant's full parking lot.

She glanced at him and nodded, still unsure how she should tell him about the conversation she'd had with his father.

"I don't believe you," he said, noting the somber look on her face. He shifted the car in park and turned his full attention to her. "You've been quiet since we left the shelter. Tell me what's wrong."

She sighed and stared into his eyes; concern and worry were etched on his face, and she knew what she was about to say would only make things worse. "Devon, promise me you won't get too upset when I tell you this."

"That's not a good way to start a conversation," he said. "But, I'll try."

"I got a phone call from your father."

He mumbled a string of curse words that would've caused Eddie Murphy and Richard Pryor to blush. Marie shook her head. "Devon," she murmured.

"What did he have to say?"

"Well," she said, chewing her lip as she considered her words. "Umm, he wants us to come to Atlanta."

"Absolutely not. The last conversation we had was the *last* conversation we're going to have."

"But, ahh, he's doing something that you should be aware of, and you're not going to like it in the least."

Devon folded his arms and narrowed his eyes at her. "What's the bastard up to now?"

"Oh, God," she moaned. "He's sponsoring a fund-raiser."

He shrugged. "So what? He lends his name to everything. If only people knew what kind of asshole they were worshiping, they would—"

"It's in your mother's name," she blurted out, dropping her head in her hands as if she were bracing for an explosion.

Devon unfolded his arms and hopped out of the car. His silence made Marie worry as she got out of the car herself. Crossing over to him and touching his shoulder, she didn't know what to expect.

"You know," Devon said quietly, "he's done a lot of things that I've ignored. There was a time early in my career where his people wanted me to participate in some event he had going on in Atlanta. I told them to go straight to hell. But this. This shit here is beyond tasteless. He wants me to show up. Well, I will. And I'm finally going to rip that mask of I-give-a-damn-about-people off his smug face. That son of a bitch doesn't have the right to mumble my mother's name, and he wants to do this?"

"Devon, no."

He faced her, anger contorting his face into something she barely recognized. "Marie, I love you and I know that you're close to your father. You love him and he loves you. But the only thing my father has ever cared about is himself and his image. He will not sully my mother's reputation to add a further feather in his cap. I don't give a damn if he's dying or not, I won't take this lying down."

She opened her arms to him and hugged him. "Is this what you're going to need to do to release the anger and find peace? Devon, I don't know what it was like for you with your father, but he's dying. Yes, he hurt you and your mother in painful ways that I can't imagine. But don't you owe it to yourself to let it go?"

"Every time I think about trying to make real peace with him, he pulls some bullshit like this. All I can do is sever this relationship, and what I plan to do at this fund-raiser will do just that." He started to storm away from her, but Marie grabbed his arm.

"Devon," she said quietly. "Calm down. Look at me." He turned and faced her, and she could see his face slowly softening. "Don't run from me, I want to help you. You're in pain and I don't like this."

He stroked her cheek and tilted his head to the side. "And what am I supposed to do?"

She closed her hand around his. "Forgiveness isn't about the other person winning; it is about you. You finding peace within yourself. You can't love if you're holding on to hate for your father," she said, her eyes bubbling with tears.

"Is that what you think?" he asked. "You don't get it. You know what it's like to have a real father."

"And that's why I know you need to see him. Maybe not at this fund-raiser, but you should talk to him, Devon."

He shook his head and squeezed the bridge of his nose. "I can't. I'm going to take a walk," he said.

She didn't know if she should've followed him or not. Instead, she headed inside the restaurant and ran for the office. Devon needed his friends; specifically, he needed Kandace.

"Alicia," Marie said breathlessly from the doorway. "Do you know where Kandace is?"

Alicia looked up from the computer, surprised to see Marie standing there. "I haven't seen her since earlier. What's going on?"

Marie closed the door behind her and sighed. "I think Devon needs her." Despite the fact that Marie wanted to be the one who calmed her man down, she knew Kandace had a deeper understanding of Devon's relationship with his father.

"Why? What's going on?" Alicia asked.

"Devon's having a tough time and I just don't know how to help him. I'm guessing Kandace does because she's dealt with his father before."

Alicia nodded. "That man just doesn't quit."

"His father called me and said he's doing a fund-raiser in memory of Devon's mother. So, you can imagine how that went over."

Alicia's mouth dropped and she snatched the phone off the hook. "I'll call Kandace."

Devon hadn't realized how far he'd walked until he passed Wendy's. It was really ironic that he ended up there since this had been the only fast-food restaurant that his mother would allow them to dine at during their adventures. Smiling, he started to go in and order a single with cheese, mustard, and extra pickles, his mother's favorite sandwich. Instead, he grabbed his cell phone and called his father.

"Son, I'm surprised to hear from you," Devon Sr. said when he answered the phone.

"That's a damned lie and we both know it. Why did you call Marie?"

"I want this war between us to end, Son. I want us to try and put the past behind us. That's why I'm honoring your mother."

"That's a damned joke. You honoring the woman you abused for years, right. You'd better call it off or I will tell the world what a louse their hero is. I will tell them why I spent the last decade avoiding you and everything you stand for."

"You don't want to do that. There's no need to air our family business."

"I've tried to handle this by just ignoring you. Obviously, you can't take a hint."

"Is this about your mother or the fact that you blame me because you couldn't keep it in your pants and that girl caught you? Get over it, Junior. She certainly has."

"You're a pathetic, lonely old man and I actually feel sorry for you. You know what, I'm not wasting my time on you anymore. When your judgment day comes, you're going to have to answer for everything you've ever done," he said, quoting his mother. He actually heard his father gasp. Devon couldn't remember how many times he'd heard his mother say those exact words to his father. Knowing that he couldn't do anything to make his father see the errors of the past, Devon felt peace wash over him. His mother wouldn't want him to spend another day angry with his father. He finally understood her last words to him. *Baby, you can only control what is in your soul.*

"I hope your fund-raiser is successful and you find the

forgiveness that you're seeking before you meet your end," he said, then hung up the phone.

As he walked back to the restaurant, his phone rang again. Though he started to ignore the call, thinking it was his father, Devon pulled the phone from his pocket. "Kandace?" he questioned when he answered.

"Where are you?" she asked.

"Heading to the restaurant. What's up?"

"Are you all right?"

Devon laughed, knowing Marie had told his friends what happened. That was sweet and a bit annoying. "Everything is cool, and why did Marie have you call me?"

"Because that girl loves you and wants to keep you on this side of sanity. You're really going to have to open up to her. It takes a lot for a woman to ask a man's ex for help."

"Kandace," Devon said, "I'm good. I'm going to go to Marie and let her know that."

"Are you sure? She told me and Alicia what your father had planned and how . . ."

"Yeah, yeah, yeah," he said. "I was pissed, ready to smash his face in and tell the world what kind of man he is. But as I walked, I felt the presence of my mother, and I really let it all go. I can't keep this anger inside me and I released it today."

"Please let Marie know that. And whatever you do, don't mess things up with this woman," Kandace said. "You need her."

"It's not often that a man can find the right woman once, but to have it happen a second time, I know what to do not to mess it up."

"Umm, that's great. I have to go, I think my water just broke," she said, then the line went silent. Devon jogged to the restaurant to share the news of Kandace's labor.

* * *

Waiting for Devon to return was driving Marie crazy. Where did he go? Was he all right? Maybe she should've followed him because she knew how upset he was.

"Marie," Alicia said as she watched her pace back and forth. "You're going to walk a hole in the floor."

She stopped and cast a sheepish glance at Alicia. "Sorry. I'm just worried about him. What if Kandace wasn't able to calm him down? You didn't see him; he was so angry and I just can't help but wonder if he . . ."

The door to the office swung open and Devon burst in. "Have you two heard from Kandace or Solomon?"

"No," Alicia replied. "Why?"

"Are you all right?" Marie asked Devon as she crossed over to him. He nodded and placed his hand on her shoulder.

"Kandace said her water broke," he said.

Alicia brought her hand to her mouth, and as she was about to call Jade and Serena, the office phone rang. Alicia grabbed the extension and Marie turned to Devon, whispering, "Are you all right?"

"I'm fine," he replied. "We need to talk about what you did."

"Look," she began. "I was . . ."

"Guys," Alicia called out. "Kandace is at Presbyterian Hospital. Jade and Serena are on the way."

"Let's go," Devon said.

"I think I'm going to my office," Marie said. Devon shook his head.

"Come on, ride with me," he said. "We can talk on the way to the hospital."

The last thing Marie wanted was to hear a lecture from Devon about calling Kandace, but what else was she supposed to do? He didn't give her much of a choice with his silent anger. Rolling her eyes, Marie decided that she wasn't going to let him make her feel bad about trying to protect him. She walked out to the car with him and noticed a slight change in his gait.

"Devon," she said. "Look, if you're upset because I went to your friends and . . ."

He took her face in the palm of his hands. "I'm not upset. I owe you an apology," he said. "I haven't let you in and that's not fair to you."

Marie blinked and sucked her bottom lip in. "OK."

"No, seriously. The last thing I wanted was to scare you or make you think that I was going to lose control. I'm done with my father, and if he's truly going to 'honor' my mother, then I wish him the best. It's the least he could do for the hell that he put her through. I can't be angry with him anymore if I expect to truly experience love," he said, then brushed his lips against hers. "And I don't want you worrying about me when all we should be thinking about is what we have between us right now."

Marie tilted her head and kissed him again, slipping her tongue between his lips as if she was showing him how relieved she was that he'd calmed down. Breaking the kiss, Devon stared into her eyes and nodded. "We'd better get going," he said.

"OK," she replied with a smile. When Marie and Devon arrived at the hospital, Jade, Alicia, Serena, and Antonio were there in the lobby of the maternity ward. "How is she?" Devon asked.

"We don't know yet," Jade said. "Solomon said there was a complication."

"Oh, no," Devon said. Marie gripped his hand, noting the pained look on his face.

Serena held on to Antonio tightly as her eyes misted with tears. "She has to be all right," she whispered.

"She will be," Antonio said comfortingly. "She's a fighter, just like the rest of you ladies, and she isn't going to leave that baby without a mother."

About an hour later, Solomon walked into the lobby and smiled at his friends. Jade and Devon leapt to their feet. "How is she?" they asked in concert.

"My wife and my daughter are just fine. I'm guessing this is the first of many near heart attacks I have to look forward to," he said as he leaned against the wall and sighed.

"So, what happened?" Serena asked.

Solomon released a breath and started telling the story. "The baby was breach. The doctor thought she would turn, but as Kandace continued to dilate, the baby didn't move an inch. Then she went into distress because the umbilical cord was wrapped around her neck. Kandace's blood pressure dropped. It was scary for a while. All of the machines were going crazy and I was standing there about to pass out."

Devon held Marie closer to him, Antonio stroked Serena's shoulder, and Jade and Alicia squeezed each other's hands as Solomon continued his story.

"I told the doctor he had to save them both, and he went on about how they couldn't do the emergency C-section if Kandace didn't stabilize, and I thought my life was going to end right there. But she did stabilize and the rest is, as they say, history."

Jade, Alicia, and Serena surrounded Solomon and enveloped him in a tight hug as they cried tears of relief and joy. As Marie watched them, she felt out of place, as if she was intruding on a private moment.

"I'm going to get everyone some tea," she told Devon.

He nodded and did everything but shove her down the hall—at least in Marie's mind.

She slowly wandered down the corridor, wondering if she was being too sensitive to what she thought was a random dismissal. After all, the woman had been his first love, and she was married to another man and just gave birth to his child. *And she nearly died. Of course Devon is going to be concerned about her. This isn't William; it's not as if you're going to walk in someplace and find them kissing.*

Marie didn't do insecurities and these feelings were new. And if she was honest with herself, she knew she'd never felt this way about anyone else she'd ever dated because she had never been in love. Never put her heart into it because she was afraid to get hurt. Now she had fallen so deeply for Devon that she was afraid that such a love would lead to pain. But Devon wasn't the type of man to play games, and he hadn't given her a reason to feel this way. Her old sabotaging self seemed to be whispering in her ear as she walked into the cafeteria. *Maybe I don't deserve a man like Devon,* she thought as she ordered tea for everyone and picked up some snacks just in case anyone wanted something to eat. When Marie returned to the waiting room, Jade and Alicia were gone. Devon told her they were visiting Kandace as he took the drinks and snacks from her hands. "You must've known that we were sitting here contemplating ordering some food."

"Well, I wanted to make sure everybody could have something they wanted," she said. Devon kissed her.

"Thank you, baby," he said as he grabbed a granola bar. Antonio and Serena thanked Marie as they took tea and two bags of chips. Marie started to ask Devon if he thought she should be there, since she was much like an outsider to the crew, but Jade and Alicia walked over to them.

"She is a beautiful little girl and Solomon is already so protective of her," Jade said.

"What did they name her?" Serena asked.

"Kiana Danielle," Alicia said and the three women laughed.

"What's so funny?" Antonio asked, then took a sip of tea.

"Nothing, except she's been carrying that name around since . . ." Serena stopped and glanced at Marie and Devon. "It's an old name we came up with in the AUC."

Marie grabbed her cup of tea and took a big gulp so that she wouldn't say something inappropriate. "They took the baby back to the nursery; Solomon said he'd come and escort us over there to see her," Jade said.

"You can wait for Solomon," Serena said. "I'm going to see my goddaughter now."

As she walked down the hall, Alicia turned to Jade and shook her head. "You see how she just automatically assumes she's the godmother," she said, then laughed.

Devon noticed how quiet Marie was and sat down beside her on the bench where she was sending e-mails from her BlackBerry.

"Hey, you," he said. "I guess all this motherhood stuff isn't your scene, huh?"

"I thought it wasn't your scene," she shot back. Marie shook her head. "I'm sorry, I guess I need a nap. I just feel like you guys have a life and a connection that I will never be a part of. I mean, you're almost leaping for joy that Kandace had a baby, but the one time we had sex without a condom, you nearly jumped out of your skin at the prospect that I could be carrying your child."

"Really? You want to do this here?" Devon asked, taken aback by Marie's attitude.

"No, I don't. As a matter of fact, let me go and leave

you with your friends. Enjoy the tea and the snacks." She leapt to her feet and stormed to the elevator. When she felt a hand on her arm, she was honestly surprised that Devon had followed her.

"First of all, I don't know where this is coming from," he said in a whisper. "Obviously, you knew what kind of friendship Kandace and I had or you wouldn't have reached out to her earlier today. Secondly, her baby has nothing to do with me. Am I happy for her? Yes. But I'm not going to be the one responsible for raising that child. That's her and her husband's job. So, what is really going on with you?"

Marie couldn't answer the question. Because she was afraid that her answer wouldn't make sense at all. She was jealous, plain and simple, and she knew she had no reason to be. Devon was right; she had reached out to Kandace when she thought he was in trouble.

"Why don't you just go back to your friends," she said. "I need to go and talk to Adriana about some business and I don't need to be hanging around here." She jabbed the button for the elevator, and Devon shook his head. But he didn't try to stop her, recognizing that whatever she was fighting with in her head, he couldn't do anything to help her until she calmed down.

Chapter 22

Two days after their disagreement at the hospital, Devon still couldn't figure out why Marie had gotten so upset. But he had grown tired of her avoiding him and not answering his calls. She had adjusted her schedule at the shelter to get there after his class was finished. After he finished his preparation work at the restaurant, he headed to Marie's office to put an end to the madness. Either they were going to work things out or it was time to stop wasting time.

Who am I kidding? I'm not letting her go, and if I have to lock her in this office until we get things right, then that's just what I'm going to do, he thought as he hopped into his car. Driving to her office, all he could think about was how empty he'd felt these past few days. As he pulled up to a stoplight, his cell phone rang, jarring his mind away from Marie.

"Yeah?" he said when he answered.

"Devon, this is Amélie Michel from Paris Dining," she said. "Bonjour."

"Bonjour," he said.

"It's been a while since we've spoken about the show," Amélie said. "Today, I'm able to make you a formal offer.

The host of our show has decided that he wants to focus on running his restaurant and no one wants to see this show end."

"Wow," he said. Since Devon and Marie had gotten serious, he hadn't given Paris a second thought.

"You say that as if Paris is no longer an option for you," she said, her voice tensing.

"Honestly, Amélie, I haven't thought about it in a while."

"*Mais non*, Devon. You're the only chef I know who can pull this show off. You have a following in Paris because of the *gâteau d'amoureux*. One cake. You have to do this. How much will it take to get you here?"

"It's not the money," he said.

"I understand that you're working with a restaurant in North Carolina, but I will buy out your contract and pay any penalties. You made your mark here. Do you know how many students have a dessert being sold in Le Bouquet des Archives? Of course, you're not a student anymore, and your talent has become world renowned."

Devon laughed underneath her compliments. "I don't know if I'd go that far. When would you need my decision?" he asked as he turned into the parking lot of Marie's office building.

"Well, we don't start the show for another ten months, but if you're going to take over the restaurant, change the menu, and remake our dessert offerings, then I'd like to have you here in the next six months."

"I have a lot of things I have to tie up here," he said, thinking about the upcoming fund-raiser, his work at the shelter, and Marie. Looking up at the office building, he thought about turning the offer down. But Paris was his absolute favorite city, and he had considered going back there. Would Marie come with him? This would be a chance for him to start over and put distance between him and his father. He couldn't start a new life if Marie wasn't a part of it, though.

"Well," she said, "I wish I could say that you had all the time in the world, but I'm going to need an answer in a month."

"All right," he said. "I will get back to you."

"*Au revoir*," she said.

After hanging up the phone, Devon sighed, wondering if he should take the next step to further his career or if he should fight for the love of his woman. The woman he wanted to spend the rest of his life with. The woman he wanted to stand beside while she gave birth to his son. The woman who made him dream of chocolate and think of nothing but tasting it all over her body.

Was he ready to give up his dream for Marie?

Marie sipped a latte with her feet up on her desk as she listened to Adriana tell her about a horrible date she'd had last night. "Girl," Adriana said. "You're lucky."

"What?" Marie said.

"No more bad dates; you have a great boyfriend," she said.

"Yeah," she said wistfully.

Adriana raised her eyebrow. "I hope you haven't messed it up with him, because he is clearly the best thing that's ever happened to you."

"Whatever," she replied. "My wonderful boyfriend hasn't talked to me since we had a disagreement at the hospital when his ex had her baby."

Adriana shook her head and tossed her empty Starbucks cup in the trash can. "And it has nothing to do with the fact that you haven't been answering his calls? I thought you were done with this craziness, Marie."

"What do you mean?"

Adriana smiled and faced her friend. "You don't want to be happy."

"Excuse me?"

"That's why you accepted William's engagement ring. That's why you're trying to ruin what you have with Devon over the fact that he's friends with his married ex," she said. "His married ex, who he's in business with." She shook her head again. "Who just had a baby, so it's not as if they can engage in some clandestine affair."

"I never said they were having an affair or that it was possible, but . . ." Marie stopped talking when she heard the door buzz. "Yes?"

"There's a Devon Harris here for you, Miss Charles," the doorman said.

"Send him up," she said as she dropped her feet and smoothed her pencil skirt. Adriana giggled at her friend.

"Should I leave or pretend that I'm busy working on a campaign?" she asked.

"Get out," Marie replied.

Adriana offered her friend a mock salute. "And in the words of RuPaul, don't—" She stopped short when the door opened and Devon walked in. "Hi," she said to him. "Marie, I'm going to meet with those club owners. It's going to be a long meeting."

Marie shook her head and muttered, "Smooth."

Devon offered Adriana a smile as she made her hasty exit. Marie looked at Devon, wondering what to say as a tense silence surrounded them like thick curtains.

"I didn't come here just to look at you," he said.

"Why are you here?"

"Either I'm here to fix a problem or say good-bye." His words stabbed her in the heart. *Good-bye?*

"I. Hope that isn't the case," she stammered. "Good-bye? Why?"

"Because, you have decided that this isn't what you want. You've been avoiding me and I have no idea why."

"Because I'm an idiot. I don't know what came over me at the hospital. Well, yes, I do. What you and Kandace shared really made me jealous."

"She's happily married. And what we had ended years ago. There's nothing for you to be jealous about or to worry about." Devon crossed over to her chair and placed his hands on the arms. "I love you. I only want you, and despite the fact that you tried to push me away, I'm not going to be that easy to get rid of, got it?"

She nodded. "I love you, too, and that really scares me."

"Don't be afraid," he said. "You have nothing to fear. Let me prove it to you." Devon captured her lips with a heated passion that took her breath away. His tongue slowly meandered the sweet crevices of her mouth as she wrapped her arms around his neck, pulling him in deeper. Devon snaked his hand underneath her skirt, reaching for her creamy center. He could feel her throbbing need as his fingers danced across her crotch. And he was—again—thankful for flimsy lace that could barely contain Marie's wetness. Pushing her panties aside, he slipped one finger inside, in and out as he kissed her, swallowing her lustful moans.

Breaking the kiss, he pushed her skirt up to her waist with his other hand, then dropped to his knees in front of her. He pulled her panties to the side and devoured her wet folds of flesh, hungrily lapping her sweet wetness and lashing her throbbing bud until she screamed out his name. "Come for me, let me taste what I've been missing." Devon's hot breath made her explode just as he'd requested. Feeling her climax sent electric currents through his body and made him harder than a Stonehenge monolith.

Gripping her hips, he effortlessly lifted her from the chair and sat her on the edge of the desk. Next, he peeled her panties off as she reached for his belt. "Protection?" she moaned.

As she unzipped his pants, Devon reached for his wallet and removed a condom. Marie snatched the package from his hand and ripped it open as he stepped out of his jeans. She slid the sheath in place, providing the barrier of protection they needed. Still, she yearned for a day when they were joined as man and wife and condoms were no longer a necessity. The thought froze her momentarily as the image of that wedding dress and Devon in a simple black tuxedo flashed in her mind. He took her face in his hands. "Are you all right?"

"Yes, yes," she said. "But I could be better." She slipped one leg around his waist, inching him closer to her desire.

He leaned into her, brushing his lips against hers as he melted with her wetness. She was hot, tight, and delectable as they ground against each other, going stroke for stroke. With each thrust, she released her fear, released her insecurities, and accepted his love.

"Oh, Marie," he breathed against her ear as he felt the oncoming of an explosion. "I love you."

Through her orgasmic haze, she cried out, "I love you, too." They climaxed together, their hearts pounding to the beat of the same love song. A few moments of silence passed before either of them could muster the strength to unwind their bodies.

"We'd better put some clothes on before Adriana or one of your clients comes in," he said, then kissed her collarbone, knowing it would make her hot.

"My clients are all online these days," she said. "I've

decided to work on social media campaigns rather than hitting the party scene every night."

Devon smiled and adjusted her skirt while pocketing her panties. "Is that so?" he said.

"Yes, and did you just . . ."

"I sure did, and if you want them back, you're going to have to join me for dinner tonight."

"I guess I will since those are my lucky panties."

"Mine, too," he joked. "On the way over here, I got a phone call that . . ."

Marie's phone rang, interrupting Devon. "I have to take this. My clients don't come by, but they call all the time. Can we talk tonight or do you want to wait?"

Looking down at his watch, Devon saw he needed to get back to the restaurant. "Tonight." She blew him a kiss as he headed out the door and she picked up the phone.

Driving to Hometown Delights, Devon thought about Paris. It had been a dream of his to work there for years, but would Marie go with him? Could he ask her to give up her business and move with him to France? Especially if they didn't have a stronger commitment. He didn't want to take his girlfriend to Paris; he wanted to live there with his wife. He wanted children who spoke French and English, who would see the *Mona Lisa* on the wall of the Louvre rather than in the pages of a book. There was only one thing he could do. Devon was going to ask her to marry him and live with him in Paris.

Now, he just had to tell the ladies that he was leaving. As he headed inside, his cell phone rang again. When he saw the 404 area code, he started not to answer, but he did.

"Yeah," he said.

"Mr. Harris, this is Dr. Harold Neiderman from Grady Memorial Hospital."

"OK."

"I have some news about your father," he began.

"You know what, you can save it. I'm not up for any more of his tricks and . . ."

"Mr. Harris, I'm sorry to tell you this, but your father passed away this morning after being admitted to the hospital last night with complaints of chest pains. We tried to save him, but due to his condition, all we could really do was make him comfortable."

Devon tugged at his ear, wondering if he was supposed to feel something or if he was supposed to say something to the doctor. All he really wanted to know was if his father had made peace with God before he took his last breath. Finally, he said, "I'm sorry to hear that."

"Well, he had instructions, but we had to notify his next of kin, and you're the person who was listed."

"Thanks for the call," Devon said, then ended the call. He sat in the car for a few minutes, thinking this was a sign for him to let go of the past and move forward in the future. He didn't have anything holding him back now. It was time for him to move on, and he was going to take those steps with Marie. That is, if she was willing to go to Paris with him.

Devon headed for the office and was glad to see Alicia and Jade in there. "Ladies," he said with a smile. "We need to talk."

"Anytime a man says we need to talk, it isn't good," Alicia quipped.

"What's going on?" Jade asked. "We were looking at the AUC reunion site. Guess who's getting honored at the reunion ceremony." She nudged Alicia, who hid her smile.

"I don't see why all of us are going to accept the award," Alicia said. "And who is this prince from Africa?"

"I have no idea," Jade said, then looked away from the computer and at Devon. "Well, what's going on with you?"

"I'm thinking about going to Paris."

"What?" Jade exclaimed. "That's been your dream for the longest time." She flung her arms around him and hugged him tightly.

"But what about everything that you've built here?" Alicia asked. "Do you really want to start over?"

"More specifically, what about Marie?" Jade asked.

Devon folded his arms across his chest. "I'm hoping she will come with me."

Alicia and Jade exchanged knowing looks. "So, does this mean there's going to be a wedding before you head to Paris?" Jade asked.

"Because no sane woman would just leave the country with a man without a ring on her," Alicia said.

Jade squeezed her friend's shoulder. "You would," she said.

Alicia smacked her lips and rolled her eyes. "Yeah, right. You know I've always been the practical one out of the group."

"If that's what you believe," Devon said. "But, yes, I'd marry her either in Paris or on the plane ride there. Problem is, I haven't told Marie about Paris yet. I want to get through the fund-raiser, first."

"You'd better tell her!" Jade and Alicia said in concert.

He laughed. "Y'all are probably right. Oh, my father died," he said, no emotion in his voice.

Jade and Alicia stared at him as if they were waiting for or expecting a breakdown. Jade asked, "Are you all right?"

Devon shrugged. "It's not as if we were close. I made my peace with him and let go of my anger. Am I going to break down and cry about his passing? I don't think so. He's been dead to me for years."

"Will there be a funeral?" Alicia asked. "Are you going or making the arrangements?"

He shook his head. "I'm sure his people will take care of that," Devon said.

"Wow," Jade said quietly. "You know, I can't blame you for feeling that way. Bless the dead, but your father was something special."

"That's one way to describe him. Listen, I don't want to talk about him. The kitchen staff can cook my menu, and you won't see any difference in the food quality."

"But we're going to miss you," Jade said. "Wait until we tell Serena."

Alicia laughed. "I bet she'll cry."

Devon shook his head, then joined in the laughter. "If you guys don't mind, let's keep this quiet for a little bit. I want to tell my staff and, of course, I want to talk to Marie about it."

"All right," Alicia said. "But how long do we have before you leave?"

"At least six months," he replied. "We still have the fund-raiser for My Sister's Keeper and more meals for me to cook for you guys."

"You'd better stock Serena's freezer before you leave or poor Antonio and A.J. are going to starve," Jade joked.

"Maybe you guys should invest in some cooking lessons for your girl," Devon said. "I'm heading for the kitchen now."

Chapter 23

Still basking in the afterglow of makeup sex, Marie decided to go home early and prepare for her dinner with Devon. Slipping behind the wheel of her new Jaguar, she smiled, thinking how her life had changed since being with Devon. The party girl was no more. She honestly didn't miss that life, either. She hadn't been on the blogs or in the papers for the wrong reasons. She thought about sending a thank-you basket to the judge who handed down her sentence those months ago. Had it not been for him, she would've never met and fallen in love with Devon Harris. Maybe they should've gone out and flaunted their relationship. They could make all the right headlines and become the darlings of the city. Nah, she wanted to keep this relationship just between the two of them. Still, she wanted one last night out. She needed to say good-bye to the party scene and leave it in hands that cared, but definitely not hers.

Just as she was about to back out of the lot, there was a banging on the trunk of the car. Looking in the rearview, she saw William standing there. "He just won't go away," she muttered as she mulled over the idea of slamming the car into him. Knowing that she wouldn't do anything but cause trouble for herself, Marie simply pulled forward and rolled her window down.

"Stalker much?" she exclaimed.

"We need to talk and I'm not leaving until we do."

"Just like I said weeks ago, I have nothing to say to you and that hasn't changed."

He walked over to the driver's side and glared at her. "You think you can just ignore me? I lost everything because of you."

"You had nothing to lose to begin with. Get away from my car before I turn you into a speed bump."

He stepped back and smirked at her. "You say I didn't have anything to lose, but you have a lot to lose. How would your new man feel if he knew the truth about you?"

"What madness have you made up in your head? Please go find Greta or someone who gives a damn to listen to what you have to say. I don't. Now. Move!"

William glared at her and shouted. "I'm going to sue you!"

Marie flipped the ignition off and hopped out of the car. "On what grounds? You're going to sue me for being stupid enough to accept your engagement ring? You're going to sue me for not seeing you for the trifling piece of crap you are? Am I supposed to write your broke ass a check to get you out of my life when you are the one who was at my event kissing your ex-wife? Or is that 'current meal ticket,' I'm a little confused. You know, I should thank you. Had it not been for you making an utter fool of me, I would've never met the man who means the world to me." She stalked back to her car, grabbed her purse, reached into her wallet, and flung a twenty-dollar bill at William. "Why don't you take this and go buy a damned clue?" Marie hopped into her car and sped away. He had one more time to try to threaten her or just show up at her business or her home and she was going to have him thrown in jail. William wanted a payday, and she would not be extorted by that loser. Still, Marie headed to her father's office to ask him how she should handle this thing with William.

As Devon headed to his car, he heard someone call out his name. He was shocked to look up at Solomon Crawford. Yes, the men had come to an understanding, but they were far from best friends.

"What's up?" Devon asked.

"I was in the neighborhood and figured I'd get Kandace some dinner since she keeps talking about New Orleans chicken," he said. "Listen, I wanted to ask you something."

Devon eyed him suspiciously. What could Solomon want with him? "Go ahead."

"Will you be my daughter's godfather? And before you say no or anything, hear me out," he said.

"Why would you want me to be your daughter's godfather? We're civil, but I'd hardly call us close."

"I know how much you love my wife. And I know the love you have for her has changed over the years. This whole circle of friends you all have here is the closest thing to a real family I've ever seen," he said. "I had money growing up, but never people who truly gave a damn around me."

"Are you sure you're comfortable with this? It wasn't too long ago that you thought I wanted to steal your wife away as soon as you turned your back," Devon said folding his arms across his chest. "And you're right, I do love Kandace. I guess it was always meant for us to be close like this. She found her happily ever after with you and I'm hoping to find mine elsewhere as well."

"I know, you and the party girl. But since I know you love my wife, I know you'll love my daughter as well. And, trust me, I think Karma is going to bite me in the ass, so I need all the backup I can get. Me, with a daughter." Solomon shook his head.

"If you're this stressed out this early, you're going to worry yourself into a heart attack by the time she's sixteen."

The two men headed into the restaurant so that Devon could prepare Kandace her favorite dish. Seeing this side of the great Solomon Crawford was nearly comical. But it showed Devon something else as well: Kandace was with the right man. The love Solomon had for his wife and daughter was tangible. Devon wondered if he'd feel like this when Marie gave birth to their kids. He wanted two, preferably two boys.

"When are you guys going to have little Kiana's christening?" Devon asked as he mixed the spices for the chicken.

"No time soon. I'm still in shock that I'm someone's father. How do I do this and not mess it up?

Devon nodded. "I say we do the opposite of what our fathers did and we should be great fathers."

Alicia walked into the kitchen and smiled. "I thought you'd taken off. Hey, Solomon," she said.

"What's up, Alicia?" he replied.

"Kandace wanted some dinner, and while I'm in here, I might as well take care of my dinner date entrée."

Solomon shook his head. "So, you and that chick are serious?"

Devon bristled. "Why wouldn't we be?"

Solomon threw his hands up. "I'm not trying to say anything, but if I can give you a word of warning."

"Uh-oh," Alicia mumbled. Devon stopped mixing and glared at Solomon.

"What?" he asked.

"I don't know Marie and I'm sure she's a nice girl. But I've seen a lot of party girls in my day, and it's a lifestyle that's hard for them to give up, and it comes back to bite you at the more unexpected times," he said. "Just putting it out there."

"Well, she has changed a lot," Alicia said. "I just read on that silly *After Dark* blog that she's now considered MIA and they're trying to see who's going to take her place on the party scene."

"And," Solomon said, "this isn't New York."

"Thanks for your concern, both of you," Devon said. "But I got this."

Alicia shrugged and tossed her head back. "I hear you, player. Oh, wait," she said, pointing at Solomon. "You used to be the player."

"And all this time, I thought you were the nice one," Solomon shot back.

"They are all evil," Devon said. "Especially the one in denial." He nodded toward Alicia as she left the kitchen.

Solomon turned to Devon once Alicia left. "So, are you going to consider being Kiana's godfather? She's going to need you to balance out those three godmothers."

"I'll do it," he said. "But it may be a long-distance job."

"Yeah, I do want to move back to New York," Solomon said. "Not sure how Kandace is going to like that."

"Guess we're in a similar position. I wonder how Marie's going to feel about moving to Paris."

"Paris? Damn. I get the feeling that she won't say no. That's every woman's dream to be whisked away to the city of lights," Solomon said. "You're right, you do have this."

* * *

As Marie drove to her father's office, her cell phone would not stop buzzing. Every time she glanced at the phone, the screen read Unknown. The only thing that came from answering a call from an unknown number was trouble. But when the phone buzzed again, curiosity got the best of her.

"Marie Charles."

"Miss Charles, it's David Cross from *Charlotte Living* magazine. How are you?"

"What can I do for you?" she asked.

"Well, I'm calling because I know that you've been seen around town with Chef Devon Harris, and I was wondering if you had any information about the funeral arrangements for Devon's father."

"What?" she asked. "His father passed away?"

"You weren't aware? According to the Associated Press, he passed away this afternoon," the reporter said. "We've tried to contact Mr. Harris, but he's not at the restaurant."

Marie ended the call and made a quick illegal U-turn and sped to Devon's loft. Was he all right? Had he left to go to Atlanta? Why hadn't he told her about his father? What if he didn't know? Then she needed to get to him before he got a call from a reporter. She made it to NoDa in record time and saw that Devon's car wasn't in the parking lot. She reached for her phone and started to dial his number when it buzzed again. Another unknown number. *What now?* She grabbed the phone and pressed the answer key.

"Yes?"

"Marie Charles?" a female voice asked.

"Who is this?"

"Helen Conover from the *Charlotte Observer.* My colleague passed your information on to me."

"I don't have any information about Devon Harris Sr.'s death. I would suggest calling one of his charities in Atlanta . . ."

"Miss Charles, that's not why I called. I have been trying to reach Chef Harris to confirm a rumor I heard about him taking over a French restaurant and becoming the face of the Paris Food Network."

"What?" Marie murmured. Paris. What other changes did he have going on that she knew nothing about?

"Miss Charles? Do you at least know how I can reach Devon?"

"I–I don't," she said as she watched Devon pull into the parking lot. She disconnected her call and hopped out of the car. Devon stepped out of the Mustang with a confused look on his face. "You're early," he said. "Not that I'm complaining."

"Devon, what's going on?" she asked. "I just found out two things about you from reporters. Pretty important things that I'd like to think my boyfriend would tell me."

He calmly reached into the backseat and removed two bags from the restaurant. "Let's take this inside, all right."

Miffed, she followed him up the stairs and inside. "Really," she mumbled as he held the door open for her.

"I keep forgetting that reporters have you on speed dial," he said. "So this is about my father?"

"And Paris," she said. "When were you going to tell me about either of these life-changing episodes in your life, or didn't I warrant . . ."

Devon brought his index finger to her lips. "I didn't find out about my father's death until I left your office. I'm still processing it, because I don't feel any emotions about his passing. So, forgive me if I didn't rush to tell you. As far as Paris goes, I haven't officially given them an answer and I was going to discuss that with you tonight over dinner."

Marie tilted her head to the side and tried to think of something to say, but she couldn't. There was no way she could be angry. "Devon, are you going to Paris?" she finally asked.

He took her hand into his and kissed it. "It depends," Devon said.

"On?"

"You."

"Me?"

He nodded and led her to the sofa. They sat down, and Devon pulled Marie against his chest. "Have you ever seen Paris at night? It's a sight that you can barely describe with words, and the smell. Chocolate, freshly baked bread, and the sweetest breezes. When I was a student in Paris, I fell in love with that city."

"Why did you come back?" she asked.

"I had to be here for my mother," he said. "And I never got a chance to go back to Paris until now."

"But what about everything that you have here?" she asked, though she wanted to ask about her and their relationship.

"Of course, I'm going to have to turn over running the kitchen at Hometown Delights, but the most important thing I have in Charlotte, I'm hoping I can take it with me."

"What, your Mustang?" she asked.

Devon narrowed his eyes at her. "Be serious for a moment. I want you to come to Paris with me."

Marie's eyes bulged. "You want me to what?"

"Come to Paris with me."

"Are you serious? I'm just supposed to leave my life

and do what?" Marie asked, leaping to her feet. "What about my business?"

"You said you're doing social media work. Can't you do that from anywhere?"

Marie paced back and forth, her mind clicking like a high-speed camera. "I can't just make this kind of decision without talking to Adriana about our business, then there's my father and . . ."

"I wish I could tell you that you had all the time in the world, but I have to let them know something pretty soon," he said.

Marie shrugged. "How can you just drop this on me and expect me to make a decision?"

"Let's be real: There's no way we can continue a relationship with that much distance between us, and I understand your apprehension, but . . ."

"No, you don't understand, because if you did, you just would stay here!" Marie grabbed her purse. "Obviously, you've made your decision. You're going and I'm not going to stand in your way." She paused and took a breath. "Paris is your dream and I can't keep you from that."

Devon leapt to his feet and blocked her exit. "You want me to stay? Just say it; I'll call them in the morning and turn them down flat."

"And live to resent me? When you described Paris, I could hear in your voice that you've always had one foot in France," Marie said. She blinked back tears and shook her head. "I guess I should get used to being without you." Marie ran out the door in a blur of sobs and tears. Devon ran after her, but she made it to her car before he could stop her. He turned around, went inside, grabbed his keys, and then got into his car to follow her. Devon reached speeds of sixty miles an hour on the city roads, trying to keep up with Marie. He finally slowed down when he saw a blue and white police cruiser near Fifth Street. Marie turned into the parking deck of her condo complex and he followed her.

He double parked beside her and hopped out of the car. "Marie," he called out.

"Why did you follow me?" she asked as she climbed out of the car. "Just go home, call the people in Paris, and tell them you're on your way."

"Is that what you really think I'm going to do?" he asked. "Marie, I don't want to lose you."

"And I can't ask you to give up your dream, and you can't expect me to . . ."

"Give up yours?" he finished. "Then I guess we have to find a way to make this transcontinental relationship work."

Marie dropped her head, sexy French women flashed in her mind. Sexy French women kissing Devon when he got the yearning late at night. "It won't work," she said quietly. "It's all or nothing, and I refuse to stand in your way to living your dream. What's holding you back?"

"Am I supposed to forget that I love you? Am I supposed to just forget what I feel and go to Paris?"

"You might not forget now. Or six months from now, but at some point when you're in your Parisian chateau, you're going to forget."

"Do you have a crystal ball in that car so that you can see the future? If that's the case, tell me if this show is going to be a success. Tell me if Paris is going to be worth anything without you there."

"Devon," she groaned. "Please, don't make this harder than it has to be."

He pulled her into his arms. "Do you think walking away from us right now is going to be easy?"

She shrugged, holding back her tears. "But it's the right thing to do."

Holding her against his chest, Devon shook his head. "I don't want to do the right thing; I want you, and if it's here or in Paris, then that's what it will be."

"No," she cried. "I don't want you to miss this chance, this opportunity that you're excited about and that's obviously getting buzz. You can't let it slip through your hands again."

"So, you want to give up? You want this to be the last time that I touch you?" He leaned into her, his lips inches from her face. "The last time I kiss you?"

Before Marie could reply, Devon captured her lips. The lie she was about to tell—yes—died in the back of her throat as his tongue danced in her mouth, bringing her temperature to the boiling point. He pulled back from her. "You want to walk away from that?" he asked, stroking her arm.

"This is so unfair," she said. "If you stay, if you go, nothing will ever be the same."

"What happens if you come with me?" The heat from his breath made it hard for her to think, hard for her to imagine her life without him.

"Devon," she said.

"Marie."

She didn't say another word; she kissed him, and he lifted her into his arms and backed against the wall. When he slipped one hand underneath her skirt, he remembered that her panties, her flimsy lace panties, were in his pocket. She was wet. She didn't want to be apart from him any more than he wanted to leave her. He needed to remind her that they were meant for each other, and apart, there would be no happiness. No dreams and no joy. Lifting her leg, he wound her around his waist.

"Tell me that you can be without me," he said, his lips so close to her ear that she could almost feel his tongue. She pressed her hips against him, making his erection nearly burst through his zipper.

"I don't want you. To. Go."

"I want you to come. Right here and to Paris," he moaned, then kissed her again. Devon suckled her bottom lip until she nearly exploded.

"Take me inside," she cried. Marie wrapped her arms around his neck and Devon nearly ran to the elevator as she stroked the back of his neck and his desire rose like yeast-rich bread.

The elevator couldn't move fast enough as Marie closed her lips against his neck. Her heat was becoming unbearable and told Devon that he wasn't going to leave Charlotte without her. As they reached her floor, Marie realized that she couldn't and wouldn't let the best thing that happened to her leave Mecklenburg County without her. Devon planted her on the floor as she dug her keys out of her pocket. With trembling hands, she unlocked the door. Once they were inside, she looked him in the eyes and said, "I can't let you go to Paris without me."

"Maybe I won't go at all, at least not to stay," he said before covering her mouth with his, coaxing her tongue into his. As he pushed her skirt up around her waist, she unbuckled his belt and unzipped his pants. Marie stroked his erection until he moaned with anticipation. Their need for each other was electric and crackled as Devon ripped her blouse open. Her breasts heaved and tingled as he caressed and squeezed them. "Are you sure you want to do this?" he asked.

"Yes! Yes," she moaned.

"I mean, moving to Paris," he said as he thrust into her wetness, ignoring the fact that he needed a condom. She felt so good around him. Tight. Hot. Wet. His. Yes, Marie was his and he wanted and needed her to be his forever. She couldn't go to Paris as his girlfriend. She was going as his fiancée, and he'd marry her in the sweetness of a Paris spring with the flowers in bloom.

Marie thrust her hips forward and reveled in the skin-to-skin feeling, wishing that she was making love to her husband. She wanted and needed him as much as she needed her next breath.

"Devon," she moaned. "Oh, baby." Marie tightened herself around him and felt him shiver with desire.

He scooped her into his arms and they fell on to the sofa. Marie straddled him and Devon looked into her eyes and smiled. "Love me," he moaned as she ground against him, milking his passion, making him shiver before he exploded inside her. Marie collapsed against his chest and released a sigh of relief. Devon stroked her back and kissed her chin while she struggled to keep her eyes open.

"Devon," she whispered.

"Yes, baby?" he replied.

"I love you," she said.

"I know and I love you, too."

"But I'm really scared about going to Paris," she said honestly.

"What are you afraid of?" He held her chin, not allowing her to look away. "Marie, if you don't want to go to Paris, don't feel as if you're forced to come. I'll still love you."

"That's not why I'm afraid. I've visited a lot of places,

but I've never lived anywhere else. What happens if you decide that you don't love me anymore or vice versa? Then what?"

"You really think that's going to happen? I'm going to love you forever, Marie Charles." Devon kissed her with a gentle passion that was as reassuring as it was hot.

Chapter 24

After Devon called Amélie Michel and accepted the position in Paris, he had to tell the ladies at the shelter about his decision to leave. Part of him wanted to wait until the fund-raiser was over, but he wanted to tell his culinary class before they read about it or heard it from someone else. He was happy that his class had been getting smaller over the last few weeks. Marie had worked her contacts to find jobs for a few of the women, and many of them had found places to live. Devon was going to send part of his salary to My Sister's Keeper so that the shelter could continue with the classes and add more staff to help the women continue on their quest to getting back on their feet.

The fund-raiser was a step in the right direction, and he hoped that My Sister's Keeper would be around to help women like Bria for years to come. As he headed inside, Bria met him at the door and wrapped her arms around him. "I have great news!" she said.

"What's that?" he asked as they broke their embrace.

"Marie's dad got my trust fund handed over to me. I was just on the phone with him. I can finally get my life together, and I have you and Marie to thank for this," she said. Bria hugged him again. "Is she with you or are you two still fighting?"

"She's not with me, but we are definitely not fighting. I wanted to talk to you ladies about some news I have," he said as he and Bria walked inside.

His students, who were milling around the shelter doing different chores and finishing up errands for the fund-raiser, smiled when he walked in. "Ladies," Devon said, "we need to talk."

"Wedding plans?" Shay asked. Though she didn't live at the shelter anymore, she was still involved in the planning of the fund-raiser.

"Not yet," he said. "I'm not going to be teaching culinary arts anymore."

The ladies exploded in moans of disappointment. "Why?" Bria asked.

"I'm taking a position in Paris," he said. "As much as I hate to leave you ladies, this is an opportunity that I can't turn down."

"So, what happens now?" Rita asked. "Is the class over?"

"I'm going to talk to Mrs. Harper about bringing the new chef from Hometown Delights in to continue the class, because I know how important this class is to all of you."

Bria and Andrea nodded. "It won't be the same," Andrea said. "We're going to miss you."

"And I'm going to miss all of you, but I expect big things from you ladies," Devon said as he walked through the students and hugged them.

"Are you taking Marie with you, too?" Shay asked as she and Devon embraced.

He smiled. "That's the plan," he said.

"Well, I hope you plan on marrying her before you go

to another country," Shay said, then popped him on his shoulder.

"Or at least asking her father for her hand in marriage," Bria said.

"You know what," Devon said, feeling as if a lightbulb had exploded in his head. "You ladies are right. I have one last assignment for us. We have a wedding to plan. I'm going to marry Marie in two days at the fund-raiser."

The ladies squealed in excitement. "Wait," Shay said. "How are we going to do this without Marie knowing? There's the marriage license and other legal details to take care of."

"We're going to need a lot of help," Devon said as he pulled his cell phone from his pocket and called Jade.

Marie smiled as Adriana told her about the six new clients they'd just landed. "Things are really turning around for us. We should have a party, kind of like the old days, but not with you getting arrested or kicked out."

Marie shook her head. "My party days are over. As a matter of fact, my time in Charlotte is coming to an end."

"What?" Adriana asked. "Are you serious?"

"Yes," she said. "Devon asked me to move to Paris with him."

"Paris? As in Paris, France? Wow. This is major. I can't believe you're leaving Charlotte. What about M&A?"

"I'm still going to do the social media part of the business," Marie said. "But you will officially become the face of the business. Look at what you've done while I was going through my legal trouble. You gave us respectability, profits have increased, and I haven't had to take my clothes off to get attention."

"Except from Devon," Adriana joked. She crossed over to Marie and hugged her. "I'm going to miss you."

"Calm down, girl, I'm not leaving for at least a month," Marie said. "Don't forget, we have that fund-raiser at Hometown Delights in two days. One more thing."

"What's that?"

"I told Mrs. Harper from My Sister's Keeper that we would do some publicity work for the shelter. Since I'm not going to be here . . ."

"Say no more, I'll handle it. Working with Shay showed me just how important that place is. I'd be happy to keep that promise for you. Just make sure you send me lots of presents from Paris. The shoes that you're going to be wearing," Adriana said. "I'm jealous."

"Don't worry, I'll share," Marie said. "Let's go and have lunch at . . ." Before Marie could finish, the phone rang and Adriana picked it up.

"M&A Events, Adriana speaking," she said. Marie smiled and returned to her tweeting. When Adriana hung up the phone, Marie turned to her and said, "Well? Are we going to lunch?"

"Actually," Adriana said. "I have a meeting; silly me, I nearly forgot. Let's meet at Nordstrom after work?"

"Nordstrom? I'm there," she said as Adriana headed out the door. Once she was alone, Marie pulled out her French-English dictionary and looked up how to say, "Does that shoe come in a size eight?"

Devon walked into Richard Charles' office, and for the first time in his life, he was intimidated. Richard's presence filled the room like water in a fish tank; it was everywhere. "Mr. Harris, what can I do for you?" Richard asked as he rose to his feet and extended his hand to Devon.

"Well," Devon said, "you can call me Devon."

"Force of habit, I'm usually dealing with clients or adversaries. What's going on? Have a seat."

Devon sat across from Richard's desk and looked down at his watch, then back up at Marie's father. "Sir," he said. "I love your daughter."

Richard laughed. "I've noticed. And I've noticed that you've been a very positive influence in her life."

"And she in mine," he replied. "That's why I'm here."

"OK."

"I want to marry her and I want to do it in two days."

Richard folded his arms across his chest and leaned back in his chair. "What's the rush? Should I be getting my shotgun?"

"Oh, no. It's nothing like that, but I'm moving to Paris, and I don't want to take my girlfriend with me. I want my wife to fly to Paris with me and share in my life there."

"Paris? You want to take my little girl to Paris?"

"And marry her, with your blessing, of course," Devon said.

Richard rose from his chair and crossed over to Devon. "You know, I love my daughter more than anything in this world. She's been my life for a long time, and over the years, I've given her everything that she's ever wanted. Marie is headstrong and she rebelled. Dated some of the biggest jerks and wannabe players in the world, and then she met you. Certainly a step up from the lot she normally aligned herself with, but Paris. That's a long way from Charlotte. However, don't think, for one second that if my baby needs me because you've hurt her, I won't be on the next flight over there to help her."

Devon nodded in deference to Richard's point of view as he stood up and looked the man directly in the eye. "I would never do anything to hurt Marie. So, when you come to visit, you won't have to bring that shotgun of yours."

Richard laughed heartily, then extended his hand to Devon. "Welcome to the family," he said as they shook hands. Then Richard's phone buzzed, signaling a call from his assistant. "Excuse me," he said as he crossed over to his desk. "Yes, Libby."

"Ms. Adriana Kimbrell is here to see you and Mr. Harris," she said.

"Send her in," Richard said, then eyed Devon suspiciously.

"I can't surprise Marie with a wedding without help," Devon replied as Adriana walked in.

"Marie is going to die," Adriana said excitedly. "Hi, Mr. Charles."

Richard nodded toward Adriana and smiled slyly. "So, how are we going to plan a wedding without my daughter knowing? Marie has to be in the middle of everything."

"I have an idea," Adriana said. "If you're doing it at the fund-raiser, all we have to do is get a preacher there and, of course you, Mr. Charles . . ."

"There is also a need for a marriage license," Richard interrupted. "Perhaps I can work some of my connections to speed that process up."

"That's a great idea, sir," Adriana said. "We're going to Nordstrom today to get her wedding dress and shoes. I know a few photographers who can get shots of the ceremony, and . . ."

Devon held up his hands. "Slow down. You seem to have everything taken care of."

"Yes, this is what I do. Now, let me see the ring," Adriana said.

"That's a slight problem, I haven't gotten one yet," Devon said. "I was hoping you knew Marie's . . ."

"You don't need to do that," Richard said. "I've been holding on to my wife's engagement ring, and I'd like you to give it to Marie. She's always loved that ring, and with it on her finger, I'll feel like a piece of my wife is there at the altar with her."

Adriana's eyes watered with tears. "That's so sweet."

"I'll line up the preacher and prepare the cake," Devon said.

"And I'll bring the ring to you tomorrow," Richard said. "This is pretty exciting. Now, you're sure Marie's going to say yes?"

"I have a pretty good indication that she will," Devon said with a smile.

"All right," Richard said. "I hate to cut this short, but I have a meeting in about fifteen minutes. You two handle the details and I'll be there to stand up for my daughter."

The two men shook hands again, and then Devon and Adriana headed out the door.

"That's a first," she said once they were out of Richard's earshot.

"What?" Devon asked.

"Mr. Charles liking a man who showed interest in his daughter. He usually finds something to intimidate him about. You're special, Devon, and lucky."

"I know it," he said. "Marie's the best thing that's ever happened to me, and I want her to know how special she is."

Adriana nodded. "And this is going to be another first, pulling the wool over Marie Charles' eyes. She's the one who's usually full of surprises."

"Why am I not surprised by that?" Devon laughed.

"So, what are you wearing on your wedding day? I think Marie should get married in a red dress, so that's what we're going to shop for today." Adriana pulled out her cell phone and called someone. Devon stood back in awe and watched her work. "He's Devon Harris," he heard her tell the person on the other end of the phone. "He's going to come in the back of the store. A nice black suit and a red tie, yep. I can't tell you that, just make it happen, Hayden. And I love you, too. Don't forget to send your donation to the fund-raiser at Hometown Delights. I hope to see you there. Smooches." With that, Adriana hung up the phone and turned to Devon. "Hayden Smalls is a personal shopper at Nordstrom, and he's expecting you. You need to be out of there before five, because that's when Marie and I should be arriving to find her red wedding dress."

"Got it," he said. "I guess I'd better head over there now."

"Then tomorrow, we get the wedding band once we see what Mr. Charles' engagement ring looks like. I bet it is beautiful."

"You're sure Marie's going to be all right with wearing her mother's ring and not having one of her own?"

Adriana nodded. "I'm sure she's going to love it. This is going to be so amazing."

After leaving Adriana, Devon headed to Hometown Delights to share his wedding plans with his friends. Looking at his watch, he knew that he was going to have to keep things short and to the point if he was going to be able to get fitted for his suit before Marie and Adriana arrived at Nordstrom.

When he arrived at the restaurant, he headed for the office and was happy to see Jade, Alicia, and Serena were there. "My sisters, what's going on?"

"Hey, Devon," Serena said. "We were just talking about you and the fund-raiser."

"Really?" he said with a smile.

"The *Observer* did a great piece on My Sister's Keeper today," Alicia said as she turned the screen toward Devon. He gave it a perfunctory glance and nodded.

"The fund-raiser is going to do more than raise money for the shelter," he said.

"What do you mean?" Jade asked. Serena and Alicia looked on with curiosity blanketing their faces.

"Well, I'm going to marry Marie."

"What?" the three women exclaimed.

"When did you two get engaged?" Serena fired out.

"Why didn't you tell us?" Alicia asked.

Devon held his hands out. "Listen," he said. "I have to go pick up my suit shortly, but this is a surprise. And there's more: I'm going to Paris."

Jade and Serena gasped. "Paris? For a visit?" Serena asked.

He shook his head no. "I've been given an opportunity to run a restaurant in Paris and to become the face of Paris's Food Network."

"And Marie's going with you?" Jade asked.

He nodded. "This isn't something that you ask your girlfriend to do, that's one reason why we're getting married."

"I can't believe you're leaving us," Jade said. "But I knew this day was coming eventually."

"I hate to leave you guys, but Paris has always been my dream," he said. Jade crossed over to him and hugged him while she silently cried.

"This is wonderful. Devon, I'm really happy for you," she said.

"Thank you," he said. "I'm going to need you ladies to help me keep this wedding under wraps."

"What do you need us to do?" Alicia asked. "This is going to be so much fun."

"I'll let you know tomorrow. I have to meet my personal shopper at Nordstrom to get this suit. We can talk about it over breakfast tomorrow, say nine o'clock?"

"All right," Alicia said. "As long as you're cooking."

"Come on, now," he said as he headed out of the office.

Chapter 25

Marie was getting tired of seeing red. "What's up with you and this obsession with red dresses?" she asked Adriana when she brought her another red dress to try on. It was the fifth one since they had been in the store.

Adriana held up the red gown, which was trimmed in lace and had a sheer tail. Marie had to admit that it was a beautiful dress. Even if it was red. "Are you telling me that you don't think this is a show stopper?" Adriana asked as she handed it to her friend.

"I didn't say that." Marie held the dress against her body and gazed at herself in the mirror. The dress was hot. But she felt as if it was a little too flashy for the fundraiser.

"I don't know if it's appropriate for the fundraiser, though. However, I only have two days to find something."

"Well, I think your job is done," Adriana said. "This dress is classy, and if you need to get it fitted, the seamstress is waiting for your orders. Just try it on and I have some shoes to show you."

"All right," Marie said, slowly falling in love with the dress as she swished around with it. She was already seeing her hairstyle and thinking of a statement piece of jewelry. Maybe she'd get a large necklace, since the neckline of the dress would show off her cleavage in a daring, yet classic manner. *Old Hollywood,* she thought as she entered the dressing room. Once she put the dress on, Marie's decision about the dress had been made. "OK, Adriana," she called out. "I defer to your sense of fashion on this one. This dress is amazing." Marie spun around, enjoying the way the dress hugged her curves like a second skin.

"Let's see it," Adriana said. Marie walked out standing on her tiptoes. "I told you!"

"You were right, Adriana. This dress is delicious."

She handed Marie a pair of silver stilettos. "And these are going to set it off!"

Marie smiled and took the shoes. "I think you missed your calling, you could be a stylist to the stars."

Adriana shook her head. "I don't think so. It was hard enough convincing you to go red."

"OK, I was wrong," she said. "This red dress isn't bad."

"Are you going to call Rodricko? Do you think he can squeeze both of us in?" Adriana asked as she glanced down at her watch.

"I think he should be able to, especially since I'm about to be his former client. You should lobby for my standing appointment. After all, the face of M&A can't have split ends, ratty roots, and God forbid, a horrible weave."

"Ah, that would never happen. But you're right, I am going to lobby for that appointment. Who's going to do your hair in Paris? Do you think you're going to like it there?"

Marie slipped into the shoes and forced a smile. She had no doubt that Devon loved her, but moving so far away gave her pause. She didn't want to admit it, but she was a little afraid. Glancing at Adriana and the smile her friend had on her face, Marie didn't want to share her fears. "I think I will," she finally said. "Paris is beautiful and I've been wanting to visit there for years, now I get to live there with the man I love."

"Are you going to miss Charlotte?"

"Charlotte is a part of me, and I will miss it and all of my friends here. But Paris, it's a dream for most people, and I'm going to get to live it," she replied with forced gaiety.

"And Devon," Adriana said.

"Oh, yes," she said genuinely. "I used to laugh when I heard women say a man was the best thing that ever happened to them, but in this case it's true. I really wonder what I was ever thinking about when I dated William. Did I tell you he threatened to sue me?"

"For what? Gaining your sanity?" Adriana laughed. "Word on the street is Mr. Franklin is so down and out that he had to get a real job because no woman would have him. And Greta has a new job. She does promotions for a strip club."

"Wow, how the mighty has fallen," Marie said as she examined the silver shoes. "Are you sure this isn't too Diana Ross from *The Wiz*?"

"No, and I'm impressed."

"With the shoe?" Marie wiggled her foot in front of Adriana.

"No, silly, with you. I just dished some dirt and you didn't have anything smart to say about it. That's not the Marie I'm used to dealing with. Devon has really made some positive changes in your life."

Marie smiled at her image in the mirror. "He really has. I will never admit this to anyone else, because it sounds so horrible, but that accident was the best thing that happened to me. It really woke me up to how stupid I was being with my life."

"You could've saved yourself a night in jail and a totaled car had you just listened to me and never gotten involved with William. And by the way, Hailey sends her love. She's decided that she doesn't want to work in the public-relations industry," Adriana said as she snapped a picture of Marie with her cell phone.

"Poor thing, but I'm not surprised," Marie said as Adriana took another picture. "My father took care of William. He served him with papers that said if he comes near me or talks to the press about me, he'll be sued for a million dollars. Something he clearly doesn't have. Um, what are you doing? What's with the pictures?"

"Old time's sake," she said with a laugh.

Devon put the finishing touches on the dessert selections for the fund-raiser when his cell phone rang. Putting the chocolate aside, he answered, "Hello?"

"Devon Harris, you have some nerve," Kandace said.

"What?"

"I guess you forgot to tell me that you're getting married," she said, then laughed. "Congratulations. I knew there was something special about what you and Marie had. I'm so happy for you."

"Thank you," he said, smiling.

"I wish I could be there, but of course my doctor has not cleared me to leave the house," she said. "And you're going to Paris. I know how much that means to you."

"Finally getting a chance to do it right," he said. "Kandace, I don't know if I've ever told you how sorry I am about what happened all those years ago."

"Water under the bridge. I guess we were meant to be

friends more than anything else. But a word of advice: Don't mess it up with Marie."

"I have no plans to do so," he said. "She means everything to me."

"I've noticed," she said, then Devon heard Kiana crying in the background. "My baby's hungry, so I have to go. But congrats again. Love you."

"Love you, too," he said, then looked up and saw Marie standing in the doorway of the kitchen.

She smiled sweetly as she sauntered over to him in a pair of silver shoes and a short trench coat. Devon dropped his phone as she untied the coat, revealing a black lace teddy that kissed her curves in a way that made his mouth water.

"Well, hello to you," he said crossing over to her and pulling her into his arms.

"I missed you today."

"If this is how you feel when you miss me, miss me every day," he said, then kissed her neck with a deliberate slowness.

"Umm," she moaned. "I just stopped by to show you my shoes."

"You have on shoes?" he quipped as he brushed his lips across her neck again.

"Funny," she moaned. "So, who was on the phone?"

"Kandace," he said, then leaned in to kiss her again. Marie brought her hand to Devon's lips.

"You were telling your ex that you loved her? Seriously?"

Devon stepped back from Marie and raised his eyebrow at her. "I can't believe that you're standing here getting upset because I told my friend that I love her."

"She's not just your friend, she's your ex, and it seems that Kandace still gets to you. Am I supposed to be her replacement? Is that why you want to whisk me off to Paris, because you don't want to see her raising her family with Solomon?"

"Are you serious?" Devon walked away from her and returned to the chocolate. "Marie, what is this really about?"

Marie dropped her head and sighed. This had nothing to do with Kandace and she knew that. When she looked up at Devon, she wanted to tell him that she was afraid, that she wasn't sure if she could handle being so far away from everything that was familiar to her. He locked eyes with her and dropped his spoon. Crossing over to her, he drew her into his arms. "Aren't you sure about us?" he asked softly, brushing his fingers across her cheek.

"I'm scared, Devon," she replied in a near whisper.

"Baby."

She held her hand up. "This is going to sound crazy to you, but who's going to do my hair? What am I going to do while you're running your restaurant and filming your show? There's only so much tweeting and status updating that I can do. And I don't want to be a burden to you, sitting around pouting—because I do pout . . ."

Devon held her face in his hands and shook his head at her. "Marie . . ."

"Maybe you should go to Paris without me at first," she said. "Make sure that you want your girlfriend tagging along when you start your new life."

Devon folded his arms and leaned back, wondering if he should tell her that he wasn't taking his girlfriend to Paris with him. "Marie, do you want me to go without you? What do you think is going to change if you're not there with me?"

She dropped her head as she tried to put her thoughts together in a coherent way. Why was she pretending that going to Paris with the man she loved was scary? "Devon,

I have never gotten to this part before," she said. "I've never been with a man who makes me want to be a better me, and someone who isn't impressed by the media version of Marie. What happens if we get to Paris and you decide I'm not what you want?"

"I know who you are. You're the woman I love and that is never going to change," he said drawing her into his arms. "Why are you having such a hard time believing that?"

She looked up at him and sighed. "I'm tripping, I'm nervous, and I keep waiting for the other shoe to drop."

"That's because you've never been with me," he said. "I got you, Marie. And if you're waiting for the other shoe to drop, just keep in mind that when you have both feet on the ground, you can keep walking."

"I've never looked at it that way," she said with a small smile. "I'm sorry."

"There's no need for you to apologize," Devon said. "I tell you what, we're going to make up as soon as I cover up the dessert. Don't move. I want to see exactly what's underneath that coat."

Chapter 26

The day of the fund-raiser, Devon felt like a nervous kitten. The conversation he'd had with Richard Charles two days ago put him at ease, but as the moments ticked down to his wedding, those words of encouragement floated out of his head.

"What's the matter with you?" Marie asked as she stood behind Devon and wrapped her arms around his waist. "You look as if you're about to pass out. Look at the tote board."

Devon smiled when he saw that they'd raised nearly one million dollars for My Sister's Keeper. He turned around and faced Marie. "You did it," he said. "Your friends really came through."

"As well as yours. It didn't hurt to have Maurice Goings and some of the other Carolina Panthers to put up their jerseys for the silent auction and make those huge donations," she said.

Devon looked Marie up and down, loving the way her red dress accented her body and made her skin glow.

Adriana waved to Devon, indicating that the pastor was ready. He turned to Marie. "We have to go and make a presentation," he told her. "And there is a form you need to sign, as well." He led her over to a small table in the corner where Richard had placed the marriage license underneath some official-looking papers.

"What's this?" she asked, giving the papers a blasé glance as Devon explained that they were papers signing over the shoes she'd donated to the auction.

"Really?" she said as she signed. "Do you think I'm going to change my mind?"

Smiling, he took the papers from her hand. "Changing your mind is not an option," he said. "Come on, let's go make this presentation."

"What is this presentation?" Marie asked as she looked down at the printed program.

"It's something that just came up," he said, taking her hand just as the music switched from thumping jazz to the first chords of the "Wedding March."

"What's going on?" Marie asked as Devon led her to the stage.

"Remember you kept talking about waiting for the other shoe to drop?" he whispered as he reached into his pocket.

"Devon?" she asked as he pulled out a velvet box. All eyes turned to the couple as they took center stage.

"I've decided that I don't want to go to Paris with my girlfriend."

"And you brought me on this stage, in front of all of these people, to tell me this?" Marie snapped, ready to bury her silver shoe down his throat.

"Yes, I wanted to bring you up here in front of all of these people and God because when we get on the plane to go to Paris, you're not going to be my girlfriend, you're going to be my wife," Devon said, then nodded toward Reverend Layton Jackson.

"What?" she stammered, tears streaming down her cheeks as her father approached her.

"I love you, Marie Charles," Devon said as he opened the box, showing her the four-carat diamond and platinum engagement ring that her mother used to wear. Marie's knees went weak as he slipped the ring on her finger. She turned to her father, who smiled his approval.

"Told you she'd love it," Richard said.

Adriana approached the stage and smiled at Marie. "And I told you this red dress was special."

"I can't believe that you all got me like this," she said. Marie glanced at Devon and smiled. "What if I'd said no?"

"Like that was going to happen," Devon replied confidently. Marie reached over and kissed him.

The reverend cleared his throat. "We haven't gotten to that part, yet," he said.

"Sorry, Reverend," Marie said.

"All right," Reverend Jackson said. "Let's get started. Ladies and gentlemen, we are gathered here today for many reasons. To help our fellow man and woman, to lend a helping hand to those less fortunate than us, and to join this man and this woman in holy matrimony."

Marie looked into Devon's eyes as he took her hands in his. "I love you," she mouthed to him as the reverend continued.

"Marriage is not an institution to be entered into lightly, without forethought and love," he said. "The couple standing before me has shown love for each other and for others. This fund-raiser for My Sister's Keeper shows the goodness inside all of us and how love extends from our hearts to the needs of our fellow man. It was that kind of love that brought this couple together and that will sustain their marriage. If anyone here has a reason why these two should not be joined in marriage, speak now or forever hold your peace."

Devon and Marie glanced out into the crowd and were happy to hear nothing but silence. The reverend nodded at Devon. "Devon, do you take this woman to be your lawfully wedded wife? Promise to love her from this day forward, and cherish her, for better or for worse, for richer, for poorer, in sickness and in health, till death do you part?"

"I do," Devon said, then kissed Marie's hand.

She wanted to melt. She'd never felt so loved and cherished. "Marie," the reverend said. "Do you take this man to be your lawfully wedded husband? Promise to love him from this day forward, and cherish him, for better or for worse, for richer, for poorer, in sickness and in health, till death do you part?"

She inhaled sharply. "I do."

"Who gives this bride away?" Reverend Jackson asked.

"I do," Richard said, then leaned in to kiss Marie. "I love you and I'm always just a phone call away." He glanced at Devon and smiled, eliciting an uproar of laughter from the crowd.

"She won't be making that call," Devon said. "Unless it's to tell you about the grandkids."

"Hey, one step at a time," Marie said with a giggle, though she couldn't wait for that day to come.

"Well," Reverend Jackson said. "I now pronounce you man and wife. You may kiss your bride." Devon pulled Marie into his arms and kissed her as if they were in the room alone. She swayed in his arms, never wanting the feeling of his lips and tongue to ever leave her mouth.

When they finally broke their kiss, the crowd applauded excitedly. Marie smiled and looked at her husband. She couldn't believe that Devon had pulled the wool over her eyes like this. "I'm going to watch you, Mr. Harris."

"I wouldn't have it any other way, Mrs. Harris." He kissed her cheek, and they walked off the stage into the crowd to shake hands with their guests.

Richard stopped the couple. "Devon," he said. "I've never liked or respected the men my daughter spent her time with. I thought she was mocking me with her choices, and she probably was. But you had to be the man my daughter was holding out for. I'm glad. Welcome to the family." Richard extended his hand to Devon and the men shook hands, then hugged.

"Thank you, sir. And know that I love your daughter more than I thought I could ever love a woman," Devon replied, bringing a rush of heat to Marie's cheeks.

"Take care of her, because she's my little girl, no matter how grown she is. I'm just happy she's finally grown up." Richard held his arms out for his daughter, and Marie hugged her father.

"Thank you, Daddy," she said.

Devon's friends walked over to the couple, Serena, Jade, and Alicia dying to see the ring. Antonio and James greeted Devon with a glass of scotch.

"Welcome to the club, brother," James said.

"I don't know what Serena's going to do with you in Paris. I guess it's time to invest in some cooking lessons for my wife," Antonio said with a smile.

"And for the last time," Serena said, "I'm going to say this: You didn't marry me for my cooking." Antonio kissed his wife's neck.

"You got that right," he said.

Devon looked at Marie and got ready to kiss her when an eruption of applause moved through the building. "A million dollars!" someone yelled out, and the band began playing "Celebration."

Devon spun his wife around. "What a night and what a beautiful site," he said.

"The flashing total on the board is lovely," Marie said, looking at the LED image with tears in her eyes.

"Oh, I'm talking about my wife in my arms," he said, then kissed her with an intense passion that made Marie's knees quake.

"Wait until you see what I have underneath this dress," she whispered when they broke their kiss.

"And on that note, we're out of here." Devon scooped his wife into his arms and they headed out the door to begin their life together as husband and wife.

Don't miss

Too Hot for TV

On sale now wherever books are sold.

Turn the page for an excerpt
from *Too Hot for TV* . . .

Chapter 1

If looks could kill, Edward Funderburke would have been dead under Imani Gilliam's icy stare. Her agent must have been losing his mind along with his silver hair for suggesting such a thing. A reality TV show?

Imani was a serious actress, not someone seeking fifteen minutes of fame, like those people who signed up for those shows. Obviously, Edward must have forgotten that. Imani was Broadway, feature films—not reality TV. Instead of getting her a part in a cheap reality show, he should have worked harder to get her the role in the reprisal of the hit play *Kiss of the Spider Woman*. According to Edward, the producers were looking for someone with more of a recognizable name, even though she had wowed them at her audition. But how did anyone think Imani would become a bankable name if she couldn't get a big role that would make her a star?

What Imani lacked in name recognition, she made up for in talent. She was the classic triple threat—she could sing, dance, and act. That should have been enough, or at least that's what Imani thought. But in this industry, sometimes it didn't matter how talented you were, which was why so many rappers and singers had lead roles in so many movies, yet only a few of them were actually good enough to pull it off.

She'd do a film with Common, but he was the only rapper who she felt deserved the screen time he received. The rest of them needed to stick to their day jobs and studios needed to put their faith in actresses and actors—people who trained to do the job.

Imani wasn't naive enough to think that the studios weren't in it for the money. That's why 50 Cent and T.I. starred alongside Denzel and Samuel L. Jackson. And if it wasn't the rappers, it was the stars who stayed in the tabloids who got all of the plum roles. Imani would've loved the chance to play the lead in *Salt*. Of course, she didn't have the name recognition of Angelina Jolie or the headlines.

Folding her arms, she glared at Edward, letting him know that she wasn't warming to the idea of doing a reality show.

"It's a really good concept, and think of the national exposure," Edward added, hoping to open Imani's mind to the notion.

"Eddie, I know you don't really expect me to say yes. I'm a real actress," Imani said indignantly, flipping her curly locks behind her ear. "These shows are for has-beens or wannabes. Maybe if you would get out of the office more often, you'd find a script for me that would give me the name recognition that I so badly need."

"All right, Imani," he said, leaning across his desk and looking her directly in the eye. "Let's be real here. You haven't worked in months, no one has sent you a script since you did *Fearless Diva* and, need I remind you, that wasn't the best vehicle that you could have taken. *Monster's Ball* could have been your breakthrough role. Halle won the Oscar for that role. You would've been great in that role and I tried to tell you that. You just think that you can do anything you want to do and you can't. It's about building a career, a portfolio that people identify you with. Those regional plays you've done, most of them have been for free and no one, not a soul, is trying to put them on Broadway. You have to do something to shake the stagnant off your career."

Imani rolled her eyes. "I didn't want to do a drama. I had just come off a dramatic role on Broadway and I needed a break," she said. "And if you gave me better advice, then maybe I would listen. You weren't too happy about the *Monster's Ball* role either; now all of a sudden it was the best thing that I ever passed up?" She folded her arms underneath her breasts and pouted.

Unfazed by her temper tantrum, Edward leaned back and propped his feet up on the desk. "You gambled and we lost. Now, Imani, I like you and I believe in your talent, but you're not one of my most profitable clients. If either of us has a plan to make any money, we have to get you out there and make your name stand out in a crowd. This is a start. I don't want to have to drop you, but you've got to do something. This show can build your image. Look at how famous lots of people who have no acting ability have gotten—all from the exposure of reality TV. We can turn that fame into big movie roles and those Broadway shows that you want."

Imani chewed on the end of her sculptured nail, pondering what he'd said to her. It had been hard for her to get signed by a reputable agent. Before meeting Edward, she'd been scammed by so-called talent agents who wanted to put her in B-list movies and soft-core pornography films.

At least Edward had done his best to get her roles in blockbuster movies and hit stage productions, even if she didn't agree with him at the moment. He'd steered her away from the typical chitlin' circuit plays that young actresses found themselves acting in and from becoming typecast as a neck-rolling, finger-wagging stereotype.

But now, he and Imani were desperate.

"Eddie, I'm trying, but these reality shows are just so beneath me, and the images that they portray are not the best. Sometimes the women on these shows are just dumb looking, slutty, or bitchy. I'm none of the above."

"It pays fifteen thousand dollars up front. It's only ten weeks and you might even get voted off before the show is over. The concept is simple. You get teamed up with a bachelor, do some physical challenges, and America votes to see if you and your partner should get married. Just make a splash and watch the scripts and offers come rolling in."

"No," she said, and then stood up. "I'd rather starve." Imani turned to her left, ready to walk out the door.

"Aren't you doing that already?" Edward called out.

Imani slammed the office door behind her. *The gall,* she thought as she headed for the subway terminal. She wanted to take a cab, but with only three dollars in her pocket and a box of raisins for dinner in her apartment, a taxi trip was a luxury that she couldn't afford. Besides, a taxi trip from Manhattan to Brooklyn would wipe out her savings in the bank—if you could call it a savings account. She barely had a hundred dollars in her checking and savings accounts combined. Calling her parents for a loan was out because the first thing her mother, Dorothy, would say is that she needed a real job and acting was a dream she needed to give up. Her father, Horace, would tell her that it was time for her to join the family business of home restorations.

She could be in charge of the interior design aspect of

it, even live in a historic home in beautiful Savannah, Georgia. Imani wanted no part of it. Her dream was to act, sing, or dance. Her career of choice was considered an insignificant pipe dream by her family. She'd graduated with a degree from the Juilliard School and hadn't asked her parents for a penny, despite the fact that she went into major debt paying for the expensive performing arts college.

Frowning as she headed to the subway entrance, Imani tried to figure out how she was going to take a free trip on the subway because she wasn't sure if she had the money to make it home. When she saw three New York City Transit officers arresting a group of teenagers who were also trying to get a free ride home, she knew she'd have to walk. She was only about two miles from her place in Fulton Ferry and she could use the exercise. Besides, the walk would give her a chance to think about the reality show.

"I'm not doing it," she mumbled to herself. By the time she had walked five blocks, her feet were throbbing like a heartbeat. "Maybe I should do it. *The Apprentice* made Omarosa a star and she's not even an actress. But then she did that stupid dating show on TV One," Imani said to no one in particular as she unsnapped her Steve Madden sandals, took them off, and flung them over her shoulder. "But," she continued musing to herself, "I trained at Juilliard. I shouldn't be subjected to this."

Imani was half a block away from her home when she decided that she wasn't going to go on the reality show. She held her head high and walked up to the door of her building, ready to prop her feet up and relax with her *Variety* magazine. Before she could put the key in the lock, reality sucker-punched her in the stomach. A pink note with big red letters was tacked to her door. "Eviction," it read. Imani snatched the note off the door. She pulled her cell phone out of her tote bag, pressed speed dial number three, and waited for Edward to answer.

"Funderburke and Associates, Edward speaking," he said.

"It's Imani. I've done some thinking," she said as she read the eviction notice for a second time. "I'll do the stupid show."

"Well, don't sound so excited about it," he replied. "What made you change your mind?"

Imani made a mental note of the thirty-day deadline she'd been given to come up with the back rent. Then she balled up the notice. "Let's just say I know this is what I need to do right now."

Storming into her place, Imani decided to watch a little television to take her mind off her current situation. But that was the wrong thing to do. As she flipped through the channels, lamenting her career, she stopped on a sitcom that she'd auditioned for.

"LisaRaye is not a better actress than I am," she exclaimed as she came across a rerun of *All of Us,* and then flipped the channel.

Next she landed on a Lifetime movie about an abused wife who'd killed her husband. As she watched the unknown actress overdramatize her lines, Imani knew that she would have done so much better in the role, had it been offered to her. She remembered that she'd once told Edward that the last thing she wanted to do was a Lifetime movie. Now, she wished that she'd never made such a crazy statement.

Then she came across her movie on the FX channel. *Fearless Diva* was a bomb, but it wasn't J. Lo in *Gigli* or Halle's *Catwoman.* If she was honest, she'd admit that it was worse. But she wasn't practicing honesty right now.

That role should have led to something, she thought as

she watched herself prance across the screen in a skintight leather catsuit. *At least my clothes were fierce.* Twirling a lock of hair around her finger, Imani critiqued her performance. She was pretty awful in the movie, but it wasn't her fault. The script was horrible and the cameraman, who also called himself the director, didn't know how to operate the camera because every scene looked as if the wind had gotten hold of the equipment.

Maybe Imani did deserve those Razzie award nominations she'd gotten. But someone had to see her potential, didn't they? As tears welled up in her eyes, Imani wondered if her family had been right about her career. Were they right to have no faith in her? Was she chasing a pipe dream that had no chance of coming true?

The phone wouldn't stop ringing at the Palmer Free Clinic in Harlem. And that was the least of their worries. The receptionist had left for lunch three hours ago and never returned. That left Dr. Raymond Thomas juggling answering calls with seeing patients, writing down appointments, and taking messages. What he didn't have time for was a game-playing prankster. "Look," Raymond said, a frown darkening his handsome face, "this is a place of business. No one here has time to play with a lowlife small-timer like you."

"Sir, this isn't a joke. I'm Elize Harrington, a producer with the WAPC Network. You're a candidate for our new reality show, *Let's Get Married.* Your name was submitted to us and we reviewed your qualifications and we want you on the show," she said, her voice in a near plea.

"Ms. Harrington, who put you up to this joke?" Raymond dropped his pen on the desk and held his finger up to the patient in front of him waiting for her prescription.

The woman sighed. "Again, sir, this isn't a joke. Our show is going to air later this year, but the ten weeks of filming start in a few weeks. We just need you to come in and take a screen test and sign a waiver."

A rush of people were vying for Raymond's attention. All at once, he had a patient trying to make a follow-up appointment, a nurse questioning him about his orders for a different patient, and the same woman who'd been waiting for ten minutes still wanting her prescription. As Raymond's head began throbbing, he silently wished he could write himself a doctor's note and go home.

He mumbled yes to the producer, told her to call his cell phone, leave the details about the show on his voice mail, and he would call her back. Raymond hung up the phone and, putting his composed doctor face back on, turned to his patient. When things calmed down, Raymond was going to get to the bottom of this reality TV show mess. It was already pushed to the back burner.

"Mrs. Wentworth," he said, taking the elderly woman's hand, "can you come back in two weeks?"

The caramel-colored woman smiled at him. "I can do that and my grandbaby, Emma, can bring me. She's real pretty and she can cook, too. Our family is originally from the south and southern women know how to do one thing better than anyone else does, and that's cook. Dr. Thomas, you don't get many home-cooked meals, do you? You're not married, are you?"

"No, ma'am," he replied with a smile, even though he wanted to push her out the door. If Raymond had a penny for every elderly woman who wanted to fix him up with her granddaughter, niece, or daughter, he would be rich enough to fund the clinic himself.

Mrs. Wentworth shook her head. "That's a shame. You need a good woman to take care of you. You're way too skinny. I like a man with a little more meat on his bones, but my grandbaby would love you."

Nurse Karen DeSalis dropped a chart in front of Raymond. "Mrs. Wentworth, I've been telling him that for years, but he doesn't listen."

Raymond rolled his eyes. Who had time for love or romance? He and his fraternity brother, Keith Jacobs, had opened the Marion Palmer Free Clinic, named for their favorite first-grade teacher, three years ago in Harlem. They'd gone to Morehouse School of Medicine in Atlanta, Georgia, together and did their residency at Grady Memorial Hospital. When their residency was over, the native New Yorkers returned to Harlem ready to make a difference. Luckily for them, they had help. Keith and Raymond received a three-million-dollar grant from the Harlem Revitalization Group to buy equipment. The city donated the building and donations from businesses helped the men with the first year's operating costs. Then September 11 happened and everything changed. As donations began to dry up, Keith and Raymond poured their savings into the clinic. They could barely pay the staff, which was why they were on their fourth receptionist in a month.

"Karen, have you seen Keith?" Raymond asked as Mrs. Wentworth walked out the door.

"He's eating lunch in the doctor's lounge," she replied. "But what about these orders?" She placed her hand on his sculpted arm, preventing him from leaving the front desk.

Raymond picked up the chart. "Discharge Loretta, give her meds for the pain, and have her come back in a month. What's the question?"

"Sorry, doc, I'm not fluent in chicken scratch."

Raymond playfully sneered at her and then broke out

laughing. "Watch the door and phones for me. Five minutes, okay?" She nodded, and then Raymond took off for the doctor's lounge, which was more like a storage closet with a dingy window.

Keith was sitting at the small table, more akin to a TV tray, eating a salad and a roast chicken sandwich. "What's up, Ray?" Keith asked, catching his partner's stare.

"You tell me, brother."

Keith stood up, stuffing the last of his sandwich in his mouth. "The only time you call me 'brother' is when you're pissed off. What did I do now?"

Raymond raised his eyebrow. "You're going to stand here and pretend that you don't know what you did? I got a call that I'm sure you know all about. Some TV producer called me about the show *Let's Get Married*."

"Finally! I'm glad they got to my letter," Keith said excitedly. "I thought all of my writing had been in vain."

Raymond was tempted to grab his best friend by the throat and choke him like a chicken ready to be plucked and fried.

"Keith, have you lost your mind? First of all, I don't want to get married, and second of all, I'm not reality TV material."

"Think about it Ray. This show guarantees people will hear of the Marion G. Palmer Free Clinic over and over again. And I'm sure the ladies will swoon over tall, muscular Dr. Ray-Ray, just like they did in college. We can't pay for this kind of publicity. It's not as if we can afford it anyway. Bro, we're in trouble. At this point, we need to do anything to keep these doors open."

Raymond shook his head. "Why don't you go on the show?" he snapped.

"Number one, Celeste would kill me; she's been trying to get me to marry her for three years. Number two, I know the limitations of my charm. I'd be voted off the first show. And number three, I don't want my momma to see me on TV like that."

"I don't want to do it," Raymond said, "and I'm not going to do it. Besides, do you actually think you can run this place without me? Do you know how busy we've been today? There's no way we can afford to have either one of us out of pocket for any amount of time."

"It's fifteen thousand just to do it. That doesn't even include the prize money, should you win," Keith said. "This is a great way for us to get some free publicity. I know one thing for sure. If we don't start getting some income coming in, the doors aren't going to be open much longer."

Raymond rubbed his chin, thinking about the clinic's finances. The books were in the red. Medicare was slow to pay for the services the clinic provided, but that didn't stop Keith and Raymond from providing quality health care to the people in the community who wouldn't otherwise be able to get the help that they needed. The clinic had never been about the two of them getting rich. They wanted to help the people who reminded them of the women who'd helped raise them. Keith's grandmother could've been Mrs. Wentworth, a hardworking woman who, as she aged, needed help managing her health but couldn't afford health insurance.

"That's a lot of money for a one-time gig. Maybe I can make myself get voted off after two episodes," Raymond said as he fingered his goatee.

Keith nodded. "See, that's the spirit. But don't be evil or anything like that. Just make yourself seem pitiful. You have to win them over if we plan to milk donations from people who watch the show."

Raymond looked at himself in the reflective material on the side of the file cabinet. He was hardly a vain man, but he knew there was no way he could make himself seem as if he were some pitiful soul who couldn't find a date. Raymond was the kind of man who made a woman's breath catch in her chest after she got a look at his creamy caramel skin, dark wavy hair, and shimmering green eyes—which had been known to put a woman in a trance if he looked at her just the right way. People often snagged him for charity fashion shows and bachelor auctions, and asked him to pose for bachelor calendars. Raymond always brought in top dollar when he was auctioned off.

"I'm going to do it, but I tell you what—you're going to pay for this," Raymond said, pointing his index finger at his friend.

Keith patted his partner on the shoulder. "All right. I knew you would see it my way. Now stop yakking and let's get to work."

Raymond took off his white lab coat. "You work, I'm going to lunch. First thing you need to do is relieve Karen at the front desk." Then he dashed out the back door.

Many people who saw Raymond walking down the street would peg him as another New York pretty boy player. Though he enjoyed having fun with the ladies, he was also hoping to experience the love that his parents had shared during their fifty-year marriage. Lorne and Helen Thomas never had much; however, what they lacked in material possessions, they made up for in the love they'd shared. He had memories of seeing his parents hugging and kissing every time either of them entered the room. Lorne had always showed his wife the utmost respect and affection, and if they'd ever argued, Raymond wasn't around. Until the end, they worked as a team, and that was the kind of life he wanted with the right woman.

Raymond was beginning to believe his woman wasn't in New York. He didn't think he was going to find her on a TV show, either. Marriage wasn't something to be entered into for the hope of a big payoff. Doing this show was not a good idea, because it made a mockery of marriage—in his opinion. If his parents were alive they wouldn't approve of him making a joke of marriage on national TV. *What am I getting myself into?* he asked himself.